Maggie's World

by

Gillian Jackson

A Maggie Sayer Novel

Published in 2012 by FeedARead.com Publishing –
Arts Council funded

A CIP catalogue record for this title is available from
the British Library.

To my wonderful family for their support
and encouragement

Chapter 1

Slowly, almost reluctantly Ellie began to emerge from unconsciousness, instinctively aware of being in a hospital, perplexed as to why, yet utterly powerless to do even the simple task of opening her eyes to find out what was going on. Perhaps the sharp clinical smell or the tinny noises reverberating in her ears had given away her whereabouts. There were voices too, hollow hushed tones which seemed to resonate, as if coming from the end of a tunnel, one of which sounded vaguely like her mother addressing a man whose words were pitched low and inaudible. Ellie wanted to rub her dry, gritty eyes but lacked the strength to do so, her hands petrified, refusing to move even so much as an inch. Ellie's mind was floating, as were the voices, drifting near and then away again, so very strange. Was it a dream? It must be and soon she would wake up in the safety of her own bed, not this scratchy uncomfortable hospital cot with its rubber mattress irritating her skin.

Someone moved closer, their breath warm on Ellie's cheek, stroking her forehead with a cool and welcome hand.

'I thought her fingers moved, look, her eyes flickered too!' It was her mother's voice again, anxious and heavy with emotion. Ellie wanted to offer a smile of reassurance, not really knowing why, but even her face refused to obey. The floating began again, drifting, meandering, back into the dream she supposed...

Suddenly a sense of falling brought panic and a tightness across her chest, making breathing difficult.

Someone was pushing, lifting, and Ellie moaned, still unable to open her weighty eyelids.

'Ellie honey, can you hear me?' a brisk no-nonsense voice asked, but the answer came out as another moan.

'We're just cleaning you up a bit sweetheart; it will make you feel fresher, more comfortable.'

It must be a nurse; the pleasant, sing-songy voice continued,

'Can you try to move for me honey? Squeeze my hand if you can.'

Making an enormous effort, Ellie was rewarded by feeling a trembling finger rise a mere inch or two off the bed.

'Get Dr. Samms' the nurse ordered, 'I think our girl's coming round.'

The dazzling white light stung her eyes, but Ellie fought against it, determined to wake up if only to find out what was going on. Turning away from the glare and managing to open her eyes a tiny fraction, the first thing which came into focus was her mother, Grace, sitting beside the bed with damp cheeks and an enormous smile. A bulky, white coated doctor flanked the other side of the bed standing with two nurses; they were all grinning like monkeys and she wished they would share the joke. Ellie could feel a modicum of strength returning to her limp body and her hands, beginning to obey now, discovered a tube plastered to her face and running into her nose. What on earth had happened? Panic once again seized her as Ellie turned to her mother.

'Mum. What is it, why am I here?' Her voice was hoarse and barely audible, it was such an effort to speak and hot tears scalded her face whilst she struggled to make sense of everything, but could remember nothing.

'It's okay Ellie love. You were in an accident and you've been unconscious for a while, but you have come back to us now so try not to worry, everything will be all right, I promise.'

The doctor gently lifted a drooping eyelid, moving closer to peer into Ellie's eyes. Holding up three fingers, he asked how many there were.

'Good,' he nodded, asking next if she was in any pain.

'I feel stiff and weak, but no pain. I'm really thirsty, could I have a drink?' Grace was there in a flash with a glass of water, helping to lift Ellie's head from the pillow in order to sip the tepid liquid. The doctor instructed the nurses in muffled tones and then after asking his patient a few more questions, left to continue his rounds, promising to be back later that afternoon. Ellie looked closely at her mother, noticing how tired and so much older than her fifty-four years she appeared.

'What day is it Mum?'

'Thursday love.'

'And how long have I been here?'

Grace took hold of Ellie's hand in both of her own, squeezing gently.

'You've been in a coma, for over four weeks.'

'Four weeks. But how, I mean, what happened?'

'It was an accident; you were knocked off your bike by a car. It's amazing there were no broken bones, only a few cuts and bruises which have all healed nicely.'

'I can't remember Mum. Why can I not remember?'

'Shh... Don't worry about it now; it will all come back in time. The doctor said it's quite common with head injuries that the memory is affected. It will take time, that's all.'

Ellie tried to relax and not worry about the accident, after all, did she actually want to remember such a

7

painful event, but the last month was completely lost and that really was scary. It had clearly affected her mother too, it was little wonder she looked so tired; her parents must have been worried out of their minds. Suddenly Ellie thought about her exams.

'Mum. Have the exam results come through? Did I pass?'

'What exams?' Grace looked puzzled.

'My 'A' levels, what grades did I get?'

Grace Watson frowned, squeezing her daughter's hand again and forcing a smile.

'Don't worry about that, you're a little confused, rest now and we can talk about it later. I've rung your dad and Phil. They're so excited and should be here anytime with little Sam too.'

Before Ellie could ask the next question, Derek Watson appeared in the doorway with a tall, grinning young man, carrying a plump little baby in his arms. Her father stood back, allowing the younger man to approach the bed and in what seemed to be slow motion, Ellie's mother rose to take the infant while the young man, his soft brown eyes wide and moist, leaned over the bed, placing his hands on her shoulders and kissed her gently on the lips. If Ellie's reactions had been quicker, she would have turned away. Who did he think he was, kissing her like that?

'Ellie.' The young man's voice trembled with emotion, 'We've been so worried, and we have missed you so much.'

Turning to her mother who was still holding the child, Ellie asked in a quiet, pleading way,

'Mum, who is this?'

The colour drained from Grace's face, looking from Ellie to her husband and then to the young man before replying,

8

'It's Phil, darling; he's been here every day with Sam...' Grace seemed to run out of words, there was an awkward silence and she mouthed something to her husband which Ellie missed. Derek leaned over to kiss his daughter; unable to speak and patted her arm before leaving the little hospital room to find one of the nursing staff. Phil sat down next to the bed and took hold of Ellie's hand; she didn't possess the strength to pull away, this was so confusing and exhausting. It was surreal; perhaps it was a dream after all and one from which she would soon awake. Looking into the young man's smiling, but anxious, brown eyes Ellie closed her own, sinking back into a place where things were not so strange.

Chapter 2

'I am not your father and you're not daddy's little princess anymore.' Mark growled angrily at Sarah.

'You are living with me now, we're married remember? Money doesn't grow on trees you know.' Each syllable of this last sentence was emphasized by his rhythmically tapping finger on Sarah's forehead and then in a heartbeat his mood changed as laughingly Mark pulled his confused wife to her feet, embracing her in a bear like hug until she could hardly breathe.

'Don't make me have to get cross with you.' His voice sounded more rational now, gentle even as he stroked her hair.

'You know I love you and only want what's best for you. But just because you were spoilt by your father doesn't mean that I'll spoil you too. I'll be the one to look after you now; you know how much Mark loves his angel don't you?'

Sarah smiled weakly, trying to wriggle free of her husband's grasp. Yes, of course she knew he loved her, he had told her often enough hadn't he? And he could be very generous, if she had pleased him. Mark was right, Sarah wasn't a child at home with her parents any more, but a married woman who would have to accept that her husband was now the one to make the decisions.

Sarah and Mark Beecham had been married for less than a year. A few settling down problems were to be expected, Sarah frequently reminded herself. Perhaps they should have discussed practicalities in more detail before the wedding, but it was such a magical time, straight out of a fairy tale. Mark had wooed her in the old fashioned romantic way, arms-full of flowers on every occasion, romantic meals out at exclusive, intimate restaurants... and so attentive. Almost from their first date he had begun to pick her up from work, not allowing her to catch the bus as usual. Each date had been planned with an almost military precision and he treated her as if she was a china doll. If Sarah was out with friends from work, Mark insisted on coming afterwards to see her safely home, the kind of attentiveness which had certainly impressed her parents who thought him quite charming and a good prospect for their only daughter. Mark soon had his feet under the table as far as they were concerned.

Sarah chided herself now for being churlish about this latest little incident, it was only right that Mark should handle their finances, after all, he was an accountant. It was yet another change to get used to, not having the kind of disposable income she'd had when single. Impulse buying would have to be a thing of the past; it wasn't worth making her husband angry over little things such as buying make-up and the odd magazine was it? Sarah had not even realised that she wasn't good with money until Mark had pointed it out.

The one change however which Sarah did secretly regret was the loss of regular contact with her parents. Theirs had always been a close knit little family unit, the three of them against the world. They were fantastic parents, who had loved their daughter unconditionally and she in return absolutely adored them. It was Mark who again had pointed out how such a close relationship with them was unhealthy for someone of her age, explaining that they needed time alone together to nurture their marriage and such regular contact with her parents would hamper this. Trying hard to understand, Sarah had honestly felt able to give time to both husband and parents, but as usual it was easier to do things Mark's way and so it had been agreed that she would visit them only once a month. Sarah though longed to invite them round for a meal, they had only been to her new home twice before, but Mark explained how that would set a precedent, giving them expectations. Sarah's hope was that in time he might change his mind. Being alone for Sarah was also a thing of the past, browsing around the shops in town or meeting friends for coffee had always been fun, a weekend treat, but now Mark insisted on accompanying his wife on all trips to town, so there was rarely opportunity to meet up with friends and he strongly disapproved of frittering time and money on coffee dates. It was so much cheaper to have coffee at home, and, he reminded his wife, they had married to be together, not waste their free time with friends. A niggling uncertainty was beginning to gnaw at Sarah, a feeling of being trapped, a feeling she tried hard to dismiss from her mind. Any girl would be pleased to have a husband who was so protective and wanted to keep her exclusively for himself, many would kill for someone to love them that way, wouldn't they? So where were these guilty, uneasy feelings coming from? Time seemed not to be her own any more, but wasn't that what married life should be like? It was bound to take a while to settle into a new pattern of living, it was just not quite what Sarah had anticipated.

****

Maggie Sayer had also been married for less than a year and was in fact Mrs Peter Lloyd, only using 'Sayer' for her work as a therapeutic counsellor. It had been a whirlwind year for Maggie and Peter, good news and bad taking them to peaks and troughs emotionally, but their love was strong and they had formed a formidable union, tackling life together, head on. Their relationship was in its infancy when the first bombshell had dropped and Peter had been diagnosed with multiple sclerosis. If he had gone with his instincts, they might never have married. It was a second marriage for both of them, Peter through divorce and Maggie having been widowed several years previously after only three years of marriage. Peter made the decision that he could not put this woman, whom he loved so deeply, through the possibility of being widowed for a second time. But Maggie's determination and inner strength had taken him by surprise, having learned from experience to grasp every chance of happiness and not be governed by the 'what ifs' of life, it was Maggie who had eventually proposed and Peter's positive answer had brought them both a fresh start. Looking upon each new day as a bonus, they confronted his illness with pragmatic determination and often with humour. Knowing there was no cure for MS, they held onto the fact that the treatments available were advancing rapidly and Peter responded well to them. He felt blessed to be able to say that there were more good days than bad.

Maggie thrived on her work. Therapeutic counselling had played a major part in her recovery from the death of her first husband, Chris. When her world suddenly fell apart, the realisation dawned as to how ill-equipped she was to deal with such life changing trauma. Counselling was helpful in navigating through the fog of bereavement, bringing Maggie to a new understanding of herself and leaving an ongoing interest in psychology and helping others who struggled with the myriad problems which life can hold. The mundane work of a clerical officer no longer appealed or satisfied, so Maggie took the bold, but rewarding step of training to be a counsellor; a change in career which brought a new sense of purpose to her life and gave an insight into the problems which many people faced in their daily living. Generally, the work was based at the local health centre with most clients being referrals from the resident GPs. She did however take on a few private clients who knew of her reputation from friends and former clients, but during the last year Maggie had tried to reduce her working hours, wanting the time to nurture and cherish her marriage. Peter was still able to work full time as a partner in a small firm of architects, but an increasing number of working hours were spent at home, cutting out the travelling and affording the luxury of a little extra time with his wife.

The variety of people Maggie came into contact with was one of the most enjoyable and rewarding aspects of the job. In the course of a typical week she might see up to ten clients with some pretty diverse issues. Therapeutic counselling was becoming almost 'fashionable', a term which perhaps undervalued its benefits. The way Maggie personally viewed this rise in counselling's profile was that health professionals and the general public were more open to talking about emotional problems than in years gone by, at last acknowledging that mental health was equally important as physical health for complete well-being. Many clients benefitted from the opportunity to express their feelings, knowing that their problems were being shared and they were truly valued and listened to. Yes, Maggie often thought that the growth in counselling, whilst undoubtedly good, was also a sad reflection on what was deemed to be a civilized society.

Chapter 3

Mark Beecham slowly grinned at his reflection in the bedroom mirror whilst knotting the day's choice of tie. A handsome man, though not in a rugged or masculine way, he was tall, a tad over six feet, with a slim frame which perhaps gave the impression of his being slightly underweight. Fine, sandy coloured hair topped an oval face, with vivid green eyes set beneath a rather prominent forehead and skin, which had an almost translucent appearance, stretched taught over his features, resulting in a rather boyish look. His grin that morning was prompted by thoughts of his new wife. Sarah was turning out to be quite malleable with perhaps a little resistance here and there, but he would soon bring her to heel. Having worked hard to move their relationship on, now that she was his, he could ease off a bit and enjoy the benefits of married life. Sarah's parents had been a push over too and Mark was confident that he had them eating out of his hand. A bit of flattery truly did go a long way in their case, and they had encouraged their precious daughter even more than he could have hoped for, which was just as well, it was getting rather expensive with all those meals out, flowers and chocolates. Still, it had been worth the effort and now it was a most satisfying feeling to watch Sarah fuss over him, behaving as a good wife should. Maybe, he thought, it was time to be a little more assertive in the financial department. Sarah had got used to wasting money on frivolities, magazines, make-up and other such rubbish, having been truly spoilt by her parents, which is what comes from being an only child. Yet it did have its advantages and there would be a tidy sum to inherit one day which was certainly something to look forward to. Yes, his Sarah was one to keep hold of, a pretty girl with curves in all the right places, he would enjoy having her for a wife, as long as there were no silly ideas about babies and giving up work, but bridges were to be crossed only when they presented themselves, weren't they?

****

Sarah frowned, scrolling down the contacts list on her mobile phone, unable to understand how all of the numbers been deleted. It was a simple phone used only for calls and texts; she had wanted nothing complicated such as an expensive blackberry or iphone. It would be quite a chore having to start all over again compiling her friends' numbers and would take time too. Hopefully they wouldn't think she no longer wanted to keep in touch; it was difficult enough finding opportunity to ring for a chat without Mark making comments about wasting time and money on gossip. Still it was her own fault; she must have pressed the wrong key and deleted the whole address book by mistake. Pushing open the heavy glass doors leading into the dentist's surgery, Sarah took the vacant seat behind the reception desk, turned to her colleague, Marie, and began to explain what had happened.

'Give me your number again, so I can put it back in my contacts.'

'I'll ring you and you can just save it, it'll be easier.' Marie replied.

The first patient of the day arrived and Sarah buzzed through to the dentist to let him know. As the waiting room filled up and the phone began its endless ringing, the mobile phone incident was forgotten as Sarah became immersed in work. For her the job was great, with two receptionists working for six dentists, their nurses and two hygienists. Days were varied with endless new people to meet and the social side of the job was good too. The dentists were a mixed bunch but all pleasant and easy to work for, and Marie and the dental nurses had become firm friends. Consequently at her hen party, the last social event Sarah had organized, most of the guests had been work colleagues with only a few friends from schooldays with whom she had kept in touch.

Mark continued the habit of picking Sarah up after work, which at first had seemed exciting, providing opportunity to show off her new boyfriend, but truthfully now, going back to getting the bus would be preferable. The ride home had always been enjoyable, relaxing even; a good opportunity to switch off and unwind after a busy day but Mark insisted it was quicker to pick her up so their evening meal could be ready at a more reasonable hour. At least he had stopped coming into the waiting room, which had been okay at first when the other girls had flirted a bit, saying how lucky she was to have such a gorgeous boyfriend, but after a while it had put Sarah under pressure to hurry out. Lately things had changed again and Mark had taken to waiting outside in the car which was something of a relief, although why that should be was difficult to understand; after all she loved Mark didn't she? Marriage was simply not working out as Sarah had expected.

****

Ellie was unaware of how long she had slept; it could have been another four weeks, although she doubted it. This time it was easier to open her eyes and in doing so there was a sense of relief that no one was

17

beside the bed so, taking the opportunity of lying still for several minutes simply gazing at the surroundings, Ellie tried to assemble her muddled thoughts. The room appeared to be a side ward with only one other bed which was thankfully unoccupied. The door was wedged open with the nurses' station in view a few yards away, where a solitary nurse was frowning at a computer screen, her nose almost touching it. Piles of dog-eared brown folders cluttered the surface of the desk and not surprisingly the nurse looked harassed. Ellie made no attempt to attract her attention, wanting a few minutes alone, to try to remember what had happened, closing her eyes again and focusing on the incomplete scraps of memory floating around her brain. Ellie's mother said she had been knocked off her bike but that memory escaped her completely; maybe knowing where the accident had happened or where she was going to at the time would jog some recollection but the images remained incomplete. It had been the last day of term at the sixth form college where, with best friends, Rosie and Liz they had sneaked in a bottle of wine to drink in the students' common room at lunch time.

'Oh no,' a sudden panic caught her, 'I hope I wasn't knocked off my bike after drinking the wine.' But Ellie was certain she'd had no more than a couple of glasses; she would never have been that stupid. A throbbing headache was starting to pound her temples and Ellie was getting frustrated about not remembering the accident. It was no good; perhaps the nurse would know the circumstances of her admission, trying to recall it herself was akin to coming up against an extremely solid and stubbornly unmoveable concrete wall. Calling out to the nurse in a voice which was barely a whisper, then trying to sit up was no easy task when it felt as if she was made of cotton wool and had very little strength to draw on. The nurse's attention shifted from the computer screen to her young patient and entering the little room with rubber soles squeaking on the polished floor, her round, plump face was split by a wide smile.

'Hello Ellie.' The grin was almost conspiratorial, 'They told me you had come round yesterday. Welcome to the world of ward thirty –two.'

Ellie instantly took to this matronly looking nurse and managed to return the smile.

'I'm Caroline,' the nurse announced and half hitched her bottom onto the side of the bed.

'Night staff nurse and keeper of the kettle, not to mention the chocolate bikkies.'

'So, what time is it?'

'1.37 am. and I think you and I are the only ones on this ward who are not sleeping.'

The nurse had a relaxed manner and Ellie watched her pour a welcome glass of water as if reading her mind and then she helped Ellie to sit up to drink. Asking next if she wanted to sleep some more or sit up for a while, Ellie chose the latter option, sleeping seemed to have been her only occupation for some considerable time. The nurse was gentle but strong in helping to lift her patient and soon Ellie was propped up with two fresh white pillows supporting her extremely weak body. Caroline seemed in no hurry to get back to the computer so Ellie took the opportunity to find out what, if anything, this nurse knew about the accident.

'Yes,' Caroline looked thoughtful, 'Four weeks is about right. I remember because you were admitted while I was on holiday. The doctor will be doing his rounds in the morning and I'm sure he will be able to tell you more about your injuries than I can, but I do know there were no broken bones or internal injuries, which is a blessing really. Your head seemed to take the entire trauma, hence the coma and the uncertainty. But now you are back with us it's looking good. You might be confused for a while but that's quite normal, things will fall into place in time.'

'My parents,' Ellie asked, 'they had someone with them who seemed to know me, who was it?'

'Wasn't here then love, but don't worry, your mum will be here in the morning, lovely lady your mum is, hasn't missed a day visiting you.'

Ellie tried not to think, it made her head hurt, but she was wide awake now and readily accepted Caroline's offer of a cup of tea. It would be a long time until Grace Watson would be back, hopefully to answer all the questions which were stacking up in Ellie's mind.

Chapter 4

Maggie's thoughts were interrupted by a tap on the office door and Sue, one of the practice receptionists and her closest friend, popped her head in.

'You haven't forgotten tonight have you?' Sue beamed, eyes sparkling with anticipation.

'Now how could I when it's all you have talked about for a week.'

Sue was cooking a meal for the four of them and making quite an occasion out of it. She and her husband, Alan, had been married only a few months longer than their friends and playing the hostess was still a novelty. Being a detective sergeant meant that Alan's shifts varied and it was quite difficult to arrange social occasions. Sue often commented how much both her own and Maggie's lives had changed during the last eighteen months or so. They had each met and married their husbands within a short time frame, a time which was fraught with difficulties, particularly for Maggie and Peter. But things had turned out well for both couples and opportunities to get together were precious times which both women cherished.

'We're looking forward to it.' Maggie smiled, 'In fact Peter's gone for a hair cut in your honour.'

'Hmm, Alan's probably having a polish too!' Sue teased her husband relentlessly about his premature balding but he took it in good grace, confident of her love for him which was evident to anyone who saw them together. Maggie had thought theirs an unlikely match at first, her friend had always been a bit of a 'man eater' who everyone thought would never settle down. Although the complete antithesis of Sue's usual type of boyfriend, Alan had swept her off her feet and she was still completely smitten with him.

'I'm leaving now.' Sue continued, 'I've an appointment at the dentist for a check up, then I'm going to pick up some goodies for tonight.'

'Oh, poor you, all that scraping and prodding, I loathe going to the dentist.'

'Me too but the most painful bit is the bill. I'm sure I'm paying for all those exotic foreign holidays he has.' Her expression was one of mock agony as she waved her fingers in a farewell to her friend.

'See you later.' they said almost in unison.

****

The dentist's surgery was only a short distance from the health centre so Sue left her car and walked, enjoying the early spring sunshine and the daffodils in full bloom carpeting the grass verges in a vibrant yellow mass. Slowing her pace, so as not to be early, Sue shared Maggie's sentiments about the dentist and didn't want to be in there any longer than was necessary. She did however have the evening ahead to concentrate on and hopefully take her mind off drills. Alan would be home early for once and Maggie and Peter were really good company and always appreciated the effort she put into cooking a meal. They were to be unwitting guinea pigs tonight as she tried out a new recipe, a rather time consuming one, so a little bit of cheating with the desert was in order, she would buy one of the gorgeously gooey chocolate fudge cakes from the bakers in the high street and serve it with rich vanilla ice-cream. Hopefully the dentist would not find anything wrong with her teeth or she would feel terribly guilty about the cake.

Entering the foyer of the dentist's surgery Sue headed for the reception desk to give her name and looking twice at the young receptionist, whose head was bent over the desk, was sure that she was familiar but Sue couldn't quite place her. When the receptionist looked up Sue immediately recognised her.

'It's Sarah isn't it? Sarah Porter.'

'Yes...but it's Sarah Beecham now, I'm married and I certainly remember you, Sue isn't it?'

'Goodness, I wouldn't have thought you old enough to be married. I used to babysit for you when we lived next door, you were only a toddler, I didn't think it was that long ago.' Both women smiled and Sue went on to ask after her parents.

'They're fine thanks, although I do miss them since I got married, I don't manage to see them that often.'

'That's a shame. You were so close, doing everything together, I remember being quite jealous of how tight the three of you were.'

'Well, things have to change when you're married I suppose.' Sarah said wistfully.

'For the better I hope. But you're not the only one to be married.' Sue placed her left hand on the desk to display her ring.

'Oh how lovely.' Sarah admired the ring.

'Mrs Hurst?' the other receptionist interrupted. 'The dentist is ready for you now.'

Sue grimaced and turned to go in, as if to a funeral.

'Wish me luck.' she said.

It was exactly as Sue had predicted, all prodding and poking, he was bound to find something wrong.

'A couple of tiny fillings Mrs Hurst, we'll soon have them sorted. Make an appointment on your way out and we will see you soon.' The dentist smiled.

23

'He may as well be rubbing his hands in glee,' she thought, 'It must be holiday time again.'

Making the appointment with Sarah, Sue took the opportunity to have another little chat.

'Remember me to your mum and dad won't you? I always had a soft spot for them; the kettle was always boiling in your house, anyone was welcome, they were such great times.'

'Yes I will. They were happy times weren't they? I had an idyllic childhood but I don't suppose I appreciated it at the time, it's been good to see you again and it seems that I'll see you in two week's time as well.'

Sue left to do the shopping for the evening meal, trying to forget about the dentist and those fillings to be endured in a couple of weeks.

The evening proved to be a pleasant and relaxing few hours. Maggie and Peter were complimentary about Sue's efforts in the kitchen and judging by the empty plates, it could be marked up as another culinary triumph. She had entertained her friends with a wickedly exaggerated version of her trip to the dentist and consequent fears for the next appointment as if it was major surgery, then the foursome took their coffee into the lounge to relax after the meal. Sue wouldn't contemplate the offers of help with the dishes, wanting to leave them until their guests had gone so that she could enjoy their conversation and company. Alan had not seen either of them for nearly a month due to some back to back shifts, covering for colleague's holidays and so was keen to hear all of their latest news, particularly about some new drug which Maggie had mentioned as a possible alternative to Peter's injections for MS.

'It sounds quite encouraging.' Peter was happy to explain.

'They're hopeful that these pills will be able to replace injections and actually be more effective too. It's a drug called Gilenya, and the results so far have been quite exciting. It's been in trials for the last four years, mainly in the north of England, Newcastle I think, and some of the patients have had symptoms disappear completely. It would be great not to have to inject anymore and even better if symptoms could be stopped altogether. One of the problems with MS is that each time there's an attack, there is a little more damage done to the brain and the spinal cord. This drug seems to capture the cells which do the damage and stores them in the lymph nodes. I suppose it's doing the same kind of job you do Alan, catching the bad guys before they can do any more harm.'

It was obvious to them all how such a drug could change Peter's life and Maggie's too. When he had first been diagnosed Peter had broken up with Maggie, doing what he thought was the chivalrous thing, not wanting her to have to go through the kind of pain she had experienced when her first husband, Chris had died. Fortunately Maggie had persuaded him otherwise and now, if this drug proved to be effective in fighting this illness it would be nothing short of a miracle and they would all naturally be delighted. Maggie added a few slightly cautionary comments, never having been one to count her chickens.

'We don't actually know if Gilenya will be suitable yet, but we've been following its progress and to our layman's eyes it seems ideal. We have an appointment with the specialist next month so its fingers crossed for that.'

Sue was so pleased that her friends had shared this potentially good news. There were times when Peter's

MS hung over them all, the elephant in the room which no one could bring themselves to mention. They wanted to show concern, but it was a difficult balance expressing it without always reminding him of the illness and what life could hold in the future. This news had turned their pleasant evening into an almost celebratory one, a good enough reason to open a bottle of sparkling wine and hand round the chocolates.

Chapter 5

The early morning hours seemed to drag for Ellie. Caroline, the night staff nurse was brilliant, bringing a welcome cup of tea and even a slice of toast. Her throat was dry and sore, but Caroline assured her that was to be expected and would soon pass. The nurse also removed the catheter which had been in place and helped to support her first unsteady steps to the bathroom. Ellie couldn't believe how weak she felt and was sure she had lost weight, which wasn't a bad thing, although a rather drastic way to do so. As the nurse helped her back into bed, Ellie noticed that they had put the wrong name above the bed. It read, 'Eleanor Graham, known as Ellie'.

'You've got that wrong,' she remarked to Caroline. 'It's Eleanor Watson, not Graham.'

'Oh, sorry love, we'll sort that one out when sister comes on duty at eight. Now is there anything else I can get you, a couple of magazines or something?'

'I could really do with a shower, is that possible?'

'Perhaps later when the day staff are here, then there'll be more pairs of hands to help you.'

'Great, thanks. I think I'll try to rest for a while, I feel as if I've run a marathon, not just been to the loo.'

The nurse smiled, and then moving back to the desk, made a few notes on Ellie's confused state of mind, anticipating an even greater shock to come for this young patient.

Grace Watson arrived at the hospital earlier than usual. Ellie had managed to sleep for a few more hours and had even eaten a little breakfast, only orange juice and cereal, but it made her feel considerably better.

Seeing her mother talking to the ward sister Ellie couldn't help but notice how unwell she appeared and she had done something different with her hair too, which didn't really help. Her mother getting older was something Ellie had never considered before, but now...it must be all the stress this accident had caused. Watching the two women talking it was noticeable that Grace appeared worried too. Perhaps they would all feel better now, this accident must have put them through quite an ordeal.

'Hi there.' her mother's voice was unnaturally high and chirpy, 'how are you feeling?'

'Much better than yesterday, I've slept quite a bit, been up to go to the bathroom and even had some breakfast.' Hopefully this positive report would erase some of the worry from her mother's face.

'That's great sweetheart. The sister told me you had been up in the night.'

'You're very early mum, couldn't you sleep?'

'Oh, I'm fine, don't need as much sleep as I used to. The sister tells me that Dr. Samms will be round this morning, he's the doctor who has been looking after you, the one you saw for a little while yesterday. We'll get the chance to ask him some questions then if you like, okay?'

'It's you I need to answer a few things for me mum. Have you brought me the results of my exams, they must have arrived by now? And who was that man with dad last night, with the baby?'

Grace's face took on that solemn expression again and her daughter reached for her hand.

'Hey mum, it's okay, I am on the mend now, and you'll soon have me back at home. I'm sorry, I must have really put you through the wringer with all this, but it'll be all right now.'

Grace took a tissue from her bag and blew her nose.

'I know sweetheart, you will be all right, I'm sure, but you seem a little confused still. The sister has called the doctor and he's coming soon, then we can have a little talk.'

'But can't you tell me mum. Did I fail my exams, is that it?'

'No my love, you did really well, three A stars and a B. Dad and I were so proud of you.'

'That's wonderful mum. I'll get my first choice at uni with those grades.'

Ellie was all smiles, really excited but it was obvious that her mother did not share her exuberance.'

'What is it mum, what's wrong?'

Before Grace could answer, Dr. Samms appeared in the doorway, a big man with a big smile.

'Well hello there.' His very presence filled the tiny room instantly commanding both women's attention.

'I can at last get to see the colour of your eyes, and a beautiful emerald green they are too.'

Ellie could not help but return his smile, his whole nature was infectious. The doctor picked up the clip board from the end of the bed, flicked over the top sheet and glanced through the notes, nodding his head as if satisfied with what he was reading.

'Everything seems to be in order. You have been up for a little walk I see, eating and drinking okay. Well done.' He drew up a chair on the opposite side of the bed to Grace, a gesture which brought him to Ellie's level, giving the desired effect of putting his patient at ease.

'One or two questions for you this morning.' He spoke kindly now in a softer voice.

'Easy ones first, what's your full name?'

'Eleanor Grace Watson.' She replied.

'And do you know what day it is?'

'Well, mum told me it was Thursday yesterday, so I reckon its Friday today.' Ellie grinned at the absurdity of the questions.

'Very good, we can try the hard ones now. Who is the Prime Minister?'

'Tony Blair.'

'And what year is it?'

'2002', this game was beginning to get tiresome.

'Ellie, can you remember anything at all about your accident?' Dr. Samms looked more earnest now.

'No, absolutely nothing. The last thing I remember is being in the common room at college with my friends and then I woke up here. I seem to have completely lost the last month of my life.' She sighed looking in the direction of her mother, shocked to see a grim expression had crept onto her face. Suddenly Ellie was scared.

'What is it? What's wrong?'

'Only one more question.' Dr. Samms regained her attention, 'How old are you now?'

'Eighteen. But something's wrong, what is it that you're not telling me?'

'It's okay, no more questions for now, but I need you to listen to what I am going to tell you Ellie and I don't want you to worry because everything is going to be fine.'

Now she was really panicking. When someone told you not to worry about what they were going to say, it was most certainly not going to be good news. The doctor began in his soft bedside voice,

'When someone has an accident such as yours and the head suffers the kind of trauma yours did, there are all sorts of things which can happen. The brain is a very complicated and sensitive organ and it doesn't take too kindly to being knocked about. One of the things which can happen is memory loss. Now I know you've experienced this because you have no recollection of the actual event. Sometimes that memory loss is more than the hours prior to the accident and in some cases the patient has no recall of several years before the event. Do you understand what I'm saying Ellie?'

A silent nod confirmed that she did and Ellie was already putting two and two together as Dr. Samms continued,

'I'm afraid that this is the case with you. Now remember this is not an uncommon thing and in most cases what is forgotten eventually comes back, so I don't want you to worry. All it means is that it will take a little longer for you to get better. In many ways you are an extraordinarily lucky girl to have no other physical injuries and it would be a good thing for you if you dwelt on the positives rather than the negatives.' Dr. Samms could see that his patient was wrestling to grasp what he had said. She was an intelligent young woman and he doubted that she would be hysterical on learning the full extent of her memory loss, but this was a difficult case and he had prepared the ward sister to administer a sedative if necessary. It was time for him to leave his patient with her mother, time for Grace Watson to fill in the blanks of her daughter's lost years.

****

Driving out to the west side of town on Friday morning, Maggie was grateful to have avoided the rush hour traffic in what was a notorious bottleneck area. Being in good time for this appointment was not accidental, as the new housing estate towards which she was heading was unfamiliar territory and Maggie had absolutely no sense of direction, frequently being known to get lost in car parks.

Maggie had been here only once before, nearly two years ago when, with Sue they had filled in a Sunday afternoon by looking around the show homes. They had both been impressed, not only with the houses but with the whole lay-out of the estate, an appealing, well planned and successful development. It was built on a designated brown site, reclaimed industrial land, bordered on one side by a protected nature reserve, criss-crossed with footpaths over several acres, which would never be developed. The contractors had been working for over four years and were well on the way to completing the five hundred or so new homes on the site. A school had re-located into a brand new building giving them space to expand their capacity in order to take in the growing numbers of children from the families' fortunate enough to move there. A small shopping precinct was cleverly integrated into the estate together with a family pub-restaurant, a hair salon and a cafe. Plenty of open spaces and cycle routes weaved through the estate among an eclectic mix of housing designs, giving the whole project a family feel. Maggie and Sue had looked in awe at the show homes, eyes on stalks at all the little 'extras' and 'upgrades' available, and at the price tags to go with them.

The morning's visit was to a private client and would be their first meeting. Ruth Duncan had heard about Maggie from a friend and had sounded quite chirpy on the phone, giving no indication of the reason she wanted to see a counsellor. The only information which had been forthcoming was that she taught at a local primary school and was the deputy head teacher. Friday mornings were reserved for preparation time with no classes to teach and would therefore be a good opportunity to see Maggie.

Stepping into the warm sunshine and locking her car, Maggie felt the gentle heat permeate her body, bringing a sense of peace and that 'good to be alive' feeling which at one time she had thought she would never experience again. It was warm for spring and the air was filled with the smell of newly cut grass, a tantalising promise of the summer to come. The Duncan's home was a three storey town house on the end of a plot which gave them a larger garden and more parking space than neighbouring properties. Ruth answered the doorbell with a warm smile, inviting her guest to step inside an immaculate home. The interior of the house lived up to expectations with a fashionably neutral decor and modern, tasteful furniture. It was every bit as beautiful as Maggie remembered the show house had been, furnished with rich textures and colours which complemented the neutral walls and carpets, but this was a comfortable, welcoming home, put together by someone with an obvious flair for design. Ruth showed her visitor into the garden room, where they sat in the morning sunshine, each with their own thoughts and feelings. The women were of a similar height and build, this new client being the younger by nine or ten years, with a fair complexion and hair, in contrast to Maggie's olive skin and auburn hair. Ruth offered coffee which her visitor declined; at the first meeting it was always difficult to maintain the balance of professionalism whilst getting alongside the client to build a relationship of trust. Was it to become a friendship or a short acquaintance? Perhaps being in the client's home blurred the distinctions even more. Maggie began with the usual verbal contracting then asked Ruth where she would like to begin.

'I have some rather difficult decisions to make,' she began 'and I need some help in sorting things out.'

The briefest of nods from Maggie encouraged her to continue.

'Perhaps it would be best to start at the beginning. Andy, my husband, and I have been married for eight years now, almost nine, and for the last six of those years we've been trying for a family. We always knew it might not be easy, I have a history of endometriosis, which I know doesn't necessarily mean that I can't conceive, in fact I have conceived, four times but miscarried after about ten weeks in every case.' Ruth paused; having begun her story with confidence, almost as if reciting someone else's history but now looking at Maggie she was suddenly unsure of where to go next. A tension was creeping into the atmosphere and her anxiety became almost tangible, all previous composure evaporated as the articulate woman began shrinking away to be replaced by a vulnerable girl in need of help; wide eyes threatening tears. Maggie smiled,

'Do you want to tell me about the miscarriages or perhaps how you're feeling right now? But please, take your time; you don't have to say anything at all if you don't want to.'

'What and sit in silence?' Ruth attempted a smile,

'If it helps,' Maggie returned the smile.

'I'm sorry; this is all a bit strange for me. The idea of talking to a counsellor and having all my problems solved seemed such a good idea at the time, but now I feel a little awkward. The truth is I honestly don't know what to do. There are such strong emotions churning around inside, it's not like me at all. I'm usually in control of situations yet now I feel so desperate and resentful of other women who have children, I see young girls in the street pushing prams, hardly more than children themselves and jealousy eats away at me. In my mind I label them as unfit mothers and I'm crying out inside at the unfairness of it all, it should be me with a baby not them! The mothers at school seem to have one child after another and treat them as if they are burdens, I get so angry with them...and then with myself for feeling this way. I know I shouldn't judge, I sound such a snob. And then there's Andy, he's been marvellous really and he would make such a great dad, he's the life and soul of any party, always the joker, but I'm letting him down, it's my body that isn't working properly not his. It might be okay now but what about the future, what if he decides to find someone who can give him a baby, or if he ends up hating me?'

'Has Andy told you that he thinks you're letting him down?' Maggie asked.

'No, not in so many words, but I'm not sure how he'll feel in the long term.'

'Do you think you could talk to him about these feelings?'

'I don't know...'

Ruth's eyes were wide and sad as she scanned the comfortable room they occupied, her gaze moving to the window. After a few moments reflection she continued,

'He's a fantastic husband which makes me feel so guilty. I have a lovely home and I know I should be grateful but I'd gladly give it all up to live in a hovel if I could only have a baby. It's like having a huge knot in my stomach, a mixture of anger and despair which is tearing me apart. I don't want all these feelings of resentment; it's not like me at all and I worry that I'm changing into a bitter person, but I can't seem to snap out of it. Andy's mentioned adoption but to be honest that scares me. Could I love someone else's child? I just want my own baby...'

****

35

Mentally re-running the conversation on her way home, Maggie felt that this was one case which needed very little imagination on her part to put herself in Ruth's shoes. She too had agonized over coming to terms with being childless, yet she recognized that Ruth's situation was rather different to her own. At forty six years old Maggie had now accepted the fact that she would never bear children, an old wound but still painful at times and it was therefore not difficult to understand some of the emotions Ruth admitted to. Remembering how as a child she had herself constantly played at being 'mummy' as most little girls do and when asked what she wanted to be when grown up, the answer was invariably 'a mummy'. With Chris, her first husband, they had planned to have children; he hoped for a boy to play football with and a girl who would turn out to be the image of Maggie, who warned him that with two females in the house he would be outnumbered and a daughter would almost certainly be able to wrap him around her little finger from the day she was born. Chris laughed declaring that to be a risk he would gladly take. Would they have made good parents? Would their children have resembled their parents? These were questions which would never be answered. Even now when Maggie had thought to be over the pain, she would occasionally see a heavily pregnant woman and would wonder how it felt to feel that new life nestled beneath your heart, to feel a tiny foot or an elbow and to endure the bittersweet pain and ecstasy of bringing a child into the world.

Suddenly Maggie found herself at home, barely able to remember the journey. Switching off the ignition and stepping out of the car, she took a few deep breaths to compose herself before seeing Peter. Consciously shifting thoughts to her world in the present, Maggie was able to smile, thinking of Peter and his two wonderful daughters, and there was little Emma too, Jane's daughter whom she loved as if she was her own grandchild. Not for the first time, Maggie counted her blessings and was grateful.

Chapter 6

It was Friday evening and they were on their way to the supermarket for their weekly shop. Sarah could sense that Mark was in a mood, but hadn't a clue as to why.

'Did you have a good day at work?' She asked, in an attempt at conversation.

'Not particularly.' The answer was flat, a monotone but Sarah battled on.

'I met the lady who used to babysit for me when I was small, Sue Hurst. She's married now too, used to live next door to us when I was little. I adored her; she was my heroine when I was all of ten years old.'

Her husband did not seem in the least bit interested so Sarah remained quiet for the rest of the journey. Shopping used to be an enjoyable experience but Mark disliked wasting time doing something as mundane as buying their food for the week. Offering to do it alone wasn't the answer either, when she had dared to suggest it the idea had been rejected emphatically, the reason given was that he didn't think she would stick to the list, and the list must be obeyed. Sarah had a few creative ideas of what she would like to do with the list, but as with everything else it was so much easier to go along with what Mark wanted. And so, dutifully trotting along beside him reading the list while he pushed the trolley was invariably the order of their task. Naturally Mark stacked the items in the trolley, as she was deemed unable to pack things in the proper way.

The store was busy and the queues at the tills long. Having finished their shopping they headed for the checkout where Mark almost ran to get a place in a line before another customer could get there. Sarah, feeling totally embarrassed, smiled a weak apology at the other shopper before moving along to wait beside her husband who was now clicking his tongue at the elderly lady in front who was apparently not quick enough in loading the conveyor belt for his liking. Sarah wanted to disappear into the ground, he was so impatient. When the ordeal was over they joined the slow moving traffic heading for home. Turning into their road, Mark announced that Sarah would have to put the shopping away as the oil light on the car had been flashing and he wanted to check the oil and water. Perhaps, she thought, this could be the cause of tonight's bad mood?

'Okay, I'll do that, and then I'm off upstairs for a shower.'

Mark didn't even help to carry the shopping inside but that was fine by Sarah, it was quite a relief to get away from him, when he was in a mood like this she much preferred to be alone. After emptying the carriers and stacking everything away, being careful to leave the kitchen tidy, Sarah went upstairs for a shower. It was heaven, standing under the hot jets of water, letting it caress her tired limbs and aching back. Hopefully they would have a peaceful evening without much to do; perhaps she could begin the new Jodi Picoult novel she had bought, Sarah was glad to have taken the time to put a casserole in the slow cooker before leaving for work that morning. A tasty meal and a glass or two of wine might soften the edges of Mark's mood. Pulling out jeans and a cosy sweatshirt from the wardrobe, Sarah sighed. These days weekends were anticipated with mixed feelings. Saturday mornings in town had always been fun, meeting friends for coffee and rummaging in the shops for bargains but things were very different now and she couldn't help but wonder why. Had Mark really changed since their wedding or were her expectations unrealistic? They had done fun things together on weekends before they were married, such as a drive to the coast with a picnic or a stroll through the woods. They had laughed together then; Mark had been attentive and worked hard to please her, was it so very wrong to expect a little of that kind of treatment now?

'Sarah!' Mark's voice sounded icily sharp as he called her name.

'Coming,' she replied, hurrying down the stairs to find him standing in the kitchen surrounded by their shopping, still in carrier bags.

'I thought you were going to put these away,' he growled. 'This ice-cream is melted, it's ruined!'

Sarah stared around the kitchen in disbelief.

'I did put it away...I'm sure I did...'

'Don't be silly, I suppose the goblins got it all out again eh? Honestly, I can't trust you to do anything right.'

Sarah was completely shocked, so certain she had put everything away, but here it was, all in the carrier bags, she couldn't understand it.

'I'm sorry; I don't know what I was thinking.'

Mark's mood suddenly softened.

'Well, don't worry about it now, I'll help you put it away, then we'll have a nice cosy evening in together, and an early night shall we?'

Sarah's heart sank; was she going mad, had she been so lost in thought that she had forgotten to put the groceries away? How could she have been so stupid?'

Maggie's Friday morning had brought the return of a former client, Matthew West, whom she had last seen over a year ago and was now rather surprised to find once again referred for counselling. Matthew was a young man, now twenty three years old, who had been the victim of a brutal assault nearly two years previously, when a group of five or six teenagers targeted him at random, leaving him with severe facial injuries which required extensive surgery. He found it very difficult to cope with the attack at the time, as a tall athletic young man, he suffered feelings of guilt at not being able to protect himself and compounded the issue by assuming he should be able to dismiss the whole incident instantly and put it behind him. Maggie had originally seen him after the assailants had been tried and received a custodial sentence; the trial and giving evidence having been an emotional time for Matthew. Maggie felt they had worked quite successfully on his issues of fear and guilt, yet here he was again, referred by his GP whose notes made reference to depression and anxiety. Could this be related to the previous incident, or had something else occurred to make him feel in need of further help?

Matthew was early, as he had been on every previous occasion and Maggie greeted him warmly. The scars had healed well and were barely visible in comparison to the last time they had met, possibly the result of successful plastic surgery, but his demeanour initially suggested anything but depression. Maggie paid scant attention to this, knowing how people often disguised their true emotions; she was never one to assume anything on appearances alone.

Following Maggie into the room, the young man suddenly flung his arms around her as if greeting a long lost friend. Managing to extricate herself from his hold she then had to face a barrage of questions about how she had been since their last meeting, questions which took her completely by surprise. This was so unlike the Matthew from the previous year. Clients in general displayed little or no interest in her personal life which was exactly the way it should be and the best way to maintain a professional relationship. It took several minutes to actually get Matthew seated and ready to begin their work on whatever issues were troubling him. Eventually, Maggie was able to ask.

'Can you remember the confidentiality of our sessions and the exceptions to it?'

'Yes, I remember, but don't worry; I'm not going to top myself or anyone else! Gosh it's so good to see you. I've thought about you a lot since we last met, I've really missed you.' Matthew was wild eyed with an unnatural grin stretched across his face. He appeared to be on some kind of high and she began to wonder if he was taking anything.

'Has the doctor prescribed any medication for you?' Maggie ventured.

'Ah, some happy pills eh? Yes he did give me a prescription, some kind of Prozac I think, but I don't know if they're doing any good.'

Noticing that his pupils were dilated and his speech seemed a little slow she went on to ask,

'Are you taking the amount he prescribed?'

'Yes, I don't mind telling you I really needed them and I needed to come back and see you too. You were so good to me; I've missed you so much Maggie, have you missed me?'

Maggie was growing increasingly wary of this unfamiliar Matthew and ignoring the last question asked,

'Are you taking anything else as well as the anti depressants, or perhaps you've been drinking?'

He looked suddenly hurt, crumpling his face into an exaggerated pout, and then let out an unnaturally high pitched laugh.

'Don't look so cross with me Maggie, I'm not drunk, see...' Leaning in closer Matthew breathed on her. There was no smell of alcohol, but his breath had a sickly sweet smell to it.

'I'm not cross, but I'm not entirely sure you are ready for a counselling session today.' Maggie was becoming increasingly aware that he was unable to talk rationally and it would therefore be inappropriate to continue when he seemed somewhat spaced out.

'Matthew,' she looked directly at him, her tone gentle but firm, 'I think the best thing now is for you to go home and come back in a week's time. Are you free to do that or will you be working?'

'Ah ha! Now there's another thing, work. I don't have a job anymore. They made me redundant. I never got back after all that other stuff last year. Redundant and only in my twenties, not fair is it?'

Maggie felt a little sympathy, remembering the physical trauma he had suffered when his jaws had been wired and his injuries had necessitated a series of painful operations, but that Matthew was a very different young man from the one today, and she wondered what had occurred to bring about such a change. This session really needed winding up, it felt all wrong and she was uncomfortable alone with him in the room so standing up, she moved swiftly to the door and opened it wide.

'Aw... please Maggie. I've only just got here.'

'I'm sorry Matthew but I really need you to leave now. Could you make an appointment to see Dr. James again before you come next week?'

Matthew wearily hoisted his tall frame from the easy chair, despondency written all over his face.

'I'm sorry. I don't know what I've done. What have I done?'

Maggie softened.

'It's nothing you've done Matthew, but you don't seem to be quite yourself today and I don't think you are ready to start our sessions yet. Please, see Dr. James and then we'll try again next week.'

Watching as he lumbered up the corridor and stopped at the reception desk, it was almost like watching an entirely different person. He had appeared drunk at first, but perhaps it was the effects of the medication. She would make a point of seeing Dr. James later today to get his take on the change in Matthew West.

Chapter 7

Ellie watched as Dr. Samms left the room, a young nurse scurrying after him and closing the door behind her. Grace Watson turned to face her daughter, swallowing hard in an effort to keep her emotions in check.

'Mum, I know something is terribly wrong. He was preparing me for something bad wasn't he? It's scaring me mum, am I going to be alright?'

Grace enfolded her daughter in a warm hug, pulling her close and rubbing her back as if soothing an infant whilst quietly trying to reassure her.

'Yes Ellie you are going to be fine, really. Don't worry about that.' Her daughter released the breath she had been holding then pulled away, asking with urgency,

'Then will you tell me please! I feel that everyone knows something which I don't and if it's about me, I want to know... I need to know Mum.'

Grace stroked her daughter's arm then took hold of her hand which was trembling with fear and frustration.

'It's okay. Don't get upset, I'll tell you.' Sitting up straight in the chair and pulling her shoulders back, Grace took a deep breath as if to draw in extra strength.

'You understand you have been unconscious for almost a month don't you?'

'Yes.' The reply was brief; Ellie wanted her mother to get straight to the point.

'Well, as Dr. Samms explained some people lose their memories after a head trauma and to a certain extent that's what has happened to you.'

'To what extent Mum? What is it that happened that I can't remember?'

'Ellie, sweetheart, your memory seems to have lost a few years. But don't worry about it; it could come back at any time.'

'A few years! How many?'

'Nearly ten, it's not 2002 its 2011.' Grace scrutinized her daughter's face searching for a reaction.

'2011, then I'm not eighteen, I am...twenty seven, twenty eight?'

'Twenty eight, you had your birthday while you were unconscious.' Grace looked sheepish as if it was all somehow her fault. Ellie sat rigid in the bed, her mind struggling to process exactly what all this meant.

'What's happened to me in those ten years Mum? Get me a mirror; I want to see what I look like!'

Grace fumbled in her bag then pulled out her compact mirror, reluctantly passing it over. Ellie stared in horror, moving the tiny mirror to examine every part of her face. It was like seeing someone else, someone familiar whom you could not quite place. Fingering her hair, it seemed longer than usual and lighter too, had she resorted to colouring it? Her brain was working at speed with plenty of questions but no answers. Turning to look at the name above the bed, she read aloud,

'Ellie Graham, I'm married aren't I?' Her eyes reflected the sudden fear of not knowing who she was, but Ellie could still put two and two together; the young man... the baby.

'Mum, tell me please, tell me everything!'

'Yes Ellie, you are married. That was your husband, Phil, who came in yesterday with your son. You are very happily married, and little Sam is a beautiful child. You have a good life Ellie, a really good life.' There was anxiety in Grace's eyes as she could only try to imagine what Ellie must be feeling.

'How can I have such a good life if I can't remember it? That man, Phil, he was a stranger, the little boy, surely I would remember having a baby?' The sobbing began. Ellie's mind was asking questions she could not answer, how long had she been married, when was Sam born, where did they live and were they really happy? At this moment happiness eluded her completely as Ellie allowed her mother to hold her while she cried; loud sobs racking her body as Grace rocked her to and fro, as if she was a child again.

****

It would be over soon, Sue kept telling herself on Monday entering the dentist's waiting room with a glum face, feeling a little sorry for herself yet at the same time chiding her attitude; it was only a couple of fillings, she was acting like a baby. Approaching the desk, her focus instantly switched to Sarah Beecham who looked in a worse state than herself, and the young receptionist was not the one about to face the dentist's drill.

'Hi Sarah, I'm back again. Are you okay; you look more worried than I am?'

Sarah lifted her head to look at who had spoken and seeing Sue, attempted a smile which didn't quite reach her eyes. A worried look was etched onto her face and she appeared somewhat older than the week before when Sue had last seen her.

'I'm fine thanks.' Her reply was quiet, subdued, 'I'm afraid we're running a little late this morning, it will be another fifteen to twenty minutes until your turn.'

Sue groaned and reluctantly went to sit in the waiting room picking up an obscure magazine, something about the rise in popularity of allotment keeping, just the sort of riveting topic to take her mind off the ordeal ahead. Her gaze more than once drifted to the reception desk where Sarah sat hunched over the seat, her face pale and drawn. Sue wondered what could possibly have happened to make her look so sad. The second receptionist called the next patient and followed him up the stairs to whatever fate awaited him, leaving Sarah alone at the desk and giving Sue the opportunity to try and engage her in conversation.

'Was it a bad weekend?' Sue asked, trying to keep her tone light.

'What?' Sarah looked up, startled by the sudden question.

'You look as if you have the cares of the world on your shoulders.' Sue used the metaphor and was shocked to realise how much like her mother she sounded.

'I'm sorry Sue; I'm not feeling quite myself today.' Her face was pale with her blue eyes set in dark circles giving Sue even more concern. A young newly married girl should be carefree and on top of the world, Sarah had been such a happy, confident child, always laughing; it was impossible not to wonder what had happened to bring about such a huge change.

'Hey, look, what time do you break for lunch? Perhaps we could meet for a coffee and have a natter, my treat?'

'I'd like that.' Sarah nodded, 'I finish at twelve.'

'Great, I should be finished here by then and I'm not due back at work until one thirty. I'll meet you in the 'Coffee Bean' on the High Street.' Smiling and a little easier in her concerns, Sue took her seat again to resume consideration of the benefits of allotment keeping.

Sue waited in a corner seat at the surprisingly quiet 'Coffee Bean', with both hands cupping her numb jaw, feeling more than a little sorry for herself. Sarah came through the door at exactly five past twelve, still looking pale and sad, prompting Sue to comment,

'Gosh, we're a couple of miserable specimens aren't we?'

The words, or possibly the lop-sided way she said them, brought about the release of Sarah's tears which had been threatening to spill over all morning.

'Hey.' Sue instinctively moved closer, sliding an arm around the younger woman's shoulders and shielding her from the view of the few other customers.

'What's all this about?'

'I'm so sorry,' Sarah began, 'You must think I'm a right idiot.'

'Certainly not, but I am concerned for you. I always remember you as a happy, confident little girl, but something seems to have changed all that.' They sat quietly for a few moments until Sue went to the counter to order their coffee, giving Sarah an opportunity to compose herself. When she returned it was to another apology.

'I'm so sorry Sue; I don't know what's the matter with me these days. I know how fortunate I am and I should be on top of the world, but I'm not. It's probably only the change in lifestyle. I seem to be struggling with being married, which is stupid. I love Mark but things aren't quite how I expected them to be.'

'How long have you been married?'

'Ten months, not long really, I suppose its early days yet.'

Sue was not so sure. She and Alan were still relative newlyweds, but her experience was nothing at all like Sarah's. Life had been nothing but bliss since marrying Alan, surely that's the way it should be? At a loss to know what to say to her young friend, and not wanting to interfere or be judgemental in any way, yet deeply concerned, Sue went on,

'Tell me about Mark. Is he as gorgeous as you always imagined Mr Right would be?'

'Oh yes, he's good looking, quite tall and slim with sandy hair and green eyes.' The words, though complimentary, were flat and spoken without the least animation, not at all how Sue would describe Alan. She did not want to press Sarah or bombard her with questions but was troubled by her friend's sadness which was so completely out of character.

'I remember how you always used to plan your wedding when you were what, nine or ten? You would grill me about my boyfriends, hoping I would get married so you could be a bridesmaid, but I was only seventeen myself.'

'I thought you were so sophisticated.' Sarah half smiled at the memory, 'You wore make-up and perfume and I wanted to be exactly like you. I remember being devastated when you moved across town and we hardly saw you anymore.'

'Life moves on, but I wish I'd kept in contact, you were the little sister I never had, and not always in a good way.' Sue laughed, 'And I was really fond of your mum and dad, such lovely people.'

'I know, they were wonderful parents, I was very lucky...' Her voice trailed off and the sadness returned, just when Sue had thought she had cheered her up a bit.

'Hey, they still are wonderful people, they are okay aren't they?'

'Yes, fine... but I don't get to see very much of them.'

'But surely you could make time? Life gets quite hectic I know, but you should always make time for family and friends.'

'Tell that to Mark will you.' Sarah spoke almost sarcastically. It seemed that Sue had struck a raw nerve and was unsure what to say next, but Sarah immediately regretted the words, and feeling disloyal to Mark continued,

'I'm sorry Sue that sounds awful. He's a good man really and does his best to take care of me; yet I sometimes feel he wants me to the exclusion of everyone else. He seems happy for us to be alone all the time, Mark has no family you see, so he can't seem to grasp how important mine are to me.'

'He must have had family at some time?' Sue asked.

'No, none that he can remember. He was brought up in care and moved around to several different foster homes, none of which worked out for him. He doesn't talk about his childhood.'

'But you would think he'd be glad to be part of your family now, your parents do like him don't they?'

'Oh yes, Mum and Dad were delighted when I found someone who made me happy, and at first Mark seemed to fit in so well. It was only after we were married that he decided I shouldn't see so much of them.'

Sue was shocked to hear that last sentence but chose to bite her tongue. If Alan had made those kinds of decisions for her... well, she couldn't even speculate as to what she would do, knowing without doubt that he would never do such a thing. Instead of saying what was in her mind, Sue stuck with an inane comment and replied,

'Perhaps he'll come round in a little while.'

What Sarah had confided made her feel decidedly uneasy. Somewhere inside this unhappy young woman was the carefree little girl she had known over a decade ago and Sue decided there and then to seek out that little girl and find out what was really troubling her. Suggesting that they meet again was an idea which seemed to appeal to Sarah but one which would prove difficult unless again it was during her lunch hour, which seemed to be the only time Sarah Beecham had to herself.

Chapter 8

Maggie guarded Friday afternoons jealously, avoiding booking any clients, private or otherwise, to give her a few precious hours of 'me' time. Sometimes she met Sue for lunch or used the time to do some shopping or visit the hairdresser. If Peter was working at home and felt up to the exercise, they would have a light lunch and then take their dog, Ben, for a long leisurely walk. The Friday after meeting with Matthew West again, she was especially pleased to find Peter in his office at home. Maggie was decidedly uneasy about the change in Matthew; he appeared to be a completely different person to the young man of previous visits. Although she would never share specifics with Peter, she could offload some of her own feelings about work and as it was a fine, dry day, they ventured out after lunch to exercise Ben and blow off the cobwebs from their working week.

Walking and talking always seemed like therapy to Maggie. They did their 'best talking' when out together, working through little problems or discussing decisions they needed to make without the distraction of the telephone constantly interrupting them.

'I had an appointment with a former client today, someone I haven't seen for over a year.' Maggie began her tale as they set off from home, choosing her words carefully.

'I hadn't expected to see him again but he's back and I'm not sure that I am comfortable about it.'

'In what way?' Peter asked, picking up on the uneasy tone in her voice.

'Well, he appears to have changed. Last year we got on really well, and I was pleased with the progress he made, but today I felt uncomfortable, he acted strangely which made me feel so uneasy that I asked him to leave after less than fifteen minutes. I thought he was under the influence of something, which could be the effect of his medication, but it seemed as if I was meeting a totally different person.'

'Does he want counselling for the same problem?' Peter knew his wife would never cut a session short without serious concerns.

'I thought it might be related. His referral notes suggested it was, but I'm going to see Dr. James before next week to see exactly why he referred him.'

'You will be careful Maggie won't you?' he asked.

'Of course, but don't worry. I'll probably pass him on to a colleague; I'll see what his doctor says first.' She knew Peter worried about her and with good reason. Before they had begun seeing each other Maggie had been assaulted by the husband of one of her clients. It had been a difficult case and the police were eventually brought in after this man had tried to scare her off with threats and even by poisoning her dog. Maggie had a tendency to play down the whole incident, typically looking for the silver lining, which in that particular case was that her friend Sue, who had supported her throughout that time, met and eventually married the detective who had handled the case. Her client, Julie, had also become a friend and Maggie had been able to help her and her children throughout a devastating and complicated time which ended with the death of Julie's husband in an explosion.

Peter squeezed his wife's hand, knowing that she would say no more about this client but pleased to know that she was taking action to ensure her safety.

54

Maggie smiled, feeling better for having shared her thoughts, even if they were a bit vague and non-specific. Reaching the edge of the copse, which was actually the spot where Maggie had been assaulted, Ben strained to be let loose. Peter unfastened the lead and they watched him run off into the trees, tongue lolling from his mouth and his tail wagging frantically in complete little circles. They smiled at this comical sight, continuing slowly around the border of trees, giving their dog time to explore territory which he must surely know intimately after the hundreds of walks they had taken there.

The topic of conversation switched to their impending house move as Maggie said,

'I'll miss this walk and I'm sure Ben will too. On the whole we have been very happy in our little home here.'

'I know, but it'll be great to have a bit more space and I'm really looking forward to having a proper home office.'

'And what's wrong with my old kitchen table?' Maggie prodded him playfully in the ribs.

'Absolutely nothing, except I've promised it to the scouts for bonfire night this year.'

She chuckled; they were both looking forward to moving into their new home together. Peter's flat had been far too small for them both with Ben and their cat, Tara, so they settled in Maggie's little terraced house after their wedding, knowing that it would be a short term arrangement. With the money from the sale of the flat, they had bought an old barn, perfect for conversion into a comfortable, single storey dwelling. It was on the west side of town, not quite out in the sticks, but away from most of the built up areas. The barn was on one of four adjoining plots they considered and the one they had eventually decided would best suit their needs. It had outdoor space, mostly comprising of a cobblestone courtyard which Maggie could envisage with huge pots of trailing geraniums and overflowing window boxes. It was bordered with a six foot stone wall on two sides, shielding it from the elements and giving a degree of privacy, with a low stone wall completing the enclosed courtyard and a double gate for vehicle access. The house faced south with views over open countryside from both the front and the back, it was perfect for taking walks with Ben and an ideal sun trap to relax and enjoy their free time. Since they had bought and begun work on their new home, the other three plots had also been sold. Two would be conversions into single dwellings similar to their own, but the largest plot had been bought by a local builder who was pulling down the old outhouses and building six new homes, all with reclaimed stone and sympathetically designed to fit in with the character of the surrounding properties. Planning permission had been granted and Peter's firm had been engaged to design the new houses. It would create a small community and as it was barely a mile from the outskirts of town they were in no danger of feeling isolated. Maggie and Peter's home was the only one which was anywhere near completion. Peter's partners in business, Richard and Charles, had drawn up their plans as a wedding gift and during the last year, the newlyweds had watched the transformation as their own little bit of history was lovingly restored, and now they could hardly wait to move in. Recent weekends had invariably been spent in choosing fixtures and fittings and now the decorators were busy with the final details, meaning that their new home was ready to be carpeted and furnished. The following day, Saturday, would see Maggie and Peter meeting the builder to look for any 'snagging' which may need attention and the carpet fitter would also be there for most of the day, fitting the bedroom carpets. They were looking forward to reclaiming their weekends and being able to furnish and add the finishing touches to their new home.

****

The side room door was open allowing Ellie to see her mother talking to Dr Samms beside the nurses' station. The doctor's wide back blocked Ellie's view of Grace so she could not see her face or pick up any of their conversation. They would surely not simply be exchanging pleasantries about the weather but discussing Ellie, which was frustrating to say the least. Doctor Samms had visited her earlier in the day, checking the notes at the end of the bed and asking how Ellie was feeling. Her answers had been rather curt having woken that morning inexplicably angry, with herself, her parents and even the doctor whom she knew was only trying to do what was in her best interests and who had been so pleasant to both herself and her mother.

Yesterday, learning the full extent of her memory loss, Ellie had been devastated and sobbed for what seemed to be hours on her poor mother's shoulder. Wild thoughts had spun through her mind at an alarming rate; she did not know who she was any more, what had happened in her parent's life during the last decade, but worse still what had happened in her own. It was inconceivable to think that she had met and fallen in love with this man Phil, married him and even given birth to a son! To the present Ellie, Phil and baby Sam were strangers; she had no memories of either of them at all. Yesterday a CT scan had been scheduled and the doctor assured her this morning that it was completely normal, but if that was the case why could she not remember a whole decade of her life?

Watching Dr. Samms talking with her mother now, Ellie regretted being so abrupt earlier, and resolved to apologise as soon as the opportunity arose. Grace Watson stepped out from the big man's shadow and moved towards her daughter's room. Ellie couldn't help but notice how her mother's expression changed from one of grave concern to a forced smile on seeing her daughter's gaze, which did not fool Ellie one bit.

'Hi love.' Grace bent to kiss her, 'The doctor is really pleased with your progress, the scan showed nothing of concern at all.'

Ellie resisted asking the question which she was heartily sick of asking everyone, that of why she had no memory. Instead she played along with her mother's forced brightness, returning a smile of her own and feigning interest in Grace's chatter about minor problems with the busses that day. When the initial conversation ran dry, Ellie looked directly into her mother's eyes and asked,

'This is what, day three Mum? What's going to happen to me?'

'You don't need to worry about that now, get plenty of rest to build your strength up.'

'I'm getting all the rest I need. What was Dr. Samms telling you?'

'I told you Ellie. He is pleased with your progress and the scan results were fine.'

'What else Mum, what about tomorrow and the day after? He must have said more than that, don't hold back on me please, I need to know.'

Grace looked away from her daughter, earnestly studying the pattern on her skirt whilst trying to frame an answer, eventually deciding that the best way was to be completely honest.

'The truth is that we don't know what to do for the best. You can stay here for another couple of days until you are a little stronger but we can't decide what the next step will be. There is simply no way of knowing when your memory will come back.'

'And don't I get a say in these decisions?' Ellie tried to sound calm, although a little of the anger from earlier in the day was surfacing again. Yes, she could understand how hard this had been for her parents and had no desire to make matters worse, but she needed to know what was going to happen in the immediate future. The frustration was again gnawing at Ellie as Grace tried to explain,

'Phil wants you to go straight home from here. He has missed you and so has Sam, it's been a terribly worrying time for him. Your dad and I thought it might be better if you came to stay with us for a while, only until you feel a little stronger and Dr. Samms has suggested some kind of psychiatric help, or counselling perhaps, which could be residential or as a day patient.' Grace's face was drawn, her eyes framed with dark circles and Ellie's heart ached for her.

'Oh Mum. It's such a mess isn't it? Is memory loss a psychiatric problem, does the doctor think I'm going insane or something?'

'No sweetheart, of course not, I think he has a dilemma; physically you'll be ready for discharge in a couple of days, but we are really not sure what will be the best course of action to take. Amnesia is a psychological issue and he thinks treatment of some kind would be appropriate. Have you thought about what you want to do next?'

Ellie rolled her eyes,

'Oh mum, I've thought of nothing else. I am apparently a wife and a mother, something I'm struggling to come to terms with, but I can't go and live with Phil, he's a stranger, and Sam seems a lovely little boy, but I don't even remember giving birth to him and I have no maternal feelings whatsoever.' Ellie was exhausted, feeling as if she was lost in a thick fog which not only surrounded, but threatened to suffocate her as well. Grace took her daughter's hand and continued,

'Phil is coming in this evening and bringing Sam. We persuaded him to give you a little time in the circumstances, but he's desperate to see you, hoping that if you spend time together your memory will come back and you can be a family again. I can't stop him coming in Ellie, he needs to try.'

Chapter 9

Phil Graham changed his son's clothes for the second time in less than an hour. He so wanted Sam to look his best, but he had a tooth coming through and the constant dribbling had again soaked the front of his t-shirt.

'Here you are Sam; the top with the giraffe on, Mummy loves this one.' Phil almost lost control then, close to tears, yet he knew he must not let go. He had promised himself he would be strong for Sam and Ellie. The tears would have to wait until he was alone when he couldn't stop them, especially at night; climbing into the big empty bed, feeling so lonely without Ellie beside him...it was almost too much to bear. But during the day Sam kept him busy, he too was missing his mother, but had adapted as children do. Of course Sam had no understanding of this nightmare they were living and Phil had to work hard to keep his baby son happy. As for himself, well he had no idea what was going to happen and when things would return to normal, or indeed if they ever would. He had hit rock bottom after Ellie's accident when it was touch and go whether she would survive and then came the wonderful news that she had come out of the coma and spoken to Grace and the hospital staff. Phil had been so happy taking Sam along to visit, only to be plunged right back down when his wife clearly did not know who he was. Ellie had stiffened when he kissed her and looked at him with such horror that once again his life seemed to be collapsing around him while he was forced to watch, powerless to control what was happening to his family, his universe.

Dr Samms had been understanding but could in no way predict how long it would take for Ellie's memory to come back any more than he could. Grace too had been wonderful and his boss at work had insisted on him taking extended leave for as long as was needed. But what would be the next step? How long could this go on? No-one had answers and it was so hard to hope when there seemed to be no end in sight. Yet by far Phil's biggest worry, the one he couldn't verbalize, was that his wife had somehow blocked the last ten years from her memory because she had been unhappy. They appeared to have everything and Sam had been very much a wanted baby, the three of them were so happy, or were they? How could Ellie not remember their wedding, the honeymoon, the birth of their child? Could she sub-consciously not want to be a wife and mother? All these terrible thoughts were swimming around his brain but he hardly dare voice them, even to himself. Phil was desolate.

****

Sarah couldn't find her purse anywhere even though it was always in her bag and today Marie was collecting for one of the dental nurses who was leaving on maternity leave and she wanted to contribute to the gift.

'Where on earth is it?' Sarah muttered to herself digging deep into the corners of her bag. Sarah always carried her purse, even when changing bags she invariably swapped her purse together with her mobile phone and diary, feeling quite lost without those three basic items.

'I'm sorry Marie; I must have left it at home. Can I give you my contribution tomorrow?'

'Yes, no problem.' Her colleague replied but Sarah felt she was letting the side down knowing Marie had wanted to shop that lunch time.

'I was going to put in ten pounds. I can bring it tomorrow so if you're able to sub me I'll repay you then, okay?'

'That's great Sarah; we'll have nearly a hundred pounds. I am so going to enjoy spending that on baby things.'

Sarah smiled trying to put the incident out of her mind and concentrate on work; she really was doing some stupid things lately which normally would be so out of character.

When Mark arrived to pick her up from work, Sarah decided not to tell him about the missing purse. It had to be at home, she hadn't been anywhere else besides home and work so there was no need to upset him, she would find it as soon as they got in. However, Mark pulled the car up outside a newspaper shop,

'I didn't have time to get my paper today, would you pop in to get one for me?' He asked.

'I, er, I haven't got any change...have you ?' She asked.

'No, get a note changed, you'll need some anyway.'

Sarah could feel the colour flush to her face. Why such a silly situation should make her feel this way she didn't know, it was as if she was a child trying to hide some sort of mis-deed.

'I've left my purse at home.' she blurted out.

'What? Are you sure? You haven't lost it anywhere outside have you? Your bank card will be in it.'

'No, I'm sure it will be at home, I must have forgotten to put it in my bag that's all.' Sarah tried to make it sound as if it was no big deal but Mark clicked his tongue on the roof of his mouth in annoyance and drove away a little too fast.

'What about your paper?'

'It's more important to find your purse. You don't seem to realise how serious this kind of thing is Sarah. Your mind is anywhere but where it should be these days.'

Sarah sat in silence for the rest of the journey home, feeling like a naughty schoolgirl.

Mark raced into the house as if it was on fire,

'Where did you leave it?' He demanded.

'It'll be upstairs in the cupboard by my side of the bed.' She ran ahead hoping to put her hands straight on it. A sense of panic began to take over when it was not on the shelf with the bag she had used yesterday and she began to scramble about, looking under the bed and anywhere else it might be.

'Have you found it yet?' Mark's voice was loud and harsh behind her, making her jump.

'No, but it must be here somewhere...'

Mark began to open all her drawers and the wardrobe, rooting among her possessions with obvious anger and showing little care. Sarah felt strangely resentful at him doing this, but was afraid to ask him to stop. After several minutes of frantic searching Mark slammed the wardrobe shut.

'I'm going down to ring the bank.' he barked, 'that is if it's not too late, anyone could be using those cards.'

'But I'm sure it will be here somewhere, I can't have lost it outside.'

'How do you know someone hasn't stolen it at work?' Mark's eyes narrowed with fury.

'I always keep it in the staff room, the public can't get it there and my colleagues certainly wouldn't take it.' The suggestion shocked Sarah.

'Honestly. Sometimes you are so naive!' With that he turned abruptly, slammed the bedroom door and went downstairs to phone the bank.

Sarah sat on the bed, trembling, not knowing what could have happened to her purse, she was usually so careful. But in truth her husband's reaction was more upsetting. Did he not realise that she felt bad enough without him heaping more pressure on her and adding to it? A little support and understanding would have been in order, but that seemed to be a thing of the past.

After a while the sound of Mark banging around in the kitchen prompted Sarah to go down and make their evening meal before he found anything else to grumble about. At the top of the stairs she heard him shout her name from the kitchen and hurried down only to be greeted by a steely glare.

'Open the fridge.' Mark ordered.

'What...?' She didn't understand.

'Just open the damned fridge!'

Sarah did, and sitting on the middle shelf in full view was her purse. She honestly did not know what to say, but Mark got in first.

'What on earth were you thinking about? I'll have to go and ring the bank again now to tell them you have found it. How does that make me look? You can be such an idiot sometimes.'

Sarah burst into tears; she simply had no idea how it could have got there. Her scowling husband marched from the room, leaving her alone while he went back to the telephone.

The evening passed in an icy, stubborn silence. Sarah warmed the casserole and they ate without conversation, she was simply too weary to make the effort even though it would be expected of her. Why could he not laugh at the absurdity of the situation instead of turning it into a drama? Surely everyone had those kinds of moments when they did stupid things, but nothing was spoiled, it was really quite funny, wasn't it?

Standing at the sink washing the dishes Sarah heard Mark come into the kitchen but was reluctant to turn and face him. She reached for the bleach from beneath the sink and began a vigorous cleaning of the bowl.

'Leave that.' Mark told her. Sarah stopped, yet still did not turn around. He moved over and circled his arms around her waist, pushing the hair away from the back of her neck to kiss her warm skin.

'You've been a silly girl again haven't you? But it's all right, I'll look after you whatever happens. Why don't you go and have a nice bath and I'll be up soon for an early night. You can make it up to me then, can't you?'

Sarah's mind began to whirl. 'What the hell does he mean, 'whatever happens?' Is he trying to make out I'm going senile or something?' she thought, but rather than make an issue of it she turned to go up stairs knowing exactly what Mark wanted and resigned to it. Sarah still did not turn to look at her husband; had she done so she would have seen the silent twinkle of laughter in his eyes and his smug smile following her from the room.

Chapter 10

'You know there is nothing we can do, don't you?' Mary Green addressed her deputy head teacher, an emphatic tone making it clear that her words were a statement as much as a question.

'But Mary you should see the child; so quiet and listless with no life in the poor little soul, and absolutely no energy. It's simply not normal for a five year old, I don't think she's eating properly either, which would explain the lethargy and she's so thin and pale.'

The head teacher could see how strongly her deputy felt about this situation, they had had this conversation before. Removing her reading glasses and giving Ruth her full attention, she continued,

'We've done all we can by making social services aware of our concerns.' Mary's voice had softened now,

'What you're accusing her parents of is neglect and you know as well as I do how hard it is to define neglect let alone prove it, and we're not qualified to give an opinion on whether the girl is mal-nourished. Leave it to the child protection team, they know the family and are monitoring the situation. Of course if you ever see signs of physical abuse that would be different, but we really have gone as far as we can go with this one.'

'Yes,' replied Ruth, her expression mirroring the concern she felt, 'I know all that, but it breaks my heart to see Lucy looking so neglected. She looks as if she needs a good bath, a hot meal and a whole heap of affection. Heaven knows when she gets any of that.'

Five year old Lucy had been in Ruth's class since beginning school the previous September. A small girl with a pale almost translucent skin, elfin face and straggling, badly cut mousey hair, she had three older brothers, only one of whom Ruth had taught and they all had a reputation for causing trouble in the school. Looking at Lucy it was difficult to believe she came from the same gene pool as her brothers. They were big boned, tough looking boys; although in fairness it could have been their short cropped haircuts which gave the impression of being hard. There had been very little parental support in regard to homework, or any interest shown in school activities but they weren't the only family to fall into the 'disinterested' category. Ruth had rarely seen Lucy's mother and there had been cause to seek her out after school on only one occasion, when the child had head-lice. Ruth had to inform the mother of the school policy of needing the all clear from a health visitor or the school nurse before being allowed back. The woman had looked at her daughter with disgust, as if it was somehow the girl's fault. Ruth had to bite her tongue and force herself to remain polite when giving advice about treating the rest of the family.

In the staff room at break she shared her concerns about Lucy with the other three teachers who were there as she made coffee.

'I have one of her brothers in my class and he's a real pain.' Jo, one of Ruth's colleagues offered her opinion, continuing,

'I had a student teacher before Christmas and he followed her around lifting her skirt up all the time. He thought it was funny especially when his pals giggled and the poor girl was distraught, but apart from sending him to Mary, there was little I could do, he enjoys the attention. I suggested the student wear trousers for the rest of the placement to spare her blushes.'

'Lucy's no trouble at all, yet I worry about her.' Ruth confided, 'I know Mary thinks I'm paranoid but the child is simply not cared for properly. Some people look after their dogs better than they do their children. It makes me so mad, these parents who go on having children without taking any responsibility in looking after them properly.'

'I think they do it for the benefits or to get a bigger council house. Do you know that child benefit for a first child is nearly twenty pounds a week now and for the rest, twelve pounds? Then there's child tax credit, working tax credit.... if they're working that is. Why work when you can make a career out of having babies?' Jo was on her hobby horse again then stopped, suddenly realising how tactless it must sound to Ruth.

'Sorry...' she began, 'I've opened my big mouth and put my foot in it haven't I?'

'It's okay Jo, I haven't given up hope of a baby yet you know.' Ruth reassured her.

'Going back to Lucy,' Meg chipped in, 'Have you ever thought it could be autism or something similar rather than neglect that makes her the way she is?'

'Yes, I've thought about that and possible hearing problems too, but the signs are quite different. Still,' it was time to change the subject, 'I shouldn't harp on about it all the time. Now, where are those chocolate biscuits?'

Driving home from work later that day, Ruth had an image of Lucy firmly fixed in her mind, looking like a waif from a Dickens' novel.

'How could a mother be so indifferent to her own child?' she thought, not for the first time, but then chided herself, disturbed by such angry feelings which were completely alien to her nature. Ruth felt like such a child herself, wanting to stamp her foot and shout at the world,

'It's not fair!' But there would always be children like Lucy with less than perfect parents, Ruth knew this yet it did not make things any easier. Coupled with their problems in conceiving, it made the job a roller coaster of emotions at the moment. Perhaps it was time to consider a change of career, yet having worked so hard to get to where she was, and until recently having always loved the job, that was not an option Ruth really wanted to consider. Being objective was the answer, reason told her, but knowing it and putting it into practise were two very different things. Analysing her thoughts was something Ruth found herself doing more and more often lately, which inevitably brought back memories of her own past and the mistakes she now bitterly regretted. Guilt flooded her mind, reminding her once again that she was far from perfect and was acting hypocritically by sitting in judgement of others. If only things had been different all those years ago she may not have been in this position today.

Deliberately steering any remaining thoughts on the subject to more constructive issues, Ruth tried to prepare herself for the evening ahead, when she and Andy had their first interview with a social worker, the result of an initial enquiry into the process of adoption. Andy was keen to start the ball rolling while Ruth still harboured reservations. Never the less, she had agreed to proceed for her husband's sake, hoping it would turn out to be an informative meeting rather than the first step to any kind of commitment.

Andy was already home having taken a couple of hours off work, showered and changed and was now pottering around in the kitchen.
'Got the sack?' Ruth asked playfully kissing him on the cheek.

'No, I resigned,' he played along, 'Told the boss I had to cook dinner for my beautiful wife and when he wouldn't give me the time off, I quit. But don't worry, he'll be on the phone in the morning grovelling, they can't function without me you know!'

'Hmm, you should be assertive more often; it's certainly put you in a good mood.'

'Sure has, so off you go and have a nice soak in the bath and pretty yourself up, then spaghetti a la Andre will be ready when you return.'

'Pretty myself up? I was your beautiful wife a minute ago. We don't have to go overboard for this meeting you know; it's only a preliminary interview.'

I know that sweetheart, but first impressions count, hmm maybe I should cook for her too?' Andy winked as she turned to go upstairs, he was buoyed with excitement about the evening ahead whereas Ruth did not want to rush things, as she had told Jo, she had not yet given up hope of having their own baby.

****

Leaving the surgery that afternoon, Maggie's thoughts were already on the evening ahead. Peter was working at home and after ringing to let him know she was on her way, he had taken the hint and offered to start their evening meal. Unlocking the car and tossing her bag into the passenger seat, Maggie was suddenly startled by a voice calling her name. Jumping and turning in one motion she was surprised to see Matthew West standing close enough to catch her arm as she turned.

'Matthew... you gave me a fright.'

'Sorry Maggie, you seemed miles away, have you finished for the day?'

'Yes. What are you doing here, have you been to see the doctor?'

'No, but I've got an appointment tomorrow. Would you come for a coffee with me?'

Maggie frowned slightly, uneasy about Matthew's presence.

'I'm sorry; I don't think that would be a good idea.'

'But why not, you've finished work haven't you?'

'Matthew, I'm your counsellor, this is a professional relationship nothing more, and so if you'll excuse me, I'm expected at home.'

Maggie was relieved when Matthew stood aside allowing her to get into the car and drive away. Not having found the opportunity to see his doctor yet, she would certainly make it a priority the next day.

****

Sue looked at the results for the third time and double checked the instructions to make sure everything had been done properly, yet what could be simpler than peeing on a stick?

'Yes.' she whispered grinning at her reflection in the mirror before turning to run quickly down the stairs to catch Alan who was already pulling on his coat to leave for work; he was on a late shift.

Flinging her arms around his neck and almost knocking him over, Sue managed to stop grinning long enough to ask,

'Guess what?'

'Err, you've found a pair of shoes which you thought you had lost?'

'No silly, I have my very own detective for finding things like that, but can you detect this?' Sue waved the strip of card with the result of the pregnancy test beneath Alan's nose.

72

'You're not!' He looked stunned prompting a loud laugh from his wife.

'I am, and your face is a picture... Daddy.'

Alan swung her off her feet, shock instantly converted into joy.

'Really, you are sure?'

'Uh huh. They're pretty accurate these days but I'll put a sample in at work tomorrow just to make sure.' Neither of them could stop grinning, work was forgotten for the moment as the news sunk in.

'Can we tell people?' Alan looked hopeful.

'Not yet, it's a bit early, let's wait for the proper test result. I think we will have to be careful how we tell some people.' Sue suddenly became thoughtful, chewing on her bottom lip.

'What do you mean?'

'I was thinking about Maggie and Peter. Mags would have made a terrific mum, it's such a shame that she and Peter didn't get together sooner.'

'I think Maggie will be thrilled for us, I can't see her being the envious sort can you?'

'No, but I wasn't thinking she would be jealous, it's bound to bring things back to her, missed opportunities and all that.'

'They'll both be delighted for us I'm sure, they have got Peter's family and his little granddaughter haven't they?'

'Yes, but it's not the same. We'll wait a while before telling them shall we?'

'Bet you can't, you share everything with Mags, I'd put money on you telling her before you tell your mother.'

'Oh you would eh? And how much money are we talking about here?'

Alan laughed as he kissed his wife on the nose,

'Fifty pounds if you can afford it.' He then bent to kiss her flat stomach,

'Goodbye Bub. Goodbye Mummy.'

'Bub? What kind of name is that for our firstborn?'

'Well until we know what sex he is, Bub is as good a name as any.' Alan grinned then finally left for work.

Chapter 11

Although not asleep Ellie's eyes were closed as once again she endeavoured to remember the accident but could still recall nothing other than being at college with her friends. Squeezing her eyes tightly shut as if trying to see into the concealed areas of her mind, frustration began to rise. The answers must be there somewhere, memories couldn't be erased without trace, well only in science fiction movies, but this was reality, a strange and frightening reality. The burbling sound of a baby startled her. Phil was standing beside the bed with Sam, wriggling and reaching out his plump little arms towards his mother, making indistinguishable noises.

'Sorry.' Phil spoke quietly, 'Did we wake you?'

'No, I wasn't asleep, just trying to remember.'

'I'm sure it'll all come back soon, perhaps when you get home and see the house and everything?' He balanced Sam on his hip whilst dragging a chair over to the bed. Ellie was pleased that he made no effort to kiss her; it would have been an embarrassing moment for them both but he had mentioned home so she decided to confront the situation straight away without any preamble.

'Phil, I'm not sure I want to come home, I mean...I don't know where home is any more. Mum and Dad's place is home to me and I think that's where I want to go.' The look of disappointment on Phil's face spoke volumes. Ellie was saddened to be the cause of such obvious pain.

'What I'm trying to say is... I can't slip back into some sort of life which I have no recollection of. You seem a really nice man and your baby is beautiful, but I don't know you, how can I come and live with you?'

'Our baby.' Phil said quietly. 'You said 'your' baby, but he's our baby and he needs his mother.'

Again, conscious of Phil's pain, evident in his distraught expression and feeling guilt at being the cause of it, she reached up to take the child, almost an instinctive move and Phil's face softened as he released Sam into his mother's arms. It was a strange sensation for Ellie who could not remember ever having contact with such a young child, but it felt good when Sam patted her face and smiled up at her with his damp little mouth blowing bubbles.

'Hey little fellow, how are you today?' Sam made what seemed to be happy noises, then began to repeat 'Da, da' as he reached again for his father.

'He's really missed you Ellie, he needs you.'

It was difficult to meet Phil's gaze.

'Tell me about our house' her curiosity about the place where she had lived for the last ten years was genuine. Ellie's interest brought a flicker of a smile to Phil's face and he began to describe their house in great detail, wishing it was not necessary but hoping that a verbal tour of their home would jog a memory; anything would be great, something to give him a snatch of hope to cling to. When he spoke of their large family room he asked,

'Do you remember choosing the colour for the walls in there? We had a shade specially mixed but you didn't like it when I put it on. You made me change the colour three times before it was right, that was the closest we came to a row in the first year of our marriage.'

Ellie lowered her head, and looking up at Phil with a barely perceptible twinkle in her eyes, asked,

'Should I apologise now or did I do so at the time?' She asked.

'Well you did eventually apologise, which I of course accepted gracefully. What I never told you was that you were right about the colour all along, it looked so much better third time round, but I was not going to admit it then.'

They both smiled; Phil at the memory and Ellie at the relaxed and amusing way he told the story. He really was a very good looking man; she could see why she had fallen for him. Strangely their conversation flowed and there were none of the embarrassing silences which might have been expected. Phil chatted comfortably about their house and the work they were doing in the garden which was surprisingly interesting, prompting questions, the answers to which she was genuinely wanted to know.

'How old is Sam?' Ellie watched the little boy snuggling into his daddy's arms, sucking his thumb on one hand while rubbing his eyes with the other, looking so tired now.

'Nearly eleven months, his birthday's not far away. I was hoping that perhaps you might be back with us by then?'

The idea came as a surprise and there was a few moments silence before her answer.

'It would be very strange for me to come home with you and Sam just yet and I don't think I could cope with the pressure of having a time limit. How would you feel if I went to my parents for a while, to see how things work out and give us both a bit of time?'

'I'd rather you came home.' Phil's face fell, reflecting his distress, 'But if that's what you want then that is what we'll do. You will come and visit though, won't you? I'm sure if you see the house you'll remember.'

'I hope so, but can we take it a day at a time, no timescales or anything?'

'A day at a time.' he repeated slowly in somewhat reluctant agreement.

****

Peter's face took on a grave expression as Maggie related the latest encounter with Matthew West.

'I really don't think you should see him again. Can't his doctor refer him to someone else?'

'I've already decided that. I'll see Dr. James first thing in the morning and when Matthew goes for his appointment later he'll be told there has been a change.'

'Good.' Peter was relieved, he sometimes worried that Maggie took on clients with some very complex issues who could potentially be dangerous. He knew that she loved her work partly because of the diversity of the problems she encountered, but he would be much happier if she could stick to bereavement counselling or at least be able to choose which clients to take on. Typically his wife was smiling again, already changing the subject and pulling yet another cardboard box into the centre of the room, intending to fill it with their books, ready for the move to their new home at the weekend.

The packing was interrupted by the door bell and Maggie was surprised to find Sue outside looking somewhat unsure, a rare thing for her usually extrovert friend.

'Hi.' Maggie stepped back for their visitor to enter, 'This is a nice surprise, you didn't say you were calling round tonight.'

'An impulse visit, Alan's on late shift and I wanted to have a chat.'

Peter immediately took the hint and went upstairs to the spare bedroom where most of his belongings were stored.

'I've plenty of sorting out to do so I'll leave you girls to your chat.'

'Sorry.' Sue said as he left the room, 'I didn't mean to interrupt your evening.'

'It's no problem; you can help sort these books if you will?'

'No, really, I can't stay long.' Sue seemed to be avoiding eye contact which made Maggie a little concerned.

'Is everything okay?'

'Oh yes, nothing's wrong... You know this visit will probably cost me a fortune.'

'Why's that?' This was really a puzzle now.

'Alan said I would tell you first, and I said I wouldn't but here I am and so he seems to have won the bet.'

'You're pregnant!' Maggie beamed.

'How did you know?'

'Oh come on, you're all on edge, which I presume is because you are worried about telling me in case I get all upset about not having children of my own.'

'Right on the head, you amaze me, but it is okay with you isn't it?'

'Of course its okay, I'm thrilled for you. You will make a wonderful mum. Is Alan pleased?'

'Yeah, like the proverbial dog. But it's early days; I perhaps shouldn't be broadcasting it yet.'

'Well I'll say nothing until you're ready but I'm so happy for you both. You know I really have come to terms with not having my own children and Peter's family is an unexpected bonus. My life's pretty good at the moment, I have no complaints whatsoever. I can tell Peter can I?'

'Of course.'

Wasting no time in sharing the good news, Maggie called upstairs and when Peter came down, Sue told him the reason for her unannounced visit. Naturally he was delighted, kissing her and making a fuss over finding her a comfortable seat while he made them all a drink.

'Oh come on,' Sue said, 'Women have been doing this for years; it's not an illness you know!'

He laughed but still went to get the drinks.

'Mine's an orange juice.' Sue told him and he gave a mock salute as he left the two women to their baby chatter.

****

The first job for Maggie the next morning was to see Dr. James about Matthew West. Like all the doctors in the surgery he began appointments at eight o'clock so she had to catch him in between patients. Relating Matthew's visit for counselling, she then told him about the incident in the car park.

'I'm probably over reacting, but something doesn't feel right about his behaviour. I wondered if he's on some kind of medication?'

'Only a low dosage anti depressant, nothing that should make him act out of character.'

'That's exactly what it is, out of character. We had several sessions last year and he was a totally different person. I don't know what has happened to change him, but I feel decidedly uncomfortable in his presence.'

'I'm not surprised. It sounds as if he's developing an unhealthy attachment, you're right to be concerned. He has an appointment with me this afternoon and I'm going to put him on Steve's list, I'll tell Matthew I have decided that it's the best course of action for now.'

Maggie thanked Simon and left him to continue surgery, returning to telephone Peter and tell him what had transpired, knowing he would be relieved. She was aware that her husband worried about her but was always mindful of her own safety; it had been a priority which was drummed into her and her fellow students during their training. The day had got off to a good start, it felt as if a weight had been lifted from her shoulders with the knowledge that Matthew's issues would be better served by her colleague, Steve.

Chapter 12

'Well, so much for keeping this pregnancy a secret. Alan knows me too well; he said I couldn't keep quiet.' Still in a buoyant mood, Sue failed to notice her friend's reaction. Sarah was saying all the right things but her heart was not in the words of congratulation.

'Are you all right?' Sue asked, suddenly aware that her news had been met with a mixed reaction. Sarah smiled, attempting reassurance, she was genuinely pleased but this inevitably prompted thoughts of her own marriage and if she was totally honest, a touch of envy in the presence of Sue's obvious happiness.

'Your turn will come you know.' Sue assured her, assuming Sarah was thinking of her own situation.

'I know, well...perhaps. I don't think I'm ready to start a family, in fact I'm not sure of anything much at the moment.'

'What is it Sarah? Would talking help, you know, a trouble shared and all that?'

The women were enjoying midday coffee together, something they now managed to do almost weekly. They had quickly resumed their friendship based not only on their acquaintance of years gone by but on a different level now, as two recently married young women. Sarah looked at Sue's concerned expression and the kindness she saw in her eyes made her look away, concentrating on her coffee cup, idly tracing her fingers around its rim.

'Hey, whatever it is can be sorted you know.' The words were sadly deficient but unless her friend confided a little more Sue did not know what else to say.

'I'm sorry, I don't mean to put a damper on your news, forget it, it's nothing really.'

'From your expression it doesn't look as if it's nothing. Perhaps sharing will help?'

'You would think I was stupid or something, in fact I feel as if I am going round the twist sometimes.'

'Why on earth would you think that?'

'Oh, it's hard to explain...I've got everything I ever wanted but I feel so low. And I really do think there is something wrong with me, I seem to be doing such stupid things these days and then I don't remember doing them. Can someone of my age get Alzheimer's?'

'Alzheimer's! I would imagine it's possible but highly unlikely. Whatever makes you think that?'

Sarah began the tale of losing her purse and finding it in the fridge.

'But that's hilarious.' Sue laughed, 'We all do stupid things sometimes, it doesn't mean you've got Alzheimer's.'

'Well... that's not the only thing. I somehow managed to delete all the contact numbers from my phone, I still don't know how but all my friends' numbers were there, then they weren't and it took me ages to get them all again.'

'Oh, I'm always doing silly things like that. I often send texts to the wrong people, it's embarrassing but it's not the end of the world is it?'

Sarah continued,

'The really strange thing was the groceries. I'm sure I unpacked them and put them all away but when Mark came in they were still in their carrier bags in the kitchen, even the frozen stuff. And he gets so cross with me when I make a mistake that I feel I have to make it up to him, you know... to get back in his good books again.'

Sue's expression changed from mild amusement to concern; this was one of those rare occasions when she was lost for words but the silence was broken as Sarah went on to confide,

'I thought being married would be wonderful, our own home and doing things together, but now I find that I don't want to do things with Mark. He's always there and at times it makes me feel as if I'm suffocating and then I'm filled with guilt, it's all so confusing. Do you think I could be having some kind of breakdown? I should be so happy and yet at times I want to run away and hide and I really miss Mum and Dad too, is that natural?'

'Of course it's natural. I must admit to being a bit surprised the other day when you told me you didn't see them very often now. Goodness, I see my mother all the time and I don't particularly like her. It is early days for you still, but perhaps you need to have a little chat with Mark to explain how you feel.'

'Huh, I've tried that but he won't budge and keeps reminding me that I'm his wife now and he has to come first.'

Sue was shocked to hear these words. It was unimaginable that Alan would ever think such a thing, let alone say it but not having met Sarah's husband it was difficult to grasp the full situation, yet she already disliked the man. Sue felt compelled to help, but hadn't a clue what to say,

'Have another try love. He could be surprised at how you are feeling and a few gentle pointers might do the trick.'

'If only it was that simple. Mark seemed to be a different man before we were married, treating me like a china doll, you know, spoiling me with little gifts and things, but that's stopped completely now. He has to have his own way in everything and expects me to do all the running about, and doesn't let me out of his sight except for work. But look, I'm sorry Sue, I shouldn't pour out my troubles on you, we should be celebrating your good news. Cheers and congratulations.' Sarah lifted her coffee cup in a toast to Sue and the new baby, but it was such an obvious effort that Sue felt saddened whilst at the same time feeling utterly useless and unable to offer any kind of help at all. At least she could be there for Sarah and provide a shoulder to cry on if that was what was needed.

****

Maggie had seen Ruth a couple of times now and was aware that she and Andy were making tentative moves towards the possibility of adoption. Travelling to their home and knowing that the couple would have had their first meeting with a social worker to learn more about what the adoption process would entail, Maggie now wondered how that initial meeting had gone.

Her client's face said it all. Ruth silently led Maggie into the lounge, her eyes swollen and face flushed, to sit at opposite ends of the sofa. After a few moments silence, Ruth attempted to speak but could manage no words as yet again the sobbing took over and the young woman dropped her face into her hands and cried. Instinctively Maggie's arm went around her shoulders whilst waiting in silence for the flow to stop. After several minutes Ruth sat up and taking a tissue from the box on the coffee table, blew her nose.

'I'm so sorry, I'm not having a good day today, take no notice.'

'You don't need to apologise, sometimes a good cry is therapeutic and can provide the release we need.' Smiling at Ruth she waited a few more moments before asking,

'Feeling better now?'

'Yes, thank you. It's stupid really, I'm sure you have clients with real problems and here I am dithering about adopting a baby when there are dozens of women out there who would swap their lifestyle for mine in a flash.'

'It's not stupid at all Ruth. This is one of the most important decisions you will ever make; you need to be certain about this. It's not the sort of thing you can enter into without weighing up all the consequences and knowing how you really feel. Would you like to tell me how the meeting went?'

'Ah yes, the social worker...well we had some of our questions answered but the evening seemed to raise a whole lot more. Andy was so excited; you would think the social worker was a stork coming to drop a baby into our laps so we could all live happily ever after. Unfortunately it's not that simple. The lady herself was okay, and explained the procedures simply enough but it seems as if they are doing us a favour and we have to measure up to their criteria and jump through all their hoops. That sounds very selfish doesn't it and in a way I suppose they are doing us a favour, but it's a two way thing surely?'

'In many ways yes,' Maggie replied, 'but they have to be as certain as possible, the same as you do, that things will work out. It's a huge responsibility for them too, although I understand it can feel intrusive at times when you're on the other end.'

'I suppose I understand that really, yet they want us to go to this meeting and on that course, then they interview our parents, our friends and anyone else who may be part of the child's life. It's like being on trial. She suggested we consider taking a child with special needs, or siblings and hinted that I was perhaps too old for a new baby and would have a greater chance of being accepted if we took two, a baby with an older sibling. It really made my head spin and has left us with so many things to consider and discuss and oh yes,' Ruth's face took on a solemn expression once more, 'She also wanted to make sure that we have accepted the fact that we will never have our own child. How can I do that? I don't want to; I know I will never give up hope of a miracle.'

'Of course you won't.' Maggie agreed softly, 'But these are all valid considerations before taking such a big decision. Perhaps their point is whether you will still feel the same about an adopted child if you go on to conceive yourself? Have you had chance to discuss all this with Andy?'

'Oh, Andy's talked of nothing else since then. I suppose he was a little taken aback by the whole process and the length of time it takes but it hasn't dampened his enthusiasm one iota and he talks about 'when' rather than 'if' it all happens.'

'Have you told him how you feel?'

Ruth sighed, relaxing her shoulders and sinking, rather dejectedly, deeper into the sofa.

'I don't want to burst his bubble, it's not as if I have decided against adopting, but I need to be absolutely sure. The most off-putting thing, probably for us both, is the issue of contact with the birth parents. I didn't know that contact is actually encouraged now. They say it's to give the child a sense of knowing where they come from and an understanding of their adoptive status but I can see it causing all sorts of problems in the future. It is hardly my definition of 'adoption' to have the birth parents still around but apparently many of them want an input into major decisions in the child's life, such as which school they go to. Can you imagine always having to get approval from these parents who have most likely been deemed 'unsuitable' to raise a child in the first place? It's ridiculous!'

Maggie silently agreed, letting Ruth vent her feelings on the absurdity of the whole process, but keeping any personal opinions to herself.

'It may be worth making a few written notes on the positives and negatives of adoption. Sometimes seeing things in black and white can help to rationalise issues. Perhaps you could do this with Andy?' Maggie ventured.

Ruth again lapsed into silence, seeming to withdraw into her thoughts as her counsellor finished the suggestion. 'If you set aside time to do this together it might give you an insight into each other's perspective.' Maggie could sense Ruth's frustration; she had reverted to the agitated state of earlier.

'Is there something else troubling you Ruth, other than the adoption I mean?'

Without warning Ruth's tears began to flow again, this time wracking her body as she rocked to and fro, as if in pain.

'I'm living a lie, and I hate myself for it, I really hate myself!'

The vehemence of the words took Maggie by surprise as she again moved closer, laying a comforting hand on her client's shoulder but saying nothing. Ruth continued to sob for several minutes with Maggie beside her, silent tears stinging her own eyes as her heart went out to Ruth.

Eventually Ruth looked up, mopping her face.

'I'm so sorry...' she began.

'You don't need to apologise for anything. And you do not have to explain anything either. Do you want to continue, or have you had enough for today? I could come again next week, or sooner if you like?'

Ruth looked tired and drawn,

'Yes, thank you,' her voice was hoarse, 'I think I have had enough for today.'

Maggie took leave, reminding Ruth that she could ring the surgery to make an appointment at any time if it would help. Her client nodded blankly and the two women parted, Ruth to crawl exhaustedly into the warmth and safety of her bed and Maggie to wonder what on earth those bitter words meant.

Chapter 13

Moving house can be a stressful time for anyone but Maggie's concerns were not simply for the practical aspects of the move, but about Peter's health too. He of course rarely complained attempting to live as normal a life as possible, sometimes to the point of ignoring symptoms, a fact which in turn added to his wife's anxieties.

'Leave the lifting to the removal men.' If she had said it once she'd said it a dozen times in the last few days. The doorbell rang and taking the offending box from her husband, she stood facing him until he moved to answer the door. As Alan and Sue came in, they immediately picked up on Maggie's vibes.

'It's okay now, the cavalry are here.' Sue grinned. 'Just point us in the direction of the work and put the kettle on.'

'Alan, could you please tell this stubborn man of mine to stop carrying heavy boxes down stairs, we are hiring a firm to do this move but there will be nothing left for them to do at this rate.'

'Sorry Mags but I'm remaining neutral on this one, however if Peter would care to direct operations I'll happily be the brawn to his brains.'

Maggie smiled gratefully knowing that Alan understood the situation and would tactfully stop Peter from over doing things, thinking, not for the first time, what fantastic friends they were.

The men disappeared upstairs to finish packing in the small bedroom which had served as more of a storage room for the last few months, whilst the women began wrapping crockery in the kitchen.

'Hey, you've done really well.' Sue commented looking at the already full, neatly stacked boxes.

'Yes, I've been packing most of the kitchen things all week; it's only the everyday things left now. I can't believe we're actually moving tomorrow, it seems as if we have been preparing for so long and now it's finally arrived.'

'You lucky things,' Sue began,

'I'm so jealous. We are thinking of moving too now the baby's on the way. The flat's hardly big enough for the two of us, I can't think how we would manage a baby, or perhaps I should say the baby's equipment, for such tiny little things they certainly need a lot of stuff.'

'Well, the builders have started on the plots near ours; we could end up as neighbours.'

'Great, instant babysitters, I must tell Alan.' Sue was laughing but her mood changed as she took the opportunity of being alone with Maggie to ask about Sarah, drawing on her friend's experience to see how best to help.

'Maggie, can I give you a hypothetical situation and pick your brains?'

'Gosh, this sounds rather serious for a Friday evening.'

'It's about a friend that I've seen a few times lately; a girl who is quite recently married but far from happy. It seems that the 'honeymoon period' ended literally after the honeymoon. Her husband appears to be rather controlling, I would even go as far as to say that she's a bit afraid of him. Anyway, the poor girl's in quite a state thinking she has Alzheimer's or something and strange things keep happening which can't be explained, not just the silly forgetful things we all do, it's a bit more serious than that. This husband seems to be moody too, one minute angry and the next all over her until she doesn't know where she's at. He also seems to resent

91

any kind of social life she might have without him, and I'm sure he keeps her short of money, it seems she has to account for every penny spent.'

As Sue spoke, Maggie had gone quite pale. The number of times she had been asked about a hypothetical situation only to find out that it wasn't someone else, but the person asking. Could Sue's marriage be in trouble? The thought was frightening; they seemed so well suited yet experience had taught her that what went on in a marriage was often so very different to what was presented to the world.

'Sue, is this really a hypothetical situation or are we talking about you and Alan? I'm not going to think any the worse of either of you, newlyweds often need a little help in settling down to such a different way of life.'

Sue threw her head back and roared with laughter.

'You don't really think I'm talking about my marriage do you? That's hilarious; surely you know that we're still dotty about each other? Our honeymoon period certainly hasn't ended...'

'Sorry Sue, I apologise,' Maggie held her hands up to stop her friend elaborating; 'You don't have to go into any details. I'm sorry if I got the wrong end of things, but for you to ask me a serious question is so rare and you would be amazed how often this sort of thing happens.' A little embarrassed at her mistake, Maggie was flushed.

'Oh no Mags, it's my fault, but yes it really is about a friend. She has confided a little of what's been happening and I don't like what I'm hearing. If Alan treated me that way I know who would come off worse! I want to help her but I'm not sure how best to do it. Each time we meet I can sense the tension, it's not right for someone in her position, these should be the best years of her life.'

Maggie considered what her friend had told her.

'You know that joke I told you once?' she asked.

'I think I know the one, but remind me.'

'How many counsellors does it take to change a light bulb? Four, one to hold the bulb and three to ask if it really wants to be changed.'

'Oh yeah I remember, is that the only joke you know?'

'It is actually, I'm not very good at remembering jokes, but anyway what I'm trying to say is, are you sure your friend wants help? Many people live in situations that seem strange to others, but they live that way by choice. Some even enjoy constant bickering and wouldn't change things if they could.'

'I see where you're going with this but I really think that's not the case and I don't know what to do. I haven't even met this husband yet, but I know I don't like him. What can I do to help?'

'You're a good friend to have Sue and perhaps that is all you can do for now. Be there for her and listen. You don't need to offer advice, let her talk through her feelings and decide on a course of action for herself.'

'That's easy to say but I think if I listen to much more I'll be tempted to go round and sort the pig out myself.'

'Yes, then you could get arrested by your husband.' Maggie couldn't resist chuckling at the thought. 'If you think it's appropriate encourage her to seek professional help. Maybe a few sessions with a counsellor will help.'

'Would you see her Maggie? She is registered with our practice.'

'If I got a referral, yes of course I would, but you know I wouldn't be able to discuss it with you don't you?'

'Yeah, I've got used to your confidentiality over the years. I'll see if I can work it into the conversation next time I see her. Thanks for that, I think professional help might be exactly what she needs. Now hadn't we better put the kettle on then do a bit more packing? I can see you being up all night getting ready for this move.'

****

Ellie said goodbye to the nurses, thanking them for their patience and kindness.

'Hey, you were no trouble; I wish all our patients were as easy as you,' the staff nurse smiled and then continued in an attempt to reassure her departing patient, 'Try not to worry too much. I'm sure things will work out. I'm sorry no-one's been able to give you any definite prognosis but this sort of injury is the most difficult to predict, take it one day at a time eh?' Hugging Ellie, the nurse returned to the ward, leaving her in the care of her parents.

Grace and Derek Watson had arrived early to pick their daughter up, knowing how anxious they all were to finally get home. After considering all the available options, Dr. Samms had eventually agreed that it would be better if Ellie was discharged and began counselling through her GP's practice rather than any kind of residential treatment. If that did not work they could always consider other avenues at a later date.

The house seemed somehow smaller than in her mind's eye but it was home and she was glad to be there. The short journey and the exertion of packing her few belongings had tired Ellie more than she expected and so she happily flopped down on the sofa while her mother bustled off to the kitchen to make a pot of tea. Derek sat with his daughter, repeating, only for about the tenth time, how pleased they were to have her home.

'I know Dad. You've both been brilliant and I really am grateful. It's going to seem strange, for you as well as me, you've had the place to yourselves for the last ten years and now you have a sudden lodger billeted with you.'

'We don't mind that in the least and I don't want you thinking you are in the way at all. Your Mum wouldn't settle if you were anywhere else but here, and neither would I, this is still your home for as long as you need it to be.'

Ellie reached over to hug her father, kissing him on the cheek. Derek was a quiet man who did not always express his feelings but she knew how much both of her parents cared for her and was so grateful to have such a loving family. However, as always at the moment, her mind slipped back to the problem of Phil and Sam. For the present this would be home but naturally Phil wanted her to visit their home and she would have to agree to it sometime soon, perhaps after the weekend, if she felt a little stronger. Grace came in with a tray of tea and what Ellie thought to be the most genuine smile to appear on her mother's face since she came round in the hospital. Derek noticed too,

'Your mum is going to love this, having you at home. There's nothing she likes better than playing nursemaid and spoiling folk. I know I disappoint her by not being ill often enough so you'll get me off the hook for a while that's for sure.'

After tea and biscuits Ellie went upstairs to unpack the few things brought with her from the hospital. Her mother had already been to Phil's to fetch some clothes which were now neatly stored in her old wardrobe and drawers. The room had not changed, for which Ellie was grateful. Spending a few minutes reflecting and moving around, touching familiar objects such as the three rather threadbare teddy bears squashed into a child's rocking chair, it didn't seem so long ago that she too had fitted into that chair, which had been a favourite place to curl up with a book when she had first discovered Enid Blyton's famous five novels. Ellie would rock furiously when reaching the climax of the stories, unable to read quickly enough, then disappointed when the much loved book was finished. Running her fingers over the satin pastel quilt which she had slept under for most of her childhood brought a warm rush to her now. The muted pinks, mauves and yellows were faded with age but still an item of comfort and one which, as a very young child, she had rubbed between her fingers each night to help her fall asleep. The clothes her mother had brought somehow didn't seem to fit into this room. They were clothes for the unfamiliar, adult Ellie, bought for someone she did not know, items which on examination felt almost like prying into another woman's life. Picking out a pair of jeans and a soft angora sweater to change into, she was pleased with how they looked and when her mother tapped on the door a few minutes later, Ellie joked that she had found the first positive aspect of memory loss, as it appeared she had gained a whole new wardrobe of clothes. Grace smiled, encouraged at even such a slight positive attitude. Perhaps being at home would be more conducive to her recovery, it was certainly more relaxing for them all than visiting at the hospital had been.

The following Monday would bring the first of the counselling appointments and both of Ellie's parents were optimistic that this would be exactly what was needed for her to remember those lost years.

Saturday morning was cold but dry and bright, a perfect day for moving house. Maggie had planned this move meticulously with the intention of making it as stress free as possible, mainly for Peter but also for her own benefit. The removal men were pleasant and efficient, working roughly on one cup of tea every two hours which suited Maggie's timetable of how the day would pan out. Sue and Alan arrived early, the plan being for the men to supervise the packing up while their wives went to the new house to ensure that everything was put in the correct place. Their job was made easier by the fact that they were moving into a new build and they'd had the keys for a couple of weeks during which time Maggie had cleaned from top to bottom and had already stocked some of the kitchen cupboards. Sue had arrived with a huge cottage pie for lunch, which she put in the new, up and running fridge, and a tin of home-made biscuits, enough for a siege.

'I'm getting worried about you.' Maggie teased, 'In little more than a year you have turned into a domestic goddess. It'll be earth mother soon; I hardly recognise the Sue I know and love.'

Sue looked suitably offended but had to smile at the truth of the words. The changes in her life had surprised her too, her whole value system seemed to have been completely overhauled and all previous priorities had been entirely shaken, yet she had never been happier. Maggie hugged Sue, yes there were changes but to Maggie's mind they served to enhance her character. Sue had always been a compassionate person with a big heart, her world had simply become wider since meeting Alan and she encompassed all those in any kind of proximity with a desire to share her happiness. They were both truly brilliant friends to have.

Peter marvelled at the efficiency of the removal men. He suspected that his wife had given them prior instructions not to allow him to do any heavy work but he didn't mind, he'd had two or three bad days of late and he was glad of Maggie's organizational skills and of Alan's practical, cheerful help. By late morning the van was full and Alan drove them both behind it to the new home. The women were excitable and quite giggly; Peter thought they had already opened a bottle to celebrate although they swore they hadn't.

It was a good time to break for lunch after which the furniture was unloaded in half the time it had taken to pack. Once the removal men left, they began to unpack some of the boxes until Maggie announced they had done enough for the day and Sue and Alan left them alone to enjoy their new home.

The lounge felt spacious in comparison to Maggie's little terraced house. They had bought new furniture for the large open plan living space and contentedly snuggled down on the sofa to relax. Their dog, Ben, had exhausted himself running around his new domain and now lay beside their feet with Tara, who was never far away, curled into his side.

'It couldn't have gone any smoother.' Peter gave credit to his wife, 'I think we are going to be very happy here.' He kissed the top of her head drawing her close. They were both tired and happy to leave the rest of the unpacking until the next day. It had gone well and Maggie shared Peter's optimism, feeling truly blessed and content with her lot in life; this house was right for them and marked a fresh start as a couple. She could picture future times they would share; Peter's daughters would come to stay, perhaps spending Christmas together, and entertaining friends without the space restrictions of the old house would be a joy. It was most certainly a good move

Chapter 14

Maggie had never come across the problem her next client was facing; in fact it was proving difficult to imagine how it must feel to have completely forgotten a whole chunk of your life. Having tried to research the problem on the internet, the case studies all had such diverse elements to them that she came away feeling more confused than ever. The session would simply have to begin in the usual way, getting to know the client and building a relationship of trust with which to work.

Ellie too felt apprehensive, having thought counselling, or therapy, was only a luxury for the rich and famous or those with drink or drug related problems, a view which could have been influenced by watching American films and television, although none in particular came to mind. But the first impression of her counsellor was good in that she seemed to be an ordinary person, easy to talk to with no starchy white coat, permanent frown or deep penetrating eyes. There was also a conspicuous lack of a couch in the cosy little room they had entered. Maggie began with the usual outline of time available, the confidentiality and exceptions which applied to their meetings, and then 'came clean' as it were and admitted to Ellie that she had never encountered a client with amnesia before. Strangely this factor reassured Ellie; it set them on a level pegging as it were, both starting at the same point of ignorance. A smile played gently on her lips as she asked,

'So where do we begin?'

'I think today is going to be an hour of getting to know each other. Maybe if you could tell me what happened to you, or as much as you remember, and what it is you are hoping to gain from our sessions together, then we will be able to form some kind of strategy to reach the goals we're aiming for.'

'To be honest I don't have any goals except for the glaringly obvious one to remember my life. I have woken up thinking that I'm eighteen years old, getting ready to go to uni and suddenly I'm twenty eight and I want to scream at the world that it's not fair. There's also the other 'little' problem of having a husband and a child who are total strangers to me.'

Maggie found herself holding her breath as Ellie concisely summed up her present situation. This poor girl must be so confused, to have lived a whole ten years and yet have absolutely no recollection of it, or of the people who had played major roles in her life was truly frightening. The enormity of the situation prompted her to wonder about her own role and exactly what she could offer this client. It was certainly a challenge and one which Maggie both relished and dreaded at the same time. She had often likened her client relationships as a journey, one in which they walked together. Her role as companion and encourager would surely be tested in this case. Ellie went on,

'Before I left the hospital there was some debate as to what form of treatment would be best for me. The doctor offered a residential place in some kind of psychiatric hospital, or being treated as a day patient there. You were the third option and if I am honest I'm afraid I chose you as the lesser of the evils, even though I haven't a clue what 'counselling' really is or how it works. What exactly do you do?'

Maggie smiled at the idea of being the 'lesser' of three evils, it was similar to winning the raffle, or was it losing?

'With most clients my role is that of being some kind of sounding board for them to bounce their feelings and thoughts around. I sometimes play devil's advocate and try to let them hear their own words and look at things from different perspectives; reflecting and paraphrasing can be useful tools in exploring feelings, and I occasionally ask questions, but there's no obligation to give an answer, I'm only asking to clarify a point or make sure I understand what is being said, it's not because I'm nosey. There are more practical things we can do too, ideas of interest to the individual, which can be used as a form of expression or therapy.'

'What, arts and crafts, throwing pots, macramé or whatever?'

'If that's of interest yes, why not? The human mind is complex and we are all so vastly different so if working with clay appeals then go for it. But you could find that literally throwing pots is much more of a release, not the best china of course. Whatever form our sessions take, you will be in charge. It is entirely up to you what we discuss and what we try and you can be absolutely honest with me, I'm not here to judge you and I certainly won't be shocked at anything you might say. Having an honest and open relationship is usually the key to sorting out issues. I don't have all the answers but hopefully we will make progress as we go along. We also don't have a time frame; usually clients are referred for a bloc of six or eight weeks and very often there is a waiting list. Dr Samms, your neurologist at the hospital, has specifically asked for an open ended time frame. He also asked that we see you straight away and I agreed that you needed to be fast-tracked as it were. So Ellie, what d'you think, will this be the lesser of the evils offered to you?' Maggie asked with a slight smile and a twinkle in her eyes.

Ellie smiled too; liking this lady already and feeling they would somehow gel. Maggie went on,

'I work in the present Ellie, the here and now. Yes, sometimes we have to look back in time but only if it's relevant to understanding yourself better. You have lost ten years of your history, but we still have today, and I have talked far too much. Do you think you could give me a rest and tell me how you are feeling now?'

'It's so difficult to explain. I feel like an eighteen year old girl, and when I came round from the coma my first thoughts were of my A levels and if the results would be good enough to get into uni. When I learned the full extent of my amnesia I felt cheated and afraid. I've done the university course, got married and even had a baby and I can't remember any of it. I had thought initially that it was all some sort of sick joke but I very quickly realised that it was true and it's not only me who is suffering, Phil, my husband and Sam, my baby son are devastated, as well as my parents who desperately want to help but have no idea where to begin. It's such a huge mess and I'm beginning to feel guilty about it all when logically I know it's not my fault. This kind of therapy would always be my first choice although I know so little about counselling. I dreaded going to a psychiatric hospital even as a day patient. Dr. Samms even mentioned hypnotherapy but I need to feel in control. If I was hypnotized it would almost be the same as being unconscious again and I need to be fully conscious and in charge of the present because I've lost being in charge of those ten missing years. Does that make sense?'

'It certainly does.' Maggie replied, 'You have a good grasp of your situation Ellie, which is very positive. I can understand where you're coming from and hopefully we can work through your issues one at a time then you can decide which course of action is best for you.'

'That sounds good to me. I've felt under pressure to do what my family thinks is right but I don't want to be carried along with what everyone else thinks. It's so important to me to be in control of my own life.'

Later that day Maggie was to reflect on her first meeting with Ellie Graham, making brief notes and trying to work out some strategy for their next session. It was going to be a strange yet interesting case, one in which she hoped not be out of her depth. In preparation Maggie had ordered a book from the internet about amnesia which should arrive before the next appointment and she also intended to see her supervisor to get another perspective on the problem. It was undoubtedly going to be a challenge and Maggie relished the thought of what both she and her client might learn.

****

Sarah actually jumped at hearing Mark shout her name from upstairs, his tone of voice clearly indicating annoyance about something. Her stomach clenched, what on earth could be wrong, they had only been home for about five minutes. At his second more urgent shout Sarah quickened her step almost tripping over the stairs on her way, anxious not to upset Mark any more than it seemed he was already.

'What is it?' Entering their bedroom for one awful moment Sarah thought they might have been burgled.

'Look at this mess!' Mark continued his rant. Why the hell didn't you make the bed before we left for work this morning? It's a bit much having to come home to this.'

'I did...or I thought I had...' Sarah could hardly believe what was in front of her. It wasn't only the bed; the whole room looked in disarray with drawers' half open and her robe and nightie thrown across the ottoman.

'I'm sure I...' Tears pricked the back of her eyes which she blinked back, not wanting Mark to see how confused she really was. They had not been burgled; the room had simply not been tidied as it usually was. It was part of the morning routine always to make the bed before going to work, yet thinking about it now she couldn't actually remember doing it. It was the same with most routine chores, such as locking the door, if you thought about it afterwards you could not always remember the actual motion, but if you went back to check, it was invariably locked.

'I'll do it now, it won't take long.'

'That's not the point. It's yet further proof that you are losing it Sarah. Do I have to see to every little detail in this house?'

'It's only an unmade bed.' Attempting to defend herself, Sarah was surprised at how her legs were actually shaking.

'Don't you dare speak to me like that, I put up with enough as it is!' Mark was furious making her regret her words.

'All I ask is that you keep the household chores running smoothly. I'll make the bed; you can go down to start dinner!'

Sarah turned to go back to the kitchen. Her legs would hardly support her and it suddenly dawned on her that she was afraid. Afraid of Mark, of her own husband.

When he came downstairs a few minutes later he went straight to the lounge to put the early evening news on the television. Sarah continued to make their meal fighting the desire to get out of the house, to walk or even run, anywhere. Not wanting to face Mark again, it struck her almost like a physical blow, *she didn't love him!*

What was happening here? Sarah had been so much in love when they married, full of hopes and plans but things weren't as she had dreamt they would be. In truth, she no longer wanted to be with Mark, but this was a marriage, they had made promises, surely these feelings should not be happening. What was wrong with her? Was she losing her mind, doing such stupid things, perhaps it was insanity in which case Mark had every right to chastise her. Maybe she did need him to look after her; maybe he was right after all.

****

'But I need to see Maggie!' Matthew West was almost shouting at his doctor. 'You don't understand, Maggie knows me, we get on so well. Please, ask her, I'm sure she'll agree to see me.'

'We have to do what we think is best for our patients Matthew and in this case I think your needs will be better served with Steve Franks. He is equally as well qualified as Maggie and I am sure you'll get on well with him.' Dr. James was trying to calm the young man who had not taken the news of the proposed change at all well. Sitting now looking like a petulant schoolboy, served to emphasize to Simon James that he had made the right decision.

'Maggie will want to see me, I know, please just ask her.'

'I have already spoken to her and she agrees with me. I'm sorry if you are unhappy about the change but if you give Steve a chance I'm sure you'll get on fine with him, after all, Maggie was a stranger when you first began to see her.' Dr James was not going to change his mind and his expression and tone of voice conveyed this to his patient.

'Steve has an opening next week, Thursday at 10.30 if that's convenient?'

Matthew's response was a resigned shrug as he stood to leave.

'You can book the appointment in at reception Matthew, I'm sure you two will get along.'

Simon could see why Maggie had brought this case to his attention. The young man did seem to have changed in temperament since he had last seen him; hopefully a male counsellor would be able to help him through whatever was troubling him at present.

Matthew waited at reception to make his appointment, frustration rising within him, making him shuffle from one foot to the other, impatient to get out of the surgery and wait to see Maggie. The appointment with Dr. James had been an early one and it was still only eight forty-five. Knowing that Maggie didn't begin work before nine o'clock, he wanted to catch her in the car park, certain she would see him, knowing that he was as important to her as she was to him even if no one else understood. Five minutes later Matthew was standing beside the large chestnut tree which shaded the car park, a spot which gave him the advantage of seeing each car as it turned into the entrance. Watching as

Maggie drove in to park against the boundary wall in a spot reserved for surgery staff and not moving until the car door opened, Matthew sauntered over as if this were a chance meeting. Maggie saw him approach and quickened her step but the place was well chosen and there was no way to avoid him. Forcing a smile of greeting, Maggie then turned towards the door, hoping he would pass by but Matthew easily caught up and swung his body directly in front of her, forcing her to stop.

'Hello Matthew. You'll have to excuse me; I'm running a little late.' Turning to continue, the path was blocked by Matthew who then grasped both of her arms.

'Maggie, please, listen to me, I've seen Dr. James and he wants me to see someone else. Could you speak to him, tell him I'm one of your patients and I need to stay with you?' He appeared agitated and Maggie was unsure whether he was angry or upset.

'I know about the change, I have already spoken to your doctor and I agree that seeing Steve would be better for you.'

Matthew released his grip on her arms and stared aghast, as if she had physically struck him.

'But why Maggie, I thought you liked me?'

'It's not a question of liking you, I generally like all my clients but ours was a professional relationship which worked for a while, but now we have decided it would be better for you to see another counsellor.'

'No!' His voice was rising attracting a few stares from patients entering the surgery. 'I need to see you Maggie. What we have is more than a professional relationship, there's a bond, you can't deny it.'

Maggie tried to take control of the situation, speaking firmly but quietly.

'The only bond was a counsellor/client one. You seem to be reading more into it, which makes me feel that a change is most certainly the best thing. Steve is a fine counsellor and a compassionate man, I'm sure you will get on well. Now I really must go and prepare for my day. Goodbye Matthew.'

This time there was no move to stop her but Matthew stood watching until the doors closed and she was out of sight. It wasn't Maggie's fault, he reasoned, she had obviously been persuaded by the others, he knew she had feelings for him even if they were unspoken. He would try again, find somewhere away from the surgery where they could be alone and talk, Matthew was sure she would come round eventually.

Chapter 15

'Why don't you give it a try?' Sue was working hard at persuading Sarah to see Maggie. It was one of their lunchtime coffee dates and Sarah had confided in her about the latest incident.

'She's really good and I'm sure it would help you. Mags is the soul of discretion, I should know, we've been friends for ages and she never talks about her clients.'

'It's not that, I'm sure she is a lovely lady but I'm scared that Mark would find out, I don't know what he would do.'

'If you're scared to do something which is for your own wellbeing then there's definitely something wrong.' Sue reached out to squeeze her friend's hand,

'I don't mean to push you into this but I am worried about you. Perhaps if you saw Dr. Williams and set the wheels in motion you would have time to think about it, there's usually a waiting list and if you felt better by the time you get an appointment then nothing's lost.'

Sarah looked thoughtful for a moment before saying,

'Okay. I'll see what Dr. Williams thinks and perhaps go on the waiting list.'

'Good, you won't regret it, I promise.' Sue was relieved that Sarah had agreed to consider counselling. Each time they met her concerns for the younger woman increased, her unhappiness was obvious and she was looking increasingly tired and ill. Sue knew Maggie would agree to see her at lunch time, she was always flexible with her working hours and it seemed that this would be the only opportunity Sarah would have without Mark finding out. The very fact that this appointment needed to be made in secret was alarming in itself, being Mark's wife didn't take away her right to make her own decisions. Sue knew what she would do if Mark was her husband.

****

Maggie had spent the evening reading up on amnesia. The book she had ordered had arrived and would hopefully provide some valuable insight into the condition to help her support Ellie. Much of the introduction dealt with the various types of memory loss but she already knew that her client was suffering from retrograde amnesia; this had been documented in the notes received from the neurologist who had referred her. Ellie's case was typical of the kind of head trauma suffered, and the prognosis varied in each case and was therefore unknown. After reading for almost two hours, Maggie felt no further forward. Ploughing through the section on how the brain makes and stores memories through a process of consolidation was all very familiar; much of this had been covered years ago in her training. Her conclusion remained the same as she had initially thought which was that the only way to help Ellie was to encourage her to live in the present, one day at a time. It was clear from this research that any kind of stress would exacerbate the condition which was obvious from an objective viewpoint, but putting herself in Ellie's shoes, stress avoidance was a tall order. Retrograde amnesia was the loss of old memories and Maggie could find no statistics on the length of time before these memories returned or any percentages of patients who never recovered them at all. Everything considered, she thought this was only mildly preferable to anterograde amnesia in which the sufferer could not retain new memories but then that was usually only a temporary amnesia. Swings and roundabouts she thought.

Feeling ready to call it a day, Maggie had just closed the book when Peter looked around the door offering a drink.

'My hero. I would love a white wine. Does it perhaps come with a neck and shoulder massage, I am so stiff?'

'I think that could be arranged.' Peter grinned and headed towards the kitchen.

Maggie's mind went back to an incident in her late teens of visiting a friend who was in hospital after a motoring accident. She had been horrified to find this friend more than a little confused. The girl would say hello, greeting her visitor normally then her attention would be distracted and eye contact broken, the same greeting would then be offered again as if the visitor had just entered the room. Maggie had been embarrassed by this, not fully understanding what had happened. The poor girl must have welcomed her at least half a dozen times and matched that number in reciting the lunch menu. This, Maggie now knew, to be anterograde amnesia, but as a young girl it was an unsettling experience and she had been so relieved when her friend's memory returned to normal a few weeks after the accident. But as for Ellie, would her memory ever return? Peter reappeared and the wine began to work its magic which, coupled with a gentle massage, had the desired effect of taking Maggie's mind completely off work.

****

The house looked the same as any other from the outside, an ordinary suburban home but even looking at it made Ellie apprehensive; would entering the house be the catalyst needed to restore her memories? She made no move to get out of the car and her father patiently allowed her to take her time. It was a semi-detached property with a blue front door shielded from the elements by a tiny porch where the remains of a clematis plant clung resolutely to the wooden trellis. The drive was neatly block paved and the windows were double glazed but not to the detriment of the property's character. All in all, it looked quite inviting, or it would have been if there had not been two strangers waiting inside who knew everything about Ellie, when she knew virtually nothing about them.

'Do you want me to come inside with you love?' Derek Watson offered.

'No, this is something I have to do by myself.' Smiling to reassure her father seemed rather ironical when Ellie was anything but reassured herself. Her parents had been wonderful, protecting her from well meaning friends who simply did not understand how difficult this was. Friends could wait but it was unfair to keep her husband and son waiting any longer.

'Only a couple of hours Dad, no more, right?'

'Okay love, I'll not be late and you can ring if you want me back any sooner.' Derek leaned over to kiss his daughter on the cheek, hearing her drawing in a deep breath before opening the car door. Ellie had no idea what to expect or how she might feel. Her heart rate increased on approaching the door and her face and hands felt clammy. Would she remember anything? Would it all come flooding back and her world once again make sense? Trying to keep her expectations low, for her own sake and Phil's, Ellie couldn't begin to imagine what he must be going through. He must have seen her arrive as the door opened before she had chance to ring the bell, his face a picture of expectation, like an excited child at Christmas.

'Hi, come in!' Phil waved to Derek in the car, who began to pull away now that his daughter was safely handed over.

'Coffee?' he asked, almost too soon.

'Hmm, please.'

'Come through to the kitchen while I make it and we can chat.'

Ellie dutifully followed Phil into the kitchen desperately trying to think of something to say.

'Where's Sam?' was her best offering.

'Upstairs, he still has a little sleep after lunch.'

'Yes...of course.'

Looking around the kitchen while Phil's attention was turned to the coffee machine, Ellie noticed it was beautifully designed, with plenty of storage and one of those islands in the centre of the room with a hob and a feature stainless steel hood suspended above. It almost looked futuristic, such an up to date, good quality space. Silly questions began to crowd her thinking; were they rich? It all looked very expensive; had they chosen this style or was it here when they had bought the house? But what was still uppermost in her mind was what her husband's expectations would be of this first visit. Taking the coffee, Ellie followed him back to the lounge and they sat on the L shaped sofa, not too close, yet not quite at opposite ends. Phil looked at her, his eyes almost pleading,

'Well... do you remember anything?' He paused then jumped in again when she seemed to hesitate.

'Damn it! I'm sorry; I wasn't going to ask that question but it's all I've been thinking about since you agreed to come over, please ignore my stupid ramblings. Tell me how you've been, how are you coping?'

Ellie didn't know what to say, knowing he was desperate for some sign that her memory was coming back. There was absolutely nothing, a complete blank, as if she was visiting this house for the first time. Aware that that was not what Phil wanted to hear, Ellie sipped her coffee, made just as she liked it, playing for time to find the right words.

'I wish I could say yes, but the truth is that I still don't remember anything. I had hoped that seeing the house would bring back something and I'm disappointed too, I really want to remember.'

It was Phil's turn to sip coffee and play for time, but he needed the time to stop himself from breaking down. Logic had told him not to expect a miracle yet he had hoped for something, nothing earth shattering, only a little something?

'Are those photographs?' Ellie tried to turn the mood around. 'Can I see?'

'Yes, please do, I thought they might......you know...'
Ellie smiled,

'It is okay to talk about it. It's not a disease and hopefully it is not a permanent condition either. Now let me have a look.' Picking up the album from the coffee table, Phil moved a little closer to look with her. The first one was of them both when she was heavily pregnant. Instinctively Ellie put her hand on her stomach wondering how on earth she could have had a new life growing within her own body for nine months and not recall a single moment of it. In her blackest moments since coming out of the coma, Ellie had thought this whole situation was one awful sick joke at her expense, a stupid idea she knew, but one that had seemed to come from somewhere in her subconscious mind as she struggled to rationalise her position.

Common sense of course told her it was all true, supported by the stretch marks and an unfamiliar reflection in the mirror. The rest of the photos were mostly of Sam, a careful chronological record of his first year of life. As Ellie slowly turned the pages, it was so strange, the photo's, some of which included her, brought the reality of this unknown life sharply into focus. Phil kept up a running commentary while she turned the pages. It could easily have been someone else's family photos, yet there was no doubt that they were hers.

'I've printed these off the computer, there are loads more, but I thought you might want to take them away with you?'

'That's a good idea, thank you, I'll do that.'

Phil smiled; so pleased to have done something right, and then he jumped up at the sound of Sam crying upstairs. Moving to go up he paused to ask,

'Would you like to come?'

Ellie silently followed Phil up the stairs and into a room at the back of the house. Sam was chattering now, standing up in his cot, watching as his daddy opened the curtains. Light flooded the room revealing such a well thought out space for a baby. Pale blue walls with prettily patterned curtains and bedding, a darker shade for the carpet and purpose made children's furniture. A mobile hung above the cot which Phil turned on making Sam clap his chubby hands together and smile, revealing four little white teeth. He was in no way perturbed at Ellie being in the room and raised his arms to be lifted out.

Downstairs again they sat in the same places, this time with Sam in between. Phil had collected several toys on his way back to the lounge and the little boy began to explore them with both fingers and mouth. He

116

giggled at those which made noises and his daddy was quick to encourage this by tickling his son until the child was actually laughing, a deep, throaty chuckle. Sam provided a welcome focus. Neither of the adults had felt it right to open up a serious dialogue about Ellie's amnesia; it was too soon, it was still an embarrassing topic for Ellie to discuss with someone she felt she hardly knew.

When Sam grew tired of the tickling game Phil picked him up and suggested they looked round the rest of the house. Ellie again followed her husband and son, aware that in each room they entered, Phil was watching for any reaction, looking for signs of recognition and hoping that his commentary would jog some memory. He gave the history of nearly every piece of furniture, recounting stories of things which had happened while they had decorated some of the rooms and chosen carpets and curtains, but all Ellie could do was smile and nod, longing, as much as Phil, to be able to say, 'yes, I remember buying that,' but in all honesty she could not and felt this every bit as keenly as her husband did. On returning to the lounge, Phil stood Sam on the floor where the little boy held himself up against the sofa, managing to shuffle his feet along the carpet towards his mother. Ellie instinctively reached out for him, marvelling at his sturdy little body and determined independence in attempting to walk. When he stumbled slightly she happily gathered him up to sit on her knee. Sam bestowed one of his toothy smiles and reached for her hair, grasping and pulling, making both his parents laugh. It was a strange feeling for Ellie; the distinctive baby smell made her want to hug the little boy closer, which she did, kissing the top of his soft downy head before untangling her hair from his fingers. The baby was happy to sit there and although still hardly believing

117

this child was hers, Ellie was delighted to hold him, an emotion which took her by surprise.

Derek Watson was true to his word and arrived well within the promised two hours. He came into the house and Sam began to pat the sofa with his hands, excited to see his grandfather who eagerly whisked him up in the air bringing the laughter back to fill the emptiness of the room. It was a happy note to end the visit on. There had been no flashes of memory, or recognition of the home once shared with this man and the boy, but it had been an encouraging visit, a cornerstone upon which to build giving them all a seed of hope to grasp hold of and begin to nurture.

Chapter 16

Sarah had made the appointment by telephone and Sue, who had been checking daily for her friend's name on the computer, wanted to be around to find out what the doctor said. It would mean a change of lunch hour, but food didn't taste quite the same at the moment and apart from a piece of toast, she hardly ate at all until the evening which seemed to be her best time of day. There was no chance for even a quick word when Sarah arrived as the doctor was ready to see her, but she had been able to flash an encouraging smile, intending to walk back to work with Sarah to find out how things had gone. Fortunately the surgery was quiet; most of the doctors chose to finish at mid-day to get a good start on their home visits. Tom Williams however made appointments up until twelve thirty and his last patient that morning was Sarah Beecham. He had not seen much of her during her adult years and the name didn't ring any bells at first until he brought it up on the computer, then putting two and two together, realised she was now married. It made him feel his age when a patient whom he still thought of as a child suddenly appeared to have grown into an adult overnight.

'Sarah, it's been a long time, how are you my dear?' His words were accompanied by a wide smile as his arm directed her to a seat.

'I'm okay thanks,' she almost whispered.

'No you're not or you wouldn't be here.' Dr. Williams grinned but was then completely wrong footed when his patient suddenly burst into tears. He picked up the box of tissues from his desk then propelling himself in his swivel chair across the few feet between them, offered her the box. Sarah was embarrassed and tried apologising between sobs but the doctor waved his hand, dismissing any kind of apology as unnecessary and then patiently waited for her to be composed enough to speak.

'That's better,' he said as she finished blowing her nose and mopping her face, 'D'you think you can tell me what's troubling you now?' His voice was gentle, the soft Scottish accent somehow reassuring. Perhaps it was the fatherly tone of his voice which had brought the tears; she had always liked this man who seemed to sense his patient's problems before they even told him.

'I know one of your receptionists, Sue, and she suggested I see you about the possibility of counselling.'

'Okay Sarah, could you perhaps tell me why you feel the need for counselling, then I'll know if that will be the right road to go down?'

'I got married nearly a year ago but I don't seem to be coping well with all the changes. I keep making silly mistakes and I've become forgetful, I'm not sure what's happening but things seem to be getting on top of me, and if I'm honest...I'm not happy anymore.' This last revelation brought the tears back again but Tom Williams waited quietly, this was his last patient of the morning, there was no need to hurry, and it was obvious that something was seriously troubling her. Sarah again pulled her emotions into check whilst searching to find the words to explain her feelings.

'There have been times lately when I have thought that I'm going mad, or possibly have Alzheimer's, is that possible?

'Well I would have to say yes, medically it is, not so much the going 'mad' as you say but there is always the possibility of early onset Alzheimer's, but it really is extremely unlikely and if that was the case then you would probably be the last one to notice, so I am pretty sure we can rule that one out. Tell me what it is that makes you feel this way?'

'It sounds so pathetic now, but I've apparently done things which I can't remember, like putting my purse in the fridge, and not putting the shopping away when I could have sworn I had. Mark, my husband, gets a bit cross at times, but generally he's good to me, I can see how I'm annoying him but he says he'll always be there to look after me.'

'And is that what you want?'

'What do you mean?'

'Do you want your husband always to look after you?'

'Well, yes, I suppose so. We were very happy, but since we married...I don't know, it's not what I thought it would be.'

'What about your parents, have they noticed any change in you Sarah?'

'No, but I haven't seen them for ages, Mark says we shouldn't set precedents by always seeing them, I'm married now and things have to be different.'

Dr. Watson slowly nodded his head. He tapped a few keys on his computer then turned to face his patient again.

'It sounds to me as if you're a little depressed. I have a few questions here which I would like you to answer for me and then we can decide what the best course of action is.'

Fifteen minutes later, Sarah and Sue were going out through the surgery gates heading for the coffee shop, about ten minutes walk away.

'Some of the questions were difficult to answer,' Sarah confided. 'He asked if I had ever had thoughts of suicide! The worst thing was that I couldn't honestly say the thought hadn't crossed my mind, not particularly killing myself, but I have felt so bad that I didn't want to wake up in the morning.'

'So what did he suggest?'

'He thinks you are right about counselling and he says Maggie Sayer has recently finished with a client so he is going to see if she will take me on straight away. He has also given me some anti-depressants, but I'm not sure I want to take those, so he suggested I get the prescription filled and keep them as a last resort in case I feel really bad.'

'That all sounds very sensible to me. So, are you happy to go along with the counselling?'

'Yes I am. I actually feel a little better for having talked to you and the doctor. Thanks Sue, I probably wouldn't have got this far without your encouragement. He also seemed to think that I would be able to see Maggie during my lunch hour... I don't really want to tell Mark what I'm doing.'

Sue gave her friend a little squeeze on her arm as they entered 'The Coffee Bean' for a quick drink before returning to work.

****

Peter woke early to find his wife already up and in the shower. Listening to the sound of running water from the bathroom temporarily disorientated him. It was similar to being on holiday and waking up in a strange room with that momentary panic before remembering where you are, but for Peter it was being in a new house which was confusing for a few heartbeats, but then he remembered and smiled at how life was panning out. This house had been designed specifically with him in mind, all on one level with an amazing office to work in and folding glass doors across the whole wall looking out onto rolling hills dotted with sheep, a spectacular view which made him feel privileged to live in such beautiful surroundings. Maggie teased that he would never get any work done for enjoying the view, but the light and the view were incredibly inspiring and Peter thought he might even get back into the designing side of the business instead of leaving that to his partners whilst he concentrated on costing and the associated red tape of being self employed.

It was only a little over two years ago that Peter had thought, even wished at times, that his life was over. Not thinking he would ever be happy again after his wife had left precipitated a self absorbed depression, drinking way too much and loathing himself for it. Now he often thought he was the most blessed man in the land. Yes, there was the Multiple Sclerosis to cope with, but even that seemed to be controlled at the moment, without a single attack for nearly six months. There were of course bad days, incredibly weary days, and initially some trouble with his eye-sight which had left him with only thirty percent vision in his left eye, but his mobility was still good and there was always hope, like the new drug trials he was following with interest. And to think he had tried to break up with Maggie, how stupid that would have been. In fairness it was for the most altruistic of reasons, she had been devastated when her first husband died and Peter honestly felt it would be the best thing for her if they parted. But at that time the future appeared to be one of disability, of being a burden which, loving her so much, he most certainly did not want to be to Maggie. How fortunate then that she had acted completely out of character and eventually proposed to him. With the kind of work she did Maggie strongly believed that a person should and could make their own decisions, yet she had taken him completely by surprise in telling him that his decision to split up was the wrong one, and that he should marry her and live each day as it came, grasping at the happiness they had in the moment, and leaving the future to take care of itself.

Maggie came out of the shower, wearing only a towel wrapped around her as she moved to the drawers to get her clothes.

'What are you grinning at?' She asked her husband, 'Have you never seen a semi-naked woman before?'

'Not one as beautiful as you!' Peter laughed, getting out of bed to hold his wife so tightly she could hardly breathe.

'Hey, what have I done to deserve this?'

'Nothing, you're just you and I love you,' was the simple answer, as he tugged the towel away from her body.

****

The phone call from Ruth Duncan was not entirely unexpected.

'Maggie? I need to see you...that is, could you come round? I owe you an apology and an explanation for my silly behaviour.'

'Of course I can come round but you owe me neither an apology nor an explanation.'

'Thanks, but I want to tell you about it, I need your help.'

'That's fine, how about after four this afternoon, is that any good?'

'Great, I'll see you then.'

Maggie was unsure how this meeting would work out but determined not to even try to guess what was troubling her client. Pulling up in front of the house she noticed Ruth watching from the window. When she opened the door her face looked pale and tired, as it had three days ago when they had last met, but this time she seemed more composed and even managed a smile of greeting, offering Maggie coffee. The coffee accepted they moved into the kitchen. Several meetings had defined their relationship as almost a semi friendship, the two women being generally comfortable in each other's company, yet Maggie of course always acted within the boundaries of professionalism. Taking their drinks through to the lounge Ruth sighed.

'You're going to hate me when you hear what I want to say today.'

'I doubt it, but if you are sure you want to tell me, please go on.'

'I'm a hypocrite.' Ruth drew in a deep breath, 'I have been pretending that I'm something I am not and I can't live with it anymore.' Tears were threatening to fall but she sniffed them back, continuing,

'When I was sixteen, I did something terrible...I've regretted it ever since but it's something which can never be undone.' Ruth was avoiding eye contact now and picking anxiously at her finger nails. Maggie nodded silently.

'I had an abortion.' Ruth lifted her head searching for the anticipated disapproval but all her counsellor said was,

'And?'

'And what...that's it, I was pregnant and I killed my own baby. Can't you see what that makes me?'

'A grieving mother I should think.'

'No, no you don't understand... I killed my baby. It wasn't for medical reasons or because I was raped, it

125

was simply because I was young and did not want a baby to spoil my life; I wanted to go to university, to have fun. Don't you see how hypocritical this is? I've been pretending to everyone, even Andy...he doesn't know!'

Ruth's tears were flowing freely now and she looked away from Maggie, staring into her lap.

'You have kept a very difficult secret Ruth and now it's preying on your mind, that's what I see. It's incredible how you have managed to hang in all these years. It happened, and as you said, it cannot be undone. What we need to focus on now is accepting it, not beating yourself up about it.'

Ruth slowly raised her eyes.

'Don't you hate me? All the things I've said about young girls who should not have babies. All the burdens I have heaped on you about my mis-carriages and everything, I'm a hypocrite, aren't you appalled by me?'

Maggie was saddened that her client should think she would judge her.

'No, I don't hate you at all. You made a tragic mistake, you did what you thought was right at the time. None of us have perfect pasts without any regrets; we all make mistakes, often repeating them over again. The tragedy is that you are letting your past mistakes colour your future.' Pausing and waiting for her words to register in Ruth's mind, Maggie's heart was heavy for her client, she could almost feel the weight of the secret Ruth had carried so long and could barely imagine how it must feel to live with so much guilt.

'What about your parents, did they know?'

'Oh yes, it was them who suggested the abortion. They knew I had dreams of a career and I suppose they thought it best at the time. If only I had known I would never have children....I suppose the abortion is the reason why?' Ruth looked totally dejected.

'That isn't necessarily the case. Your gynaecological problems seem to be in carrying a baby to term, who knows if that baby would have mis-carried or not? Blaming yourself does no good at all.'

'But what am I going to do? I have been petrified that Andy would find out from one of the doctors. They had access to my medical notes and there was no way I could seek treatment and hide the abortion from them. I've been so scared that one of them might say something when Andy is with me. Do you think I should tell him?'

'That's a big question Ruth and one that I can't answer for you. You know Andy better than anyone else which puts you in the best position to anticipate his reaction. But you also need to look at what is best for you at the moment. Keeping this kind of secret for such a long time is taking its toll on you now. Can you keep it up? Do you want to keep it up?'

Maggie let her words hang in the air for a few moments. Ruth was obviously distressed and she could only imagine the torment her client was facing. The human mind has the capacity to work so swiftly at times and she knew that Ruth must have so many conflicting thoughts racing simultaneously through her brain, the different scenarios, the 'what-ifs', the regret, the fear, guilt and shame. It would take time to process these thoughts and Maggie did not want her to rush into any decisions she might later regret, so after a few moments she spoke again, her voice quiet and even,

'You began today by telling me that you have been pretending, that you felt as if you are a hypocrite. Why do you feel like that? Who have you been pretending to?'

'Well, everyone I suppose.'

'And what is it that you've been pretending about? Do you not want to have a baby or consider adoption?'

'No, no it's the abortion I've been pretending about. I desperately want to have a baby, you know that Maggie.'

'Yes, I know. But what I see now is a woman who is accusing herself of living a lie, someone who is beating herself up over a mistake in the past when she was little more than a child herself, and which is causing bitter regrets but cannot be changed. To my mind that's a terrible waste.'

Ruth had flopped back in the chair and was looking totally exhausted. She closed her eyes and remained motionless for several moments, finally opening her eyes to look at Maggie.

'I've been a fool haven't I?'

'Not in the least. You are struggling with a difficult present which is triggering memories from your past, painful memories, bringing back old wounds and regrets. It's amazing you have managed to get this far without breaking down; that's a testimony to your strength of character and I admire you for that.' There was a silence in the room, but not an uncomfortable one, as both women reflected on what the other had said, Ruth gazing out of the window as if the answers to her problems were to be found there.

'What am I going to do? Should I tell Andy?' Ruth spoke first.

'To state the obvious, these are not easy questions. Only you can make those decisions, but it may be better to leave it for a day or two until you have had time to think it through a little more.'

'Oh Maggie, I've done nothing but think about this for over a year now, no, perhaps since I was sixteen. But one thing I do know is that having told someone, it feels a little better, well, not better, but lighter maybe.'

Maggie took her leave shortly afterwards. Ruth needed time alone to reflect, but she had insisted that the surgery be called if things became too bad. Her client was certainly calmer when they parted and, hopefully, on her way to making the right decision.

Chapter 17

The next morning, a memo from Dr. James was waiting on Maggie's desk, asking her to let him know if she would be free for a meeting regarding Matthew West. Her heart sank, she had tried not to think about Matthew lately, knowing that he was now one of Steve's clients and his interests would be better served by this change. Waiting in reception until Simon's patient left, Maggie nipped in to arrange a time to meet later.

'Would noon suit you?' The doctor asked. 'I assumed you would be free and I'll have finished morning surgery by then. Steve's coming in too.'

'Things are not good with Matthew then?' A frown appeared on her face.

'I am afraid not, but it's nothing for you to worry about. His first session with Steve didn't go too well, so I thought a case conference was in order.' A tap on the doctor's door announced his next patient so Maggie was unable to learn any more, the subject would have to wait until noon.

Steve Franks was already engaged in conversation with Dr. James when Maggie entered the room. Both men looked up and smiled as she took the remaining seat, pulling it closer to complete the little circle. Steve held a pad of paper and a pen, intending to take notes, which somehow gave the meeting greater import.

'Maggie,' began Simon, 'We thought it would be best if Steve started with a briefing on his session with Matthew to get you up to speed and then perhaps we can brainstorm how we are going to handle things from here.'

Steve took over; he was a slightly built man in his early fifties, the thick lenses of his glasses giving him a scholarly appearance and his earnest expression was a reflection of concern for his client.

'I had my first session with Matthew West yesterday. Now obviously this meeting today raises questions of confidentiality and could seem to breach Matthew's confidences, but I did tell him that I would be sharing some of the things he told me with colleagues, the reason being my concerns for his safety and possibly others too.'

Maggie groaned inwardly. How could such an intelligent, personable young man with his whole life ahead of him come to this? What had happened to change him? But then no one knew what other people's lives were like, you would have to walk in their shoes.

Steve continued.

'Matthew didn't look good right from the outset, quite distracted and antsy and when he spoke it wasn't too coherent. The only time he seemed to perk up was when he talked about you Maggie, and then he became quite animated. It seems pretty obvious that there is some kind of fixation here and he was under the misapprehension that the two of you were engaged in a relationship of sorts.'

Maggie gasped, shaking her head in horror.

'Don't worry, we know it's all in his mind, no-one's questioning your professionalism here at all. Matthew was quite open about his 'love' for you, and it seems that in his mind those feelings are reciprocated. I came to the conclusion that he has been dabbling in some kind of substance mis-use, which he more or less admitted, and it's now getting out of control causing him to live in his own fantasy world.'

Dr. James chipped in to the conversation at this point.

'Steve's asked him to see me again and it's my intention to stop his anti depressants and talk about some sort of program to help with this addiction.'

'There is something else Maggie,' her colleague continued, 'While he was talking about you and this imagined relationship, I pointed out that you were happily married, which seemed to almost topple him over the edge. He really lost it then and began to sob, declaring his life no longer worth living. It was an obvious shock to find out that you were married.'

'Of course, it would be. When I saw him nearly a couple of years ago I was single, but I can't honestly say I ever discussed my own circumstances, he must have assumed...'

'Or found out from some other source, not hard to do. My concern is that he seemed absolutely flawed by this news, I fear he may be unbalanced enough to do something rash to himself or possibly even you Maggie. You need to be vigilant and take extra care with your personal safety.'

Maggie nodded, unable to think of a response. Simon chipped in again,

'There is a residential program which I think could be the answer. Matthew's a bright young man, if we could sort out his addictions I'm sure he would.....'

Simon didn't get to finish the sentence as Laura, the practice manager, flung the door open in obvious panic.

'There's a man outside the surgery shouting for Maggie, he's acting really strange, shall I ring the police?'

The three occupants of the room were on their feet immediately, following Laura into reception, they did not need to be told who it was.

Tom Williams who was watching Matthew through the glass doors, turned as the trio joined him asking,

'Isn't that your patient Simon?

'It certainly is, how long has he been there?'

'We noticed him about half an hour ago but thought he was waiting for someone until the shouting began.' Laura explained.

132

Matthew's appearance was dishevelled as he paced up and down the path opposite the doorway, he had stopped shouting but his jaw was still working as if muttering to himself. He was clearly agitated, nervously wringing the bottle of water in his hands, screwing the top off and then on again, waving his arms wildly at times.

'Should I go...'

'Don't even think about it Maggie, in fact I think it would be better if you moved back a little, so he won't be able to see you.' The senior doctor then looked at his two male colleagues,

'Which one of you will do it?'

Simon and Steve both began to volunteer at once, but Simon made the final decision,

'I should be the one, he's probably still upset with you from yesterday's session, I'll try to calm him down, see if he'll come in to talk.'

As Simon went through the doors, Matthew stopped pacing and began shouting again.

'It's Maggie I want, not you. Stay away, don't come any nearer!'

Simon stood still and spoke calmly and quietly,

'You can't see Maggie now Matthew, I've explained it all to you. Come inside where we can talk, come on, please.' He inched forward.

'No! Stop there!' Matthew sounded in pain. Simon halted, giving his patient time to calm down, but that was something he was not about to do. Grappling with the water bottle again, he removed the top completely and poured the contents over his head. Throwing the bottle down Matthew reached into his pocket and pulled out a cigarette lighter. It was then that it dawned on Simon that the bottle was full of some kind of accelerant, not water and now the young man was drenched with the fluid. Looking back anxiously at his colleagues, Simon was unsure what his next move should be. Tom had already told Laura to dial 999.

'Which service?'

'All of them!'

Maggie was trembling,

'I must go out, he's going to kill himself!'

Tom placed a restraining hand firmly on her arm,

'No, it's too dangerous.' Then he slowly went outside himself, leaving Steve to steer Maggie away from the doors. Tom Williams moved slowly to stand beside Simon.

'Matthew, isn't it?' His soft Scottish burr sounded reassuring. 'Why don't you come in and we can have a wee chat, see if we can sort things out?'

'No, keep away from me! You all pretend to care but you don't, you're liars, you are all the same, even Maggie!'

Matthew West was not going to give anyone chance to pacify him; he was a desperate man, unbalanced and unable to think rationally. With the smallest of movements, a simple flick of his thumb, a spark ignited the liquid with which he had soaked himself. White and blue flames engulfed his body, licking around his form like a deadly blanket, eating through his clothes at speed and scorching his flesh. Within seconds Matthew became a human torch, his feral screams pierced the air and his face contorted with pain and anguish as he fell to the ground, writhing in agony.

Steve, who had been standing with Maggie in the foyer, grabbed the fire extinguisher from the wall, hurrying outside in an attempt to save Matthew. Laura had appeared with a fire blanket and Steve and the two doctors did their best to douse the flames. It had all happened so quickly, no sooner had the flames licked around Matthew's body than he was on the floor, thrashing wildly about. The men overcame the flames but it was too late, the thrashing had ceased and his pain was over.

Two police constables cordoned off the surgery whilst a couple of receptionists hovered at the car park entrance to turn away any patients arriving for afternoon surgery as Laura tried to cancel others by phone. Sue had come back from lunch to find the whole area resembling a circus, but the only tent covered the horridly burned body of Matthew West.

Sue was briefed rather hurriedly by Tom Williams then dispatched to her friend's office to find a very distraught Maggie. Steve had been doing his best to comfort her but was relieved to hand over to Sue, who asked him to telephone for Peter to come and take his wife home.

At the sound of Sue's calm and welcome voice, Maggie again burst into tears,

'I should have gone out to him' she sobbed, 'He was shouting for me.'

'No Maggie, you should not have gone to him, if you had there would probably be two bodies out there now instead of one.' Sue's voice was firm, authoritative and in her heart Maggie knew she was right. Steve came back into the room carrying a steaming mug of tea for Maggie and giving her the welcome news that Peter was on his way. Twenty minutes later the police allowed her to go home after noting their address in order to interview her later as a witness. Never had she been so pleased to see Peter, his arms giving her the strength and support her own body lacked. As they left the surgery, with instructions from Tom to have a large brandy, Maggie couldn't bear to look in the direction of the tent, being very much aware of the horror it concealed. They travelled in Peter's car; leaving Maggie's to be collected tomorrow, what was now her greatest need was to be at home with her husband and the comfort of familiar surroundings. Within minutes of their leaving, DS Alan Hurst arrived at the scene having been called by the uniformed officers to take the lead in the inevitable investigation.

****

'Yes, there'll certainly be an investigation.' Alan Hurst answered his wife's question later that evening.

'I know there were a number of witnesses but the coroner will need reports on what led up to the incident. His next of kin would normally identify the body but in this case the injuries were horrific, so they were spared that. I sent the uniforms to the lad's flat to have a look round and bring back his toothbrush.'

'His toothbrush, what on earth for?' Sue scrunched up her face.

'DNA, it's the quickest and easiest way to confirm identity, we should have the results in the morning. I'll leave interviewing Maggie until later tomorrow, we've seen his parents, and naturally they are devastated. Suicides aren't always as straight forward as they seem and all aspects have to be taken into account. We will need to establish West's state of mind and look for any probable causes which may have contributed to unbalancing him. The PC's will have a look round his flat for signs of possible drug misuse and they'll check his computer, mobile phone, that sort of thing. Because Maggie has been involved with him recently she'll most likely be called as a witness at the inquest, not only to the actual event, but to his recent state of mind.'

'That will be awful for her, she's feeling bad enough as it is, attending the inquest won't be easy, still I'm glad

136

that you're on the case, it will make things a little better for her. Mags has had so many knocks in life, but she has some sort of inner strength which always helps her bounce back, and of course there's Peter to support her now.'

Chapter 18

Joyce Patterson had been Maggie's supervisor for more years than she cared to remember. A short, plump lady, sixty two years old but with no thoughts of retirement in the near future, she had a soft spot for Maggie, knowing the younger woman's background and the way in which helping others had helped greatly in overcoming the loss of her young husband. Joyce's periwinkle eyes, usually flashing with a mischievous sense of humour, today held compassion and empathy for her younger colleague. It was two days since the tragic suicide of Matthew West and Joyce knew something about how Maggie would be feeling, indeed the whole incident had taken her back over twenty years, to a place and time at the beginning of her own career and a similar experience to the one Maggie was in now.

Peter had driven his wife to the appointment which was in Joyce's own home where she regularly met with the three counsellors to whom she offered supervision and support. It was obvious that Maggie had not been sleeping; dark, heavy eyes and a sallow complexion was quite the opposite of the radiance Joyce had noticed of late. But this was exactly what she would expect. One of the reasons counsellors had supervision on such a regular basis was because of the intensive work they undertook. To spend each working day listening to the problems of clients from all walks of life could prove to be a heavy burden and counsellors themselves were not immune to becoming depressed and despondent, the same as anyone else. Supervision sessions enabled them to offload some of the difficult issues they faced and to use their supervisor as a sounding board, which in effect brought another perspective and fresh insight to the issues they were involved with. Two heads were most certainly better than one in many instances. Maggie sipped a welcome coffee while Joyce waited for her to speak.

'I can't help blaming myself,' were the first, not unexpected words, 'But I know what you're going to say.'

'Oh good, we can just have a coffee and chat about the weather then.' The mischievous twinkle reappeared. Despite her feelings, Maggie smiled; she admired Joyce, liked her enormously, and was in fact dreading her retirement, hoping to persuade Joyce to continue with supervision even when no longer taking clients of her own.

'Did I handle it well, or could I have done better, that's what I keep asking myself. Perhaps I was too quick to pass Matthew on to Steve, to dismiss him because it was proving difficult?'

'You handled it extremely well; we talked this issue through a few weeks ago when Matthew first turned up again as a client. It was a classic case of transference, he had been hurt, and felt people didn't care and looking back, remembered that you were the only person who had shown him any regard. You did the right thing; he was obviously under the impression that any feelings for you were reciprocated, so when you cut that first session short you acted appropriately, and again on the car park on both occasions. I think we'll find that the inquest will reveal some kind of substance abuse, you had suspicions as did his doctor and Steve. Matthew was ill; he simply did not know what he was doing.'

'But perhaps if...at the end, when he was shouting for me...should I have gone out then?'

'No Maggie, most certainly not. The doctors did the right thing in keeping you back. The young man's mind was confused; he was acting irrationally and could very easily have taken you with him.'

Maggie listened. With her head she knew Joyce was right but her heart couldn't accept it, that whispering inner voice kept saying she should have, could have, done something. Her objective, professional voice was saying it was not her fault, but her heart worried that this was a cop out, an excuse to get rid of the feelings of guilt and blame. Joyce looked on, sensing the inner struggle and wanting to reach out to help. Here was one of the best counsellors she knew, genuine and caring, walking the extra mile if she felt it would help her clients; there were too few Maggie's around in Joyce's opinion.

'Okay.' Joyce said with authority, 'A bit of role play seems in order here.'

'Oh no, I can't do that now, I've always hated role play.'

'You can do it, you need to do it.' Joyce gave a little smile. She too was not a fan of role play; her own therapeutic techniques were, the same as Maggie's, eclectic; most counsellors' pull a little bit from several therapeutic theories to develop their own style. Role play seemed to associate mainly with the Gestalt school of thought with which neither woman was entirely comfortable.

'Swop chairs.' Joyce stood and waited for Maggie to do the same. 'Good, now, you know how it goes, I'm Mags and you're Joyce.'

Maggie rolled her eyes but was thinking one step ahead. Knowing what her supervisor was doing she had to admit, only to herself of course, that it was a clever move; even the physical change in places could be effective and her mind was already taking on the role of supervisor.

'My client has killed himself and I feel responsible...I think that perhaps I could have saved him.' Joyce spoke the words without drama but in a quiet concise way, much as Maggie would do. It was working already; Maggie's mind had slipped effortlessly into the role of supervisor and was quickly working out how she could make Joyce understand that she was in no way culpable.

'Why do you think you could have saved him?' she asked.

'I was there when he killed himself, he was calling for me but I didn't go out to him.' Joyce was good, Maggie felt compassion for her, but then, it wasn't for Joyce, it was for herself. She continued in the role of supervisor,

'Would you have been in any danger if you had gone to him?'

'Well yes, he set himself alight with petrol or something... I suppose he might still have done it had I been with him.'

'Okay, I get the point.' Maggie broke the role play, reverting to herself. 'I know all the arguments and I have tried to be objective, yet I can't help feeling bad about it all.'

'Of course you do. You give so much of yourself to your clients that when things go wrong it's bound to bring up negative emotions. But you know, don't you, that you played this one by the book, it is what we do Maggie and no one can guarantee a good outcome. It will take time, but you must look after yourself. If you had been injured, how would that new husband of yours have felt? You have a duty to work with caution and I can't see anything at all that you need to reproach yourself for. Look at the statistics, suicide is the greatest cause of death for young men in the UK. There have been far too many deaths over the years in Iraq and Afghanistan, but over the same period of time, suicide in young men has been even more common. I'm not saying that Matthew's death was inevitable but you did all you could possibly do, referring him to Steve was the right move, you knew it at the time and you know it now. Keep hold of that thought, you did the right thing.'

The session with Joyce had helped to a certain degree and Maggie's colleagues had also been quick to emphasize that she was in no way to blame and had acted in a professional manner. It would take time but Maggie would get there in the end, perhaps she should engage in role play more often, giving herself the benefit of her own experience. Sue often said she should give herself a good talking to!

Maggie was grateful that Alan was the investigating officer in Matthew's case, it made things seem less formal and gave the opportunity to ask questions without feeling she was being too much trouble. He had come the following day, late in the morning. Peter was at home too and they took the statement over coffee, Alan explaining everything he could to give them a greater understanding of the whole process of the inquest and the police's own investigations. The statement had been made and Maggie duly signed it, glad to have it over with. All this had been yesterday, the day after the incident and now, having spent time with Joyce, who always made her feel better, Peter had returned to pick her up and they headed home to have lunch and hopefully a quiet afternoon.

Alan was sitting outside their new home waiting for them to arrive. Maggie looked at her husband wondering if he had been expecting their friend, which he had not. Peter unlocked the door and they went in. Alan began by asking how Maggie was; her reply being that she would be much better if she knew that the visit was a social call.

'Not exactly,' Alan replied with a rather sheepish grin, then getting straight to the point, went on,

'The lads who did the search of Matthew West's flat found quite a collection of photographs. They thought it best if I went to see for myself and decide whether their find was relevant.' Alan could tell his friends were working this one out, why would he have come to tell Maggie if it did not involve her? He continued,

'They were all of you Maggie, obviously taken without your knowledge, mostly outside the surgery with some in the High Street and other public places. West must have been following you for some time.' Maggie felt suddenly quite sick. She had no idea that Matthew had been following her; it was difficult to believe, but apparently true.

'How many is 'quite a collection' Alan?' Peter asked.

'It ran into the hundreds.'

Maggie gasped; however had he managed to take that many without being noticed, and why? Shaking her head, utterly perplexed and not knowing what to say, they both listened as Alan continued,

'By hundreds, I mean that's how many he had but several of them were duplicates, he seems to have taken them, probably on his mobile phone, then printed copies, several of each shot, and displayed them on a wall in his bedroom.'

Peter shook his head sadly, thoughts of what might have been flashing uncomfortably through his mind. Maggie was stunned, not knowing what to say, it all seemed to resemble some kind of horror film where a fixated maniac collected photos for some sinister kind of shrine. Sinking back into the sofa, Maggie suddenly felt cold, all strength draining from her. For one awful minute she was glad that Matthew was dead, then instantly ashamed at such a dreadful thought. From then onwards she could not seem to take in much more of what Alan was saying, he and Peter were talking but Maggie was elsewhere, suddenly exhausted and wanting nothing more than to curl up and go to sleep.

****

Ellie was disappointed that the appointment with Maggie had been cancelled but the receptionist who rang explained that her counsellor was taking a week off due to bereavement and would almost certainly be back the following week. It was strange that after only one meeting with Maggie, Ellie somehow knew that these sessions were going to be her life line, that one hour a week would be her time, a time when she would be able to be completely honest with Maggie, who had claimed to be unshockable, surely an asset in that kind of work. It was also a time to discuss those strange, unsettling feelings with someone who did not know her and therefore had no expectations, someone she didn't have to be wary of hurting. Ellie had hoped to see Maggie before the next big step she was embarking upon, which was babysitting for Sam but it was not to be so she simply had to get on and do it. Phil had lost so much time at work and really needed to get back. Grace, in her quiet comforting wisdom had suggested a compromise, and it had been decided that Sam would come to their house where Grace and Ellie could care for him together while Phil went back to work. For Ellie, this was a much better arrangement than having

144

sole charge of Sam; although he seemed a very placid baby, she had no experience of looking after such a young child, or none that she could remember. Phil arrived at eight o'clock sharp, juggling two bags in one hand with Sam held precariously on his hip with the other. His cheerfulness seemed out of place so early in the morning and once again Ellie had the uncomfortable feeling that those around her were watching every reaction, whilst pretending to act normally. Sam was eager to be down on his feet so his daddy stood him against the sofa, allowing him to steady himself and the little boy soon had everyone in the room smiling. Grace and Derek began to chatter to their grandson, so completely smitten with him while Ellie was left to see Phil out. There was an awkward moment when he moved forward to kiss her goodbye, then stopping himself in time; handed over a key to their house instead, should she want to take Sam back there. Ellie said nothing, knowing that was unlikely, it would feel like intruding, yet she accepted that at some point in the future she would have to go there again, and not only to visit.

'How about a shopping trip?' Grace suggested. 'Phil's left the car seat and we've got Sam's pushchair, what do you think?'

'Yes, why not?' It seemed a much better idea to Ellie than staying in for the whole day. So a little over an hour later, mother, daughter and son were wandering down the high street. The shops were still relatively quiet, which made pushing the chair an easy exercise, Ellie imagined that she would hate having to push Sam through a crowded town centre. Derek had driven them to town, leaving them to the shops whilst he bought a newspaper and installed himself in a favourite coffee shop to pass the time.

'It's a treat to be out shopping with nothing in particular to buy, just a good browse around.' Grace said. Ellie nodded, thinking of all the time her mother must have spent at the hospital and all the worry it must have caused.

'Then let's treat ourselves to something nice, Marks and Spencer's do you think?'

'Why not?' Grace replied and they headed off to her favourite shop.

The day went well; the two women treated themselves to some of the new season's fashions and couldn't resist a cute little pair of dungarees for Sam. They then trawled the food hall, buying some steak to prepare a meal for early evening for them and for Phil when he came to collect Sam. Ellie enjoyed the day much more than she had anticipated and Sam seemed to enjoy being with his mother and though he obviously loved both grandparents, she was the one he reached out for when he wanted picking up. It was a wonderful feeling, one which caught her completely by surprise so that when it was time for Phil to take their son home, Ellie felt a pang of something she could not quite identify. Later, as she went to bed, she was tired but buoyed by the enjoyment of the day and the anticipation of seeing Sam again in the morning.

The following day proved to be equally as pleasant. Ellie took Sam out in the pushchair, giving Grace and Derek time and space to themselves, something which had become a rarity during the last couple of months. They headed to the park, spending time feeding the ducks and then going into the playground where Sam enjoyed the swings, chuckling that deep throaty laugh which Ellie loved to hear. This was all going so well; when with Sam she was engulfed by such an overwhelming feeling of love towards him which must surely have come from the time before the accident. This type of bonding took more than a few visits to develop. Thinking over this on the way home as Sam slept in the pushchair, Ellie was encouraged about her relationship with Phil. Surely, she reasoned, if she could feel this way about their son, there was hope for her marriage too. Turning into the drive of her parents' home Ellie made a decision, one which would certainly please Phil. From tomorrow she would look after Sam in his own home, in their home. Ellie was surprised at how good making this decision felt, could it be a sign of turning some sort of corner and with these feelings about Sam could it simply be a matter of time before it was the same with Phil?

Chapter 19

Sarah's first session with Maggie had been delayed for a week although knowing that most people had to wait much longer to see a counsellor made her less upset. She had arranged to take an extra half hour for lunch each Wednesday which would be made up by only having a short break the next day, which enabled Sarah to attend the surgery without Mark finding out, something she dreaded happening. The last few months had been horribly like living on a knife edge, being constantly worried about what Mark would find to criticize next and when his temper would flare up again. Friends at work had begun to notice a difference in her; Marie had even asked if she was pregnant as she appeared so pale and tired.

'Goodness no.' Sarah laughed it off, 'I think I've caught some kind of virus, that's all.' Sarah left to check something in the stock cupboard, deliberately preventing her friend from pursuing such an awkward conversation. Marie accepted that her colleague was not pregnant but certainly didn't believe it was a virus, and now, learning about Wednesday lunch time arrangements, became convinced something was seriously amiss.

Now that Maggie was back at work, Sarah's counselling could begin. Taking a seat in the waiting area there was hardly time to think about the hour ahead as an attractive, pleasant woman approached her almost immediately.

'Hi, its Sarah isn't it?' She asked.

'Yes'

'I'm Maggie, please come through.'

148

Sarah dutifully followed, sitting where Maggie motioned, a little apprehensive about what would be expected of her now that she was actually here. Maggie began by explaining the confidentiality clause and the exceptions to it and then asked if Sarah would care to tell her a little about herself.

'You know I'm a friend of Sue Hurst don't you?'

'Yes, I do, but whatever you share with me here won't be discussed with anyone outside, with the exceptions I've mentioned, but even then certainly not with Sue.'

'Oh, I wasn't worried about that but I thought maybe I should mention it.'

'Thank you Sarah, I appreciate that. Now I really don't know much about your situation, even Dr. Williams only gives me the bones of a referral so I can begin with no pre-conceived ideas about a client. So, if you could perhaps tell me a little about yourself and what has brought you here today, or if you prefer, you could start by telling me how you are feeling right now.'

Sarah quietly began to explain her situation. Taking Sue at her word about how good counselling would be, she held nothing back, relating all the incidents which had caused the concerns about her sanity and even admitting that she was beginning to be afraid of Mark. It was so good to talk; things had been bottled up for too long and although she had confided to some extent in Sue, this was different. There was a sense of relief in verbalising these recent events and the room felt soothing, a safe place to be in, conducive to sharing with this concerned looking lady. The fears of dementia, after so many stupid things she had done recently, were brought out into the open and it made her feel easier in herself for expressing them fully. Maggie listened quietly, noticing that her client's voice was at times heavy with emotion, and only speaking herself

149

occasionally, to clarify a point. Sarah eventually stopped and glancing at her watch was surprised to see she had been talking for over half an hour. It was a good start, she had been open and honest to a point which most clients took several weeks to reach and Maggie already felt some kind of reasonable grasp of the situation. One or two things Sarah said about her husband flagged up warnings which would be noted down and perhaps explored in future sessions in an effort to help her client look more objectively at her marriage. On the whole, it had been an excellent start and as the two women parted, Sarah headed back to work feeling more relaxed than she had done for quite some time.

'Hi!' Marie greeted her. 'You've had a lady looking for you but she didn't want to leave a message.'

Sarah was surprised yet grateful that Marie's first comment hadn't been about the reason for a long lunch hour.

'Did you get her name?'

'No, she seemed in a hurry to get off.'

'It wasn't my mum was it?'

'Not unless she gave birth in infant school, this lady wasn't much older than you.'

Sarah was puzzled as to whom it could be but was at least saved Marie's version of the Spanish inquisition. If it was a friend, and she had hardly seen any of them recently, then she would probably ring or call back later.

****

Maggie was glad to be back at work although the week off had, admittedly, done her good. Peter too had managed a couple of days off which, after hours of talking through the issues surrounding Matthew's suicide, were spent enjoying their new home and exploring the area around it with Ben, in an attempt to familiarize themselves with their new surroundings. Matthew West was a troubled soul, whom she had tried to help, and her failure would always be a source of sadness, but slowly Maggie was beginning to accept the fact that she had done no wrong. It had been a shock to learn about the photographs but pondering this, it seemed to be yet another indication of how disturbed Matthew had become. There was of course the inquest still to face and Maggie knew she would most probably be called to give evidence, the thought of which was troubling, but her colleagues would be there and Peter had offered to attend if she wanted him to. So until then the only sensible thing was to keep doing what she did best, throwing herself wholeheartedly into her work. As they walked, they chatted about other things too, Maggie appreciating how wonderful it was to be part of a couple again. Having spent so many years on her own after Chris died; it was still a novelty to have someone to share even the mundane aspects of life with, knowing that Peter was interested and would do anything to make her happy.

Maggie's latest client, Sarah Beecham, presented quite a challenge. Having talked openly about her husband's moods and anger, it appeared that Sarah somehow accepted this behaviour as normal and perhaps even as her fault. Maggie's initial perception was that of a husband who was slowly eroding his wife's confidence whilst convincing her that she was to blame. From what the young woman had said it appeared to be an abusive relationship, so far not physical abuse but Mark certainly seemed to be controlling Sarah's life, causing unhappiness and confusion. Maggie had made a few notes after their first hour together and had already begun to think about how best she could serve Sarah's needs.

****

Each morning Sue had taken to staring into the bathroom mirror, sideways on, to check if she was beginning to show; smoothing the tiny bump always brought on a feeling of warmth and contentment.

'The toast's getting cold!' Alan shouted from downstairs. Sue quickly finished dressing then jogged into the kitchen to join him.

'Argh, no butter on mine,' she stopped him just in time, 'I can't face anything but dry toast, I thought you'd got that by now.'

'Sorry, force of habit. What took you so long up there?'

Sue stood up, turned sideways and proudly said, 'See, a bump, bub's growing already.'

Her husband shook his head,

'I'll never understand women, you spend all your time wanting to be slim and worrying about putting on weight then as soon as you are pregnant you can't wait to be fat.'

'But it's a good fat, it's a sign that our baby's growing and getting stronger.'

Alan smiled and began spreading his toast with lashings of butter.

'Ugh!' Sue ran off to the bathroom again leaving Alan free to spoon on the thick cut marmalade.

****

'How are you Maggie?' Ellie was quick to express concern at the beginning of their second meeting.

'Hey, that's my opening line.' Maggie smiled then added, 'But I'm fine, thanks for asking. Now, how are you?'

'Do you know things have been going really well? Since I last saw you I've been looking after Sam while Phil went back to work. At first I had him at mum and dad's house; I needed their support, but for the last three days of the week I went to Phil's...no, to our house and looked after him there. He is such a lovely smiley baby and we had such a great time together. I'm incredibly fond of him, this week has been magical, I've hardly thought about my situation, Sam's just occupied my time and my thoughts completely.'

'That's great Ellie. And are you going to continue looking after him?'

'Yes. I'm actually surprised at how much I want to. Do you think this must be some kind of bond which was there from before the accident, it can't have happened overnight can it?'

Maggie looked thoughtful, pausing for a moment before replying,

'I really wouldn't know the definitive answer to that, but common sense would support the theory that there is some kind of existing bond somewhere in your subconscious mind. You know how strong your feelings for him are, what do you think?'

'I honestly feel as if I am Sam's mother now. I'm protective of him and hurt when he hurts and I simply couldn't imagine life without him and that's only after one week. I think you are right; this type of bond surely wouldn't exist after only a few days. Yes, we'll go with common sense and say the feelings are from somewhere inside, from the times I've spent with him in the past even if I can't remember them.'

'So, what about Phil, have you had any of the same kind of feelings for him?'

'Now you're thinking what I've been thinking Maggie. I keep telling myself that if I can love Sam, perhaps I could love Phil again too. It's your common sense theory again isn't it?'

Maggie smiled; Ellie seemed to be one step ahead of her.

'It is of course rather different,' she said, 'but it seems feasible and perhaps with time you will re-discover your feelings for Phil too. It is important though that you take things slowly, from what you have said he's not putting you under any pressure, which is good, but you must remember not to put yourself under pressure either. Phil loves you and I'm sure he will give you the time you need, don't you think?'

'Oh yes, he's been great. In some ways we do resemble a married couple, I go round each morning to look after Sam and have a meal ready for him after work which we share together. Then I go back to my parents. I have thought about staying but I've chickened out I'm afraid.'

'I think it's still too early. This is what I mean about putting pressure on yourself, there are no time scales here Ellie, take a tiny step at a time. You could look upon it as being courted all over again. Why not try an evening out together; you're not stuck for a babysitter are you?'

'Yes, I think I might enjoy that, he is rather handsome, and perhaps I could fall for him all over again.'

'Well you did once, so I would think that is a very likely possibility.'

Ellie decided this second session had gone well. Maggie was an ideal person to share her thoughts and feelings with. She had been honest from the start about her lack of experience in cases of amnesia, but together they seemed to toss around ideas and theories which was exactly the sort of help Ellie wanted. Their sessions didn't feel as if they were a medical appointment, they seemed to have already made progress and her memory loss no longer seemed such an insurmountable problem anymore. Ellie decided to collect Sam from her parents and take him back home, picking up something special for dinner on the way. Perhaps when Phil came home she would surprise him by asking him out on a date. Ellie smiled at the thought of Phil's face, she knew he would be delighted.

Chapter 20

It had been ten days since Matthew West's death and the coroner's inquest was scheduled to begin the following morning. Alan was making another official visit to see Maggie and update her with what was happening.

'Inquests are always open to the public so you can attend if you want to, but tomorrow is a mere formality. We haven't finished our investigations yet so all that will happen is an official opening of the inquest, then I'll put in a request for more time and proceedings will be adjourned with a later date fixed.'

'If I'm not needed then I won't go.' Maggie was in no way looking forward to the time when she would have to give evidence and could see no benefit attending the hearing if it was only a formality.

'That's what I thought,' Alan smiled. 'I'll only be asking for another week at most, so the full inquest shouldn't be too far ahead and you will have to attend then. But don't worry Mags, even though it is part of official proceedings it's kept as brief as possible. By then we should have all the answers we need and the evidence will be presented, witnesses called and the coroner will rule on what he hears.'

'Will you ring me when you know the date so I can book the time off work?'

'Of course, you'll know as soon as I do. I can pick you up to take you if you like?' Alan offered. Maggie looked at Peter, who answered for her,

'Thanks Alan but I'll be going too so I can take her.'

Sarah's weekend had got off to a bad start. When she woke, Mark was already up, so, looking at the clock, seven o'clock was far too early to get up on a Saturday, she decided to turn over and have another hour. That's when the banging started from downstairs, nothing specific or easily identified but Mark had to be responsible for the noise and that made her uneasy. Closing her eyes and hoping to ignore it and sleep a while longer, the noises grew louder, almost as if he knew what she was doing. The vacuum cleaner suddenly burst into life making Sarah jump up in a sudden panic. Grabbing her dressing gown she rushed downstairs to where her husband was vacuuming the hall carpet.

'I was going to do that when I got up,' Sarah said sensing Mark's bad mood.

'And when would that be?' He switched off the cleaner and looked at his wife through angry eyes.

'It is Saturday, weekends are for pleasure as well as cleaning,' she ventured. For one minute Sarah thought her husband might explode.

'If you think I can relax when the house is in this state you had better think again. Perhaps you can lie in bed 'til all hours, but I certainly can't!'

'But it's only seven o'clock Mark.'

'It's well after eight. You'll be expecting me to bring you breakfast in bed next!'

Sarah was now close to tears and trembling, not knowing what to say.

'I must have misread the clock.' Her voice was hardly a whisper as she turned to go back upstairs and into the bathroom. Locking the door and sitting down on the toilet, she put her head in her hands and cried.

'Why? Why is he treating me this way?'

After a few minutes Sarah discarded her nightie and stepped into the shower letting the warm water run over her now puffy face, massaging life into still tired limbs. Washing her hair and scrubbing vigorously at her body, a mixture of anger and fear began to rise within her.

'This isn't like me,' the tears came again, angry, frustrated tears and Sarah sat down in the shower, hugging her wet legs and sobbed like a little girl.

When Mark heard the water running in the bathroom he climbed the stairs to their bedroom, picking up the clock at his wife's side of the bed he moved the hands forward to the correct time, smiling at how quickly Sarah had assumed the mistake to be her own. Going back downstairs, he put the vacuum cleaner away and went into the kitchen to wait for scene two to begin.

Sarah towelled herself dry then went back into the bedroom to dress; her eyes went automatically to the clock which now read eight forty-five. Pulling on a pair of jeans and a t-shirt she told herself that it was a simple mistake and even if she had slept until eight, or even nine, it would be okay, it was the weekend. Why did Mark always have to make an issue of every little thing? The tears were replaced by a measure of anger now, simmering below the surface. Dare she talk to Mark and attempt to explain how she was feeling?

'Why not?' The anger rising inside was giving her strength, 'it's about time I stood up for myself, and I can't take this much longer.'

Heading for the kitchen, Sarah was determined to confront her husband; she would sit down, in case her legs gave way, and ask him why he had changed so completely towards her.

'Hi.' Mark smiled, 'I've made your breakfast, there's only the toast to do.'

Sarah was completely wrong footed, was this the same man who had scowled at her less than an hour ago?

'Mark' her voice came out rather tentatively, 'Can we talk?' Sarah remained at the kitchen table.

'Of course sweetheart, what's on your mind?'

Now she was really worried.

'Why were you so cross with me before?'

'Was I? When'

'You know when, you were quite angry when I got up.'

'I wasn't cross darling; I was teasing, sleepy head.'

'No you weren't and it's not the first time either.' Sarah was feeling somewhat bolder now; it was time to address this with her husband.

'I can't seem to do anything right these days, you get so angry with me and I don't know why or what to do about it.' Tears were threatening again.

'Hey, where's all this come from? I don't get angry with you, you must be imagining things. You know how much I love you. I wouldn't hurt you for the world.' Mark moved to Sarah's side wrapping his arms around her. The tears flowed again as he stroked her hair, whispering loving words. It was so utterly confusing. Was it all imagined? Sarah had felt unable to trust Mark and his moods anymore, but could it be she who was losing it, was it really all in her mind?

****

Driving to the Duncan's house on a bright June morning, Maggie wondered if they had reached any decision about adoption. It was over two weeks since Ruth had told Maggie about her abortion and although they had not met during that time they had spoken on the phone and Maggie was aware of how quickly things seemed to be happening for this particular client. Ruth

159

had tried to contact her counsellor the day after the revelations but Maggie had been unavailable due to the appalling suicide she had witnessed, so it wasn't until the following week that she had been able to bring her up to date. Ruth had taken the decision to tell Andy about the baby conceived and aborted in her teenage years, having come to the conclusion that it would be almost impossible to continue along the route of adoption until she had finally confronted this episode from the past. It was also proving difficult to match Andy's enthusiasm whilst harbouring this emotionally crippling secret, so she had told him on the evening after her last meeting with Maggie. Although feeling completely drained from the hour the two women had spent together, Maggie's reaction had somehow encouraged Ruth to open up to Andy. Having expected some kind of disapproval, if not verbally then a subtle change of attitude perhaps, for Maggie to be so calm and accepting, even to the point of empathy for her pain, was staggering. Possibly it was this which convinced Ruth to waste no more time in telling Andy, who had sat beside his wife at her request on arriving home from work, with a rather puzzled expression at her melancholy demeanour. Later that evening he admitted that his first thought had been that she had some serious illness, or had decided not to go through with the adoption. Andy had listened very quietly, his gaze not shifting from her face until everything had been said, after which he slumped back onto the sofa without comment. Ruth remained beside him for as long as she could bear the silence, then rose to go to the kitchen and prepare a meal. Standing tearfully at the sink, wondering if her marriage was still intact, she became aware of Andy entering the room.

'Why Ruth?' were his only words.

'I was sixteen, I didn't realise what it was I was doing...'

'No, not that, why did you not tell me before?' He sounded so sad, so disappointed that the tears began to fall yet again.

Andy held her close, stroking her hair and kissing the top of her head.

'I would never hold that against you. I love you Ruth, you're my world. My regret is that you didn't tell me years ago, it wouldn't have made any difference to the way I feel about you.'

Ruth had related all this over the phone, sounding like a different woman, confident and in control again, the woman Maggie always knew had been there. After hearing all that had transpired, Maggie asked if Ruth felt there would be any benefit in Andy joining them for their next appointment. They had been left to ponder this and driving to their home now, she was unsure if she would be seeing her client alone or if Andy would be joining them. Ruth invited her in with a conspiratorial smile and a nod towards the room where her husband sat and after a brief introduction, left to make coffee, an offer which Maggie accepted to create an opportunity of a few words alone with Andy. Never one to make small talk, especially if the client was paying by the hour, she asked if he was comfortable about talking to her. Andy seemed completely at ease, smiling and replying that he was happy to do whatever it took to help himself and his wife decide their next step. Then probing gently into his own feelings on adoption, Maggie was left in no doubt about his enthusiasm and commitment to adopting a child.

When the coffee arrived, the three settled comfortably to begin what was to be a fruitful dialogue about their options. They had taken Maggie's advice to draw up a written list on the pro's and con's of adoption which gave them a great starting point for their time together. Many of the issues they had noted were ones which Ruth had previously raised and Andy was happy to share his thoughts on them too. The couple seemed completely at ease with one another which, Maggie thought, was most likely a result of their recent difficulties, she so often found that couples were drawn closer together in such circumstances.

'What surprised me was the whole length of the process.' Andy admitted, 'I can see the need for safeguards but I understood that they were crying out for people to adopt...and some of the checks on extended family and friends seem a bit over the top, after all, we are the ones who'll be bringing the child up and will have the greatest influence.'

His wife was nodding in agreement, taking up the theme,

'We have children at school whose parents don't seem in the slightest way concerned about their welfare let alone their education. They can go on having babies with no one assessing their suitability or interviewing their families. There's one little girl in my class and you should see her. At only five years old I dread to think what kind of life the poor little soul has had already. She appears totally uncared for, underfed and is so listless and timid. I could scoop her up and bring her home with me!' Ruth was quite animated with concern for the girl, her eyes bright and cheeks flushed.

'Well, you have just answered number three on your list.' Maggie smiled.

'What do you mean?'

'Number three on your list of concerns is whether or not you could love someone else's child as if it was your own. You are showing rather a lot of passion for someone else's child at the moment.'

Ruth reddened even more but the words hit home. If told she could have Lucy as her own child tomorrow, there would be no hesitation.

'I can vouch for that.' Andy added, 'She feels more than a teacher's concern for some of those kids.'

'I'd never thought about it that way.' Ruth became quite pensive.

'Well if you think about it now, it might help you resolve one of those issues at least.'

Talking through some of the other points they had noted, Maggie felt they were making steady progress. She chipped in at times to reflect what they were saying, rephrasing their words to help them look at things from a different perspective, or suggesting points they may not have considered. On the whole this young couple were impressive and seemed to be drawing closer to working things out. Throughout their discussions it became apparent that neither wanted to do anything with which the other was uncertain or unhappy about, which in itself was an obvious relief, especially for Ruth who seemed the more cautious of the two. Maggie suggested that time was perhaps going to be the answer and they needed to take things slowly, one decision at a time until they were sure of each next step. Her role seemed to be turning into one of an observer as the couple decided to attend the four day training course which the social worker had suggested, another step forward, but not an irreversible one. Maggie took leave of a very contented couple, fixing another appointment at Ruth's request.

As Maggie reflected on her time with the Duncans, it was apparent that in Andy's act of forgiving his wife, Ruth had finally been able to forgive herself, lifting a huge burden which must, at times, have been almost unbearable.

Chapter 21

Things were going so well for Ellie; life was once again enjoyable and she could almost see the funny side of amnesia which was certainly not the frightening black hole it had appeared to be when she woke up in hospital. Sam had effortlessly wormed his way into her heart and Ellie loved him with a passion that surprised her, one which she acknowledged must be a mother's love, strong and enduring. Phil had been astounded when asked out on a date; he had nearly choked on the coffee he was drinking, causing his wife to burst into fits of laughter, with Sam joining in as if he too understood the joke. Phil looked happier than he had for months and rather handsome too, she couldn't help but notice. Grace and Derek were delighted to babysit seeing this as a major step forward for their daughter and son-in-law, one that instilled such much needed hope for the future.

Ellie had made a special effort with clothes and make-up, effort which was rewarded by the look on Phil's face as she arrived with her parents on Saturday night. They kissed their son goodbye then set off to enjoy a meal at a restaurant which Phil assured her was her favourite. It was a balmy evening; the scent of stocks heavy in the air as they parked the car and walked through a walled garden to the country pub which they had visited many times before. Ellie was struck by the idyllic setting, from the bright summer blooms in the borders to the gentle sound of running water from the stream hidden from sight by the high red brick wall. She felt totally relaxed; exchanging smiles with Phil and leaning in close to hear what he was telling her. This was apparently the venue where they had celebrated their last wedding anniversary, which, it suddenly struck her, she had no idea of when it was, or even Phil's birthday. There was so much to re-learn but tonight was not the time to worry about that, it was a time to enjoy herself and the company of this handsome, attentive man by her side. When she chose the medallions of beef with Cumberland sauce, Phil grinned.

'What? What's so funny?'

'You always choose that when we come here,' he laughed and Ellie thought how relaxed he seemed, the anxious, ever present look had tonight been dispelled, replaced by a more mellow expression.

The meal lived up to expectations and the conversation had been easy and light. It was a time to forget their problems, to enjoy the moment, which Ellie was certainly doing. At times she even found herself flirting with Phil, enjoying his light hearted mood and the obvious pleasure the evening was giving him.

'We should do this again.' She suggested.

'We do, or rather we did. Every month we made a point of having an evening out, just the two of us. Your parents were always happy to babysit and it was good to be alone together, but I have to confess, it was your idea.'

'Ah, so I've always been the sensible one it seems.' Ellie reached across the table and squeezed Phil's hand. It felt good, natural, their fingers fitting comfortably together. Phil lifted her hand and kissed it, she did not pull away and this simple act filled her with a warm glow of hope, an anticipation of a happy future rather than a fear of what might be around the next corner.

Phil almost suggested his wife stay the night but stopped himself from doing so, knowing that such a huge decision had to be made by Ellie herself. The evening had gone so well and he would have to be content with that. It could have been any one of the many dates they had been on in the past and for the first time in months he had a positive sense of expectancy, being able to relax and let time work its healing magic. Over the last couple of weeks when Ellie had begun to look after Sam, her love for their son became evident, and Phil marvelled at how quickly this bond had developed. This, he decided was a good sign, if that love for their child was still somewhere in her subconscious mind then surely the love they had shared must be somewhere in there too. If only he knew how to bring it all back, how to make her love him again. Yet he acknowledged it was still early days. Dr. Samms had cautioned him to be patient, to give his wife time, which he was working so hard to do. Their night out had certainly been a step in the right direction and Phil clung on to the hope that he would at some point have his wife back again.

****

'I'm so pleased for you; it sounds as if you had a fantastic time.'

Ellie had just finished telling Maggie about the date with Phil, an event which she had described with animation, the life was back in her eyes and her whole appearance was so much better than it had been for weeks.

'Will you make this a regular date; it sounds as if it has been in the past?'

'Oh yes, I so enjoyed the whole evening. It had all the excitement of a first date, I felt like the eighteen year old me again, only this time I know I'm not a teenager.'

'That's really good and it leads me nicely into a suggestion I have to make. I've given your situation a lot of thought and I think you know I have tried to research the condition, but there is no way for us to know how this is all going to work out. In films and books the memory always comes back, in fact I think in everything I've seen or read, another head trauma has brought the memory back. Now I am not suggesting that I whack you over the head with a blunt instrument, I would probably get struck off, but I have been toying with an idea.' Maggie was choosing her words carefully. Her client seemed much stronger than when they had first met and it was obvious that she was being determinedly pragmatic about her life at present. Ellie's expression was open and interested so Maggie continued,

'I was going to suggest that you try to forget about the amnesia.' She realised the pun when Ellie laughed out loud.

'I know, it sounds ridiculous, but let me explain. The first time you came to see me you were distressed and confused which isn't in the least surprising. But I have watched you change in a relatively short space of time. What you have achieved already is remarkable and you can give yourself a huge pat on the back for progress so far. However I think you know that what we are working with here has no definitive outcome, that is, we don't actually know if you will ever recover your memory.'

Ellie's smile had faded and listening to her counsellor she was once again looking quite solemn.

'You are an intelligent lady, you understand that there is no definitive prognosis, so rather than letting this hang over you, or consume your whole life, what I want to suggest is that you live your life from now on, like that saying on plaques, *Today is the first day of the rest of your life.*' It seems to me that you have been doing remarkably well; I know your love for Sam has returned and hopefully your feelings for Phil will come back too. But what I want you to consider is taking each day for what it is. Let Phil court you all over again, it sounds as if you could be falling in love with him for a second time already and why not? Yes, there will be practical things to consider, things you may have to re-learn but you have wonderful family support, use them, and don't worry about those lost years. If they come back then great, but if not, you still have a lifetime ahead of you to make hundreds of new memories.' Maggie began to study her client's face in an attempt to read any reaction to this suggestion. Ellie was silent for a few moments but then slowly smiled at Maggie, nodding her head.

'I think I could run with that idea.' The animation returned and she continued enthusiastically,

'Do you know, I think to some extent I have already started to do that. The other night felt as if it was a first date and Phil is pretty good company, I could fancy him. I did actually consider staying overnight with him but I chickened out again.'

'Good, you still need to take things slowly, if you are treating this like a new relationship there's no need to rush things. Enjoy the experience, not many people get the chance to fall in love with their partner all over again, so take your time. Naturally Sam has to be considered too but it sounds as if he's already got his loving mummy back.'

'He sure has, I'm besotted by him, one grin and he's got me right where he wants me. I couldn't bear to be without him now.'

'Quite an innovative idea Maggie, perhaps you should begin to document this case, it's a rare dilemma and it could be a useful case history.'

Maggie had finished telling Joyce about the latest session with Ellie. It was, as her supervisor suggested, an interesting case from an academic perspective. Perhaps she would note their sessions in more detail in future, anonymously of course, but it would be interesting to see how things developed.

'So, how are you coping yourself?' Joyce's primary concern remained for Maggie's welfare.

'Oh, I'm doing okay really. The inquest was opened and adjourned; Alan warned me that was how it would go as they needed more time to investigate. I found it a little creepy to learn that Matthew had not only been following me but taking photographs, you'd think I would have noticed that wouldn't you?'

'Not really. I shouldn't think any of us would have been aware of such behaviour. We are generally so wrapped up in our own little worlds, busy with our lives, dashing from one responsibility to the next. You would probably have to be paranoid to notice being followed; almost looking out for it and you had no reason to do that.'

'I suppose so. I wasn't really aware how far Matthew's obsession had developed; perhaps I would have been paranoid then.'

'You seem much calmer, less agitated.'

'I am and it's mainly thanks to the wonderful support I've had from you and Peter and my friends. It's times like this when I really appreciate how fortunate I am, thanks Joyce, you have been great.'

'It's no more than anyone would do and that sounds rather like an acceptance speech for receiving an Oscar, am I missing out on something?'

Maggie laughed, Joyce's sense of humour always kept things in perspective.

****

After a most confusing weekend Sarah had been glad to get back to work, silently acknowledging that this had become her escape from Mark. She was meeting Sue at lunch time and really looked forward to seeing her and was so pleased that they had come across each other again and been able to pick up their friendship once more. Sue made her laugh, but also had a compassionate side which made Sarah feel safe as if there was someone to turn to if she was ever in trouble, Sue was a woman who spoke good old fashioned common sense, a rare commodity her mother would have said.

Marie had taken an early lunch hour and returned to staff the reception desk in good time for Sarah to meet Sue.

'That friend of yours is over the road.' Marie remarked, taking off her jacket,

'You know, the one who came in the other day asking for you.'

Sarah jumped up moving quickly towards the door, keen to see who it was. Marie opened the door and together they looked across the busy road, up and down the street but saw no one except the postman and an elderly gentleman walking his dog.

'That's funny,' Marie said,

'I'm sure it was the same woman, wearing that same green raincoat.'

'Not to worry, if she wants to see me it appears she knows where I work. I'll be off now. I'm meeting a friend for lunch.' Sarah thought Marie was probably mistaken, if it had been the same person who had enquired after her last week surely she would have come in again.

Sue was waiting at the coffee shop.

'I've ordered our drinks and a couple of Panini's, my treat.'

'Oh Sue, thanks, but you will have to let me pay next time, you always beat me to it.'

'Naturally bossy, that's me, so watch your step girl!'

Their order arrived and they began to eat whilst catching up on events since they had last met. Sarah talked about the session with Maggie and how comfortable she had been in her company.

'I suppose I felt as if I already knew her, you have talked about her so often that it seemed as if I was meeting a friend.'

'Maggie's so easy to get on with and has a knack of making everyone feel as if they matter, which to her they do. I think it's probably because she's seen difficult times in her own life which consequently makes her so genuine. Anyway, you don't want to hear Maggie's life story and I want to know how you have been getting on.'

Sarah wrinkled her nose, trying to choose the right words for a reply; Sue had become someone with whom she could be completely honest.

'If you want to know the truth, I'm really struggling. Some days I really don't want to go home after work, silly I know but I never know what kind of mood Mark is going to be in.'

'It's not silly at all, he sounds like a right pig to me, and he certainly doesn't deserve you.'

'Don't mince your words will you?' Sarah smiled. 'You see, I say these things and I really feel that Mark is unreasonable, but perhaps I'm not being fair to him, maybe it is me that's a bit crazy.'

'Nonsense, you are as level headed as the rest of us and always have been. From some of the things you have told me he's the one who's crazy, doesn't he know that slavery was abolished years ago?'

'Now look, I have coloured your judgement and you haven't even met him. I have to confess though that sometimes I do mess things up. On Saturday morning I didn't get up until after eight o'clock but I had looked at the clock and could have sworn it was only seven, so I know I'm doing some pretty stupid things lately, enough to try Mark's patience.'

'My goodness, even eight o'clock on a weekend is too early to get up, Alan and I...well, perhaps I'd better not go there!' Sue's eyes widened with mischief as she raised her eyebrows and grinned across her coffee cup but Sarah's smile was weak as she confided to her friend,

'That's another thing; I'm getting to the point where I don't want him to touch me. Surely that's not normal for someone my age? I feel that sex with Mark is a duty, something I have to do to keep him sweet.' Whatever was in the bottom of her cup was now holding her attention and Sue, who was never usually stuck for words, remained silent for a few moments. When Sarah didn't look up, her friend reached out and covered her hand,

'That's not how things should be Sarah, you should never feel obliged to have sex or agree to it because you're afraid of him. Look, tell me to butt out if you want but he seems to be controlling you. Maybe this is something you could share with Mags. I'm not an expert in this kind of stuff, but I can sense that this husband of yours has some pretty odd ideas of what a marriage should be.'

'I have done it again haven't I? I am sorry Sue, I didn't intend pouring out my troubles to you. Let's talk about something more cheerful shall we? Tell me how you've been, everything okay with the baby is it?'

Sue was happy to change the subject and began chattering on about morning sickness and her strange cravings for peanut butter and gherkins which soon managed to lighten Sarah's mood as she laughed at the way Sue described the latest examination at ante natal clinic.

'It was for a full examination by the gynaecologist, these things are so embarrassing, anyway the nurse left me in a cubicle telling me to remove my trousers and knickers saying there was a sheet on the chair with which to cover myself. 'The sheet' however, turned out to be a pillowcase! Well, look at me, a pillowcase isn't going to spare my blushes is it? The nurse apologized afterwards but the damage was done, I could be mentally scared for life!'

Anyone watching them or listening in to their conversation would simply see two good friends sharing their lunch break together, which of course is what they were. In fact that is exactly how they appeared to the lady in the green raincoat who had followed Sarah into the cafe and was seated close enough to watch her target whom she had been studying with growing interest.

Chapter 22

Peter needed a break, a breath of fresh air to waken him up. Working at home was great but he had neglected to turn off the central heating which made the house far too warm and coupled with the absolute quiet it was not particularly conducive to work. Ben was always game for a walk and as soon as Peter mentioned the word his tail began thumping on the floor. Tara of course had no interest in going out; she had taken to staying out all night of late which worried Maggie a little as they had sighted a fox in the nearby field. But Tara was a cat who was used to staying out and Peter assured his wife that she could probably outrun any fox or certainly find a nearby tree to climb. Stepping into the sunshine gave Peter an instant lift as he drew in a long breath of honeysuckle scented air and paused to admire his new home in its stunning setting. It had been a good move for both him and Maggie, a new start in a place they had chosen together. Peter could hardly believe how his life had turned completely around and often felt he should pinch himself to make sure it wasn't a dream. Of course he had his health problems but the Multiple Sclerosis was proving to be manageable at present and although no one could predict how he would be affected as time went on, he was grateful for each good day and especially grateful to Maggie who had steadfastly refused to let him shut himself away and destroy their relationship when it had so recently begun. Peter took the path towards the back of their home, a public right of way which was hardly used by anyone except the few who lived nearby. The path led nowhere in particular and after about a mile looped back on itself which was probably why keen walkers didn't use it, but for their regular walks with Ben it was perfect and gave a great view of the back of their house when they turned to complete the loop and head back home.

The late morning sunshine was comfortably warm with a gentle breeze to temper its heat. Peter and Maggie were soon to have a couple of weeks holiday for which they had planned to travel no further than her parent's home in Scotland followed by a visit to his daughter, the latter being only a fifty mile round trip. They would consider a holiday abroad later in the year, but for the summer they would enjoy pottering at home, tending the small garden and enjoying their new surroundings. Ben certainly approved of their recent move; he had much more space indoors, although Peter suspected he hadn't quite become accustomed to one level living yet and occasionally appeared to be searching for the staircase. The walks for Ben were every bit as good as at Maggie's last home and he probably had more exercise with Peter being so often at home. Having completed their usual circuit, Peter felt refreshed by the light exercise and as he unlocked the front door was just in time to answer the telephone, the caller ID informing him that it was Jane, his elder daughter.

'Hi Dad, I'm glad I've caught you.' She always sounded chirpy on the telephone if a little breathless. I've been to the doctors this morning and...it's good news, I'm expecting another baby!' Her father could almost feel the warmth of her smile coming through the telephone.

'That's wonderful, well done.' Peter hardly needed to say more, Jane chatted on about dates and decorating their little bedroom, so clearly delighted as Peter was too. After all the details were passed on Jane excused herself to make more calls to pass on their good news and Peter went into the kitchen to make coffee, deep in thought about his daughter. Jane was a career mother, having chosen to stay at home with Emma, their first child who was now two years old, quite prepared to go without the luxuries many of their generation expected as standard, with the result that they were one of the happiest families Peter knew and he proudly admired the decisions they had made. Jane loved being at home caring for Brian and Emma and a new baby would most certainly bring even more happiness. He would ring Maggie soon, hopefully catching her on a lunch break, knowing she would be thrilled for them. There were times when Peter's heart ached for his wife who had never had the chance to be a mother but refused to complain, ever the pragmatist. He was of course delighted with the way she had taken to his daughters and little Emma in such a natural, genuine way. Emma loved her new grandma, each visit seeming to strengthen the bond and both of his daughters had readily accepted Maggie, seeing the change she had made to their father's empty life. It couldn't be easy for Mags seeing other women with their babies and now there was Jane and of course Sue who was also expecting. Still, Maggie would want to know Jane's news, he would ring knowing the response would be one of genuine pleasure for his daughter, perhaps it would also help in some small way to take her mind off the inquest the following day.

Maggie rang Jane later that evening to offer her own congratulations and ask about all those little details which men never think to ask. The baby was due in September when Emma would be almost three; an age which they agreed was perfect for the role of big sister. Jane had not yet told her daughter thinking it was too long a time for her to wait but Emma was such a bright little girl that it was likely she would hear comments about the baby and her lively mind would demand answers to the never ending questions which were always on her lips. Maggie agreed that it probably wouldn't be long before she knew there was something her parents were not telling her and then the whole world would know.

****

The inquest was at nine o'clock the following morning. Maggie had anticipated a bad night with little or no sleep, but had actually slept soundly, not waking until hearing the early morning sounds of Peter up and about. After showering and dressing she sat down to breakfast accepting the coffee Peter offered, but unable to face anything other than a slice of toast to eat, nibbling with little enthusiasm. Seeing the concern in Peter's eyes, Maggie reached for his hand,

'It's okay love, I'll be fine, especially with you to hold my hand and Alan as back-up. Once today is over we can put all this behind us and perhaps plan that holiday we have been talking about.' Being 'fine' was perhaps not quite the whole truth, but at least the end of this sorry affair was in sight and whilst Maggie knew she would never forget Matthew West, today would hopefully bring some answers as to how or why he had changed so dramatically.

Alan was waiting outside the coroner's court to meet them, smiling a welcome and ushering them in to seats at the side of the surprisingly small room. Maggie had not known quite what to expect; the title 'court' conjured up a picture of a legal courtroom with a raised bench for the judge, seating for a jury and 'the dock' for the accused. Of course she had realised this would be

178

different, there was no jury, no accused, and the coroner himself sat behind a table which also accommodated a clerk whose job it was to take minutes. The only thing which was as Maggie had expected was the atmosphere, a solemn almost reverent silence which spoke of the gravity of the proceedings. A couple whom she supposed to be Matthew's parents were at the other side of the room and Alan had moved over to have a word with them. The lady was very red eyed and dabbed at her face with an embroidered handkerchief whilst her husband concentrated on what Alan was saying, nodding gravely in understanding. Her heart went out to them, they had lost their only child, and her own feelings about the incident were nothing in comparison to their loss.

The coroner did not have a gavel; he began by loudly clearing his throat which had the effect of gaining the attention of the dozen or so people in the room. Outlining the reason for the hearing and thanking everyone for their co-operation, he then asked for DS Hurst to give evidence. Alan stepped forward to a slim podium on which he placed a thickly bound notebook. Maggie half expected a lawyer or some other legal figure to appear and fire questions at him and was somewhat relieved when the coroner simply asked him to recall the sequence of events from the day of Matthew's death. Alan spoke clearly and concisely, fluently summarising what he had found on arrival at the scene and how his investigations had proceeded since then. Maggie felt her face colour when Alan began to relate what had been found at Matthew's flat, conscious that both Mr and Mrs West looked directly at her and unable to imagine what they must be thinking. Naturally the photographs were discussed, the coroner asking Alan to be more specific about the quantity and subject of them. There had also been several syringes and other drug related paraphernalia found, which didn't surprise Maggie even though Alan had never mentioned it. When all the facts were set out clearly the coroner thanked Alan and asked the family if they had any questions. Matthew's mother kept her head down, sobbing quietly whilst his father stood briefly and declined to question Alan. The coroner addressed the room,

'Having established the facts of Matthew's untimely death we will move on to try to establish his state of mind and the circumstances leading up to that day. For this we will hear briefly from various health professionals, so could I first ask for Dr. Simon James please.'

Simon moved to the podium and the coroner asked questions to ascertain his relationship as Matthew's GP and what his professional opinion was of Matthew's state of mind in the months leading up to his death.

Simon was prepared with a list he had printed out of appointment dates going back two years to the time when Matthew had been viciously assaulted in a random attack by a group of teenagers and left with severe facial injuries. He presented a brief summary of the treatment Matthew had received at both the surgery and the hospital which included several painful operations to set and wire the bones in his face to allow them to heal. After describing the physical injuries, Simon went on to relate the concerns he had at the time about Matthew's mental health and how he had arrived at the conclusion that counselling would be the best course of action to help him accept what had happened. Maggie's name was again mentioned, Dr. James being quick to say how both he and Maggie had been pleased with the progress made due to those counselling sessions. Finally Simon brought things up to date by telling the court how

Matthew had approached him more recently, claiming to be depressed and asking for counselling again. He began to describe the first session which had been cut short, but the coroner stopped him at that point asking if perhaps Maggie would take over to tell the room firsthand what had happened.

With her legs turning to jelly and with hands visibly shaking, she somehow managed the two or three steps to the podium. Simon smiled reassuringly as he moved aside, allowing her to take his place and Maggie stood grasping the wooden structure as if it were a life raft. Her voice was barely audible but she found the coroner to be most sympathetic and his questions phrased simply and kindly. Maggie described the original counselling sessions after the assault, remarking how well they went and how much benefit Matthew seemed to draw from them. Continuing the account, her professional side seemed to take control and her voice became steadier when moving on to relate the last appointment with Matthew when there appeared to be something wrong, causing her to finish the session in only a matter of minutes. The next encounter with him had been in the car park where he had appeared to be waiting and asked her to go for a coffee with him. Maggie stuck to the facts not expressing opinions, moving on to the second meeting in the car park, the one when she had actually felt threatened by Matthew. Pausing and thinking she had covered everything, the coroner proceeded to ask about the photographs, specifically whether she knew Matthew was taking them. Maggie's voice began to tremble again as she shook her head, almost whispering a shocked 'No'. The coroner seemed to sense her discomfort and smiled.

'I'm sorry to have to ask such things Ms Sayer, but we need to establish as many facts as we can.'

181

In spite of this apology, Maggie still felt uncomfortable, wondering why on earth it was relevant whether she did or did not know he had been photographing her. Surely he didn't think she had in any way encouraged him?

The final questions related to Matthew's actual suicide, ones she again could answer factually knowing that Dr. James, Dr. Williams, Steve and Laura would all be answering those questions in the same way.

It was a relief to be excused and to sit down beside Peter who smiled, taking her hand as she audibly sighed knowing the ordeal was over and particularly relieved that again Matthew's parents had chosen not to ask any questions of their own. The proceedings seemed to move at a much quicker pace now and it was not too long before she was outside, gulping in the warm fresh air and gladly turning away from the coroner's court.

The official verdict was, as expected, suicide whilst the balance of Matthew West's mind was disturbed. It was a sad case; the mis-use of drugs was cited as a contributing factor as was the original assault Matthew had suffered. It was over and Maggie was relieved but before she had gone far her name was called and on turning round she found Mr and Mrs West hurrying towards her. Maggie's heart sank as she wondered what she could possibly say to them, this might be over for her but his parents still had to live with the sadness; the untimely death of a child is a heavy burden to carry.

'Ms Sayer,' Matthew's father began, 'We wanted to thank you for all you did for our son. After his assault last year you really helped him get over it. Perhaps if he had come to you sooner this time things might have worked out differently, but we know you did your best and we are really grateful for that.'

'Thank you, I am so sorry for your loss, Matthew was a lovely young man.' Her words were hollow and inadequate she knew, but it was all she could offer. The West's turned away and moved silently towards the car park.

'Come on, I'm taking you out for lunch.' Peter steered his wife towards their car. She had taken the whole day off, not knowing how she would be feeling after the inquest and an afternoon with Peter was the only thing which appealed at that time.

Over lunch Maggie talked about the inquest. The experience was over but she needed to tell someone how she was feeling. In time her supervisor, Joyce, would be her confidant but she also needed to talk to her husband. The verdict had been expected, even the part the drugs had played in his death was not a surprise and they had been glad to hear Alan tell the coroner that the case was not closed in that they were trying to follow the trail of drugs to find the source which Matthew had used.

'The verdict might have been suicide but there was culpability involved in his death. The drug supplier and even the thugs who had beaten him so viciously have some responsibility. They sparked the chain of events leading to Matthew's state of mind, when the coroner said his mind was unbalanced, I was aware that there had been external factors in that. I suppose they pushed him by their actions and by the time he got to Simon and me, he was too far over the edge.' Maggie sighed, then turned to look at Peter and smiled.

'I think you're right,' he said, 'Matthew's obsession with you was perhaps his own way of escaping from the way he was feeling. He was crying out for help, but as so often happens, he went about it in the wrong way.'

'Hey, that's a pretty good summary; perhaps you should be doing my job?' Maggie smiled; her first unforced smile of the day.

****

'I don't want to know.' Sue told the nurse who was applying cold jelly to her stomach before switching on the ultra sound scanner.

'Are you sure?' the nurse asked, 'It helps with the shopping and hubby will know what colour to paint the nursery.'

'I'm sure, and so is *hubby*.' Sue hated that expression and was a little miffed that the nurse was questioning her choice. Whether they had a girl or a boy, this baby was more than welcome, both she and Alan were completely besotted with the idea of a baby. Parenthood was at the heart of every conversation, and every decision they made was with their new addition in mind. 'Bub' was growing, this was the second scan, Alan had been there for the first one and they had talked about nothing else for almost a week. To see the tiny embryo nestled in her womb and to hear its heartbeat was nothing short of incredible. They had bought two copies of the image, one for Sue to take to work and one for Alan, they both boasted quite unashamedly, this baby was everything to them.

'There, see...that's the backbone and a leg there, look!' The nurse sounded so excited that Sue decided to forgive her for any earlier crimes and twisted her head to get a better view of her baby.

As soon as she was out of the hospital, Sue rang Alan but the call went to voicemail which was half expected, he was at the coroner's court today with Maggie and didn't know how long the case would take.

Leaving a brief message to say everything was fine, Sue knew her husband would ring back when he had the chance.

Chapter 23

Maggie had not seen Ruth Duncan for a couple of weeks now. An earlier appointment had been cancelled as the couple were offered a place on a four-day course run by social services for prospective adopters. They had jumped at the chance rather than wait another three months for the next one and now Ruth wanted to talk about it and explore the options with the help of her counsellor. Maggie was quick to notice the relaxed and happy appearance of her client, a return to the confident woman from their first meeting.

'I know the course was close enough to travel daily,' Ruth explained 'but we decided to make it a bit of a break too and stay in a hotel.'

'Good idea, time to relax and talk as well. And what about the course, was it helpful?'

'Mostly, yes; it was certainly informative in outlining procedures and we now know exactly what we'll be letting ourselves into in that respect. And perhaps we have a better understanding of why the process is how it is, although there are still things that I simply don't agree with but will have to accept if we go ahead with this.'

'Such as?' Maggie prompted.

'Well, they try to put a positive spin on it really, saying that today there is so much more support after adoption than there ever used to be and they don't leave you alone to get on with it and so on... but I, rather cynically, thought that this would mean constant monitoring, big brother is watching sort of thing. I have this hang up about adoption not really being adoption if you can't make decisions without consulting social services, or even the birth parents! But the last day lifted

186

my hopes when experienced adopters joined us and we could ask questions to get an idea of how it works in practise. The couple we spoke to suggested that the post adoption support is more of an optional thing. There are monthly 'drop-ins', newsletters, seminars and social events but it's up to us how much or how little support we need. I found that rather comforting.'

Maggie nodded, understanding Ruth's frustrations with the system. If her client could overcome that, she would be almost there.

'How about Andy, is he still keen?'

'Oh yes, keen as mustard. But we're talking more about it now. It was a good idea for us to see you together, it made a big difference. I suppose we're still conscious of wanting to please each other but now that some of the issues have been verbalized it's easier to be more open. We've kept the list too and now as we look at it there are several points we can tick off as being resolved or accepted, so we are definitely making progress.' Ruth continued to talk, moving away from adoption issues to unburden herself of one or two problems at work. The school where she taught was in a deprived area with many social problems. Teaching was often only a part of the job, much of her time being taken up with general welfare problems. Recently Ruth had begun a breakfast club for those pupils who came to school without having eaten for one reason or another. The head was happy to spend a little of their precious budget on fruit and cereal and the initiative seemed to be paying off with pupils being more alert and better behaved during classes. Even truancy figures had improved. Ruth was also trying to get a reading group off the ground in an effort to encourage parents to spend time reading to their children. The school library had been made available for children and parents to borrow books for home reading but the project was slow in taking off. As with many initiatives apathy was the greatest stumbling block and she was constantly trying to think of new ways to make her efforts appeal to parents. Even when the children's enthusiasm was fired up if there was no support from home it would inevitably fizzle out.

Before their session ended Ruth switched topics again, sharing some upsetting news from earlier in the week. Andy's mother had been visiting and casually mentioned that his cousin was pregnant. Ruth was gripped by the familiar pangs of envy whilst trying to be pleased about the news but her mother in law continued by saying how disappointed the couple were, they already had two children and this pregnancy was looked upon as an 'unfortunate' accident, a phrase which made Ruth bite her tongue; such an accident for her would be a dream come true.

As Maggie travelled home some of the afternoon's conversation replayed in her mind. Ruth's drive and enthusiasm was impressive, the concern for her pupils was heartfelt and a credit to her, it seemed that these initiatives were making a real difference to the school. What a great mum Ruth would make. It did seem unfair that so many women who would make excellent mothers were denied the chance because of fertility problems. Maggie could think of several known to her personally, but of course there was never any guarantee that life would be fair.

****

Sarah Beecham hurried to the health centre for a second counselling session, feeling somewhat guilty, as if embarking on a clandestine meeting with a lover and hoping not to bump into anyone she knew. It was a relief to find Maggie waiting in the lobby so they could go straight through to her office, sparing Sarah the dreaded waiting in reception. A brief reminder of the confidentiality clauses gave Sarah a moment to catch her breath, after which Maggie asked what kind of week it had been.

'Pretty average really. Life's become somewhat of a routine lately which at least ensures that I don't make too many mistakes to annoy Mark.'

'And is that important to you, not to annoy Mark?'

'It makes for an easier life.'

'Sarah, I wondered what you would think about doing a little exercise to help us explore aspects of your life and how you feel about it?'

'What kind of exercise?'

'Well, I wondered how you would feel about drawing?'

'I'm not very good at it.'

'You don't have to be, it is what you draw that matters not how well you do it.'

'Okay, I'll give it a go.'

Maggie was encouraged at Sarah's willingness to try new tactics and moved to the desk, opening a drawer to return with a pad of plain paper and a handful of coloured felt tipped pens and placing them on the coffee table. Sarah watched every movement with only a hint of suspicion in her eyes.

'What I have in mind,' Maggie explained, 'is for you to draw a house. But not any old house; this is you, your life as you see it today. So, you could draw a house with open windows and doors, a garden flooded with sunshine, a yard, flowers, trees, anything you want, this is your house, your life. Put into it whatever you think is appropriate'

'Fine, that doesn't sound too difficult.' Sarah picked up the black felt pen and after studying the paper for only a few moments, set to work, asking,

'Are you going to watch me?'

'Do you want me to watch you?'

'No, why don't you draw one too?'

Maggie chuckled quietly,

'All right then, I will.' Retrieving another pad of paper from the desk and sitting opposite her client she proceeded to draw her own 'house'. There was a comfortable silence between the women. Maggie of course had no intention of showing her own efforts; she rarely disclosed any personal facts to clients. After a short time during which the only sound was the squeaking of felt tips on paper, Sarah sat back.

'There,' she said, placing the pad on the table. Maggie stopped her own endeavours slipping the pad under the cushion on the seat.

'May I?' she asked, picking up the drawing when Sarah nodded permission.

The house was tall, more of a sky-scraper, all in black with no other colour in sight. The windows were small and very dark and Maggie could see no door and no light in any of the windows.

'It's very tall Sarah, do you know why?'

'I'm not sure... it takes up less space I think, less of a footprint and it doesn't intrude on other people's houses.'

'And the windows, they are quite small and dark aren't they?'

'Yes.'

'So, is there no one at home?'

'No, I mean yes, I am at home, in there.'

'I can't see you Sarah, there are no lights on. Where are you?'

'In the attic, at the top.'

'But why have you not put the light on?'

'Because I don't want to be found.' This last statement was barely a whisper. Sarah stared at the picture she had drawn and the tears began to flow silently. Maggie waited a few moments before asking,

'And are you happy living in this house Sarah?'

'No! I want to go back to my old house, where I grew up.'

'Do you want to tell me about your old house, or draw it perhaps?'

Without waiting to reply Sarah turned to a fresh sheet of paper and began to draw again. This house was as different as it could possibly be to the first effort. Large open windows let in sunshine, bathing the whole structure in light. Sarah drew quickly, almost frantically, using all the colours Maggie had placed on the table, the images childlike and simple with a large yellow sun filling the top right hand corner and a huge bright orange front door standing open, welcoming the world, inviting anyone and everyone to enter. A blue picket fence circling a garden was swiftly sketched enclosing brightly coloured flowers, with daisy dotted grass and a tree smothered in pink blossom. The outline of two other houses flanked this one at a quirky angle, creating the effect of a personality, a happy caricature, offering an open invitation to enter. Rarely had Maggie found this exercise presenting such a distinct contrast which was so telling of her client's current situation.

'Is this your house too Sarah?' Maggie asked.

'No, not any more but I used to live there... and wish I still did.'

'Sarah,' Maggie spoke softly, 'You are an intelligent woman and I think you know what this suggests. If the first house, the house that is you, is such a dark and unhappy place, is there anything you could do to make it more like the second house, the one you grew up in, the one that is such a happy house?'

'I'm not sure there is anything I can do.'

'But if this house is you, or yours, don't you think you can alter it?'

Sarah didn't answer, dropping her head as if it was too heavy to hold up anymore and looking down into her lap with an almost imperceptible shake of the head.

After a few moments silence, Sarah looked up and attempted to smile at Maggie.

'Sorry, I'm feeling a little melancholy today.'

'Any particular reason?'

'Only the usual silly things, I overslept at the weekend which put Mark into a foul mood, although later he seemed to have forgotten about it. I sometimes wonder if it's me reading too much into things, I honestly don't know anymore.'

'Have you tried to talk to Mark about his moods?'

'Well, that's the thing really, I did try after the over-sleeping episode and he didn't seem to know what I was talking about. It's all so very confusing, I can't seem to get anything right these days.'

As their time together ended Sarah declined to take the drawings with her as she hurried back to work. Maggie studied both pictures, holding them side by side. Such clear disparity was a concern. Instinct told her that Sarah knew exactly what was wrong with her life but somehow she lacked the courage to admit it let alone address it. Any remaining confidence was being continually undermined and Maggie was almost sure her husband was controlling her, but the girl herself either couldn't see it or did not want to see it. Sarah had expressed doubts about her own sanity and after only two sessions Maggie could hardly judge such issues, but Dr. Williams had certainly discounted any serious mental health issues, so she was inclined to think the problems were most likely connected to the marriage. The question for Maggie would be whether or not Sarah wanted things to change. If during the course of their sessions it became obvious that she did, then Maggie's role would be one of support throughout the transition period. If however her client did not want to make changes in her life then Maggie would have to accept that decision and her role would be the same with a different goal of helping Sarah to work out how to achieve happiness with these life choices. Perhaps by next week this young woman would have reached some decision and made choices which would present clear goals to work towards.

Chapter 24

Ellie returned from the park feeling quite tired. The heat of the sun which seemed to be getting stronger each day had sapped her energy and if Sam remained asleep as he was now, perhaps she might take the opportunity to lie on the sofa and rest for a while herself. Unlocking the door and then turning to assess the best way of getting the pushchair over the step without disturbing Sam, Ellie's attention was drawn to the figure of a man hurrying towards the house, trying to catch her attention before she went inside. He waved as he jogged closer, giving her no alternative except to see what he wanted.

'Can I help?' The man offered, bending down to grasp the wheels of the pushchair. Ellie had no choice but to let him help lift the sleeping baby over the door step but she then swiftly wheeled Sam inside, away from the door and stood blocking the entrance to keep this stranger out.

'Ellie, don't you know me?' he clearly knew her or her name at least.

'It's Dave, I live at number 40, see, just over there.'

Ellie looked in the direction he was pointing; so far any contact with their neighbours had been avoided, anticipating the difficulties of explaining that she no longer knew them. Half smiling in an effort to make light of the situation she said,

'Hi Dave, I'm sorry but actually I don't remember you, I've not been too well lately.' Ellie attempted to retreat, taking a couple of steps backwards into the house.

'So it's true then, the amnesia I mean?'

'Yes, it is and I am really sorry but I must go and see to Sam now.' As Ellie tried to close the front door, Dave put his foot inside, pushing her back until she almost toppled over.

'Hey, don't do that! Please go, I'm busy.' Fear was rising in her chest but Dave only moved further into the hall.

'Come on; don't try to tell me you have forgotten our little arrangement? Thursday mornings, as soon as Phil is out at work, you remember that don't you?' Standing way too close now; she could feel his breath on her face and see the smug expression as he reached out and held both of Ellie's arms, pinning her back against the wall. Fear prevented the scream which seemed stifled inside, fear for herself and Sam but mostly by what this man Dave was implying with his words. Physically Ellie began to tremble and a knot in her stomach was rising as if she had actually been punched. Could she really have had some kind of arrangement with him? Surely not? Tears were threatening to fall but all she could do was hold her body rigid and hope and pray that he would go away. Dave touched her face,

'Hey, don't get sentimental with me now. This amnesia thing might fool everyone else, but I know you better than that. How about we get reacquainted while the little man's asleep?'

Pulling her right hand free Ellie slapped him hard across the face and was surprised to see a trickle of blood run down from the corner of his mouth.

'You bitch!' he shouted, waking Sam who began to cry at the sudden noise. Dave released his grasp, glaring at her with dark angry eyes.

'Okay if that's the way you want to play it I'll go for now, but I will be back tomorrow, Thursday as usual? And don't think you can get out of it by not being here

195

or I might have to tell that doting husband of yours what his wife is really like. You've never turned me down before, in fact you are the one who made the first move, so don't think you can go all righteous on me now; until tomorrow then.' Dave turned and walked out, deliberately slamming the door, causing Sam to wail even louder.

Ellie was trembling and felt suddenly very cold even though the sun was streaming in through the windows. Managing to lift Sam from the pushchair and collapsing onto the sofa, she held her son and rocked to and fro as they both cried. Sleep was no longer an option for Sam or for Ellie. Their tears had dried and the little boy was now busily toddling around the room from chair to sofa using anything he could to help steady his still wobbly legs. Ellie had barely moved, frozen with fear from the encounter and terrified to think that there might be any truth in this man's accusations. Surely not, why would there be, when, as everyone kept telling her, she was so happily married?

The next few hours were an effort. Sam needed feeding after which he thankfully settled down for a nap. His mother however could not eat or rest for the fearful thoughts which were filling her mind. When Sam woke up Ellie rang her parents asking them to come as she was feeling unwell. Grace and Derek readily came to take charge of their grandson which was always a delight, naturally concerned for Ellie but accepting that it was only a bad headache so Derek drove her home with instructions to go to bed and leave everything to them.

Ellie did go to bed but knew she wouldn't sleep. Even the comfort of a warm bed, usually a place of refuge, could not stop the dreadful thoughts from crowding in on her. Dave was a horrible man, this was obvious even from such a short meeting and she was certain, well almost certain that she would never embark on a relationship with a man like that, or any other man. It suddenly occurred to her that she was afraid. Having so recently begun to find her life again and enjoying every aspect of it, it was now suddenly all in jeopardy and could all be lost, Sam, Phil and even the respect of her parents. But what could she do? Telling anyone was inconceivable, what would she say? Ellie had lost ten years of memories and was only now coming to terms with all the implications and was ready to begin a new life and stop fretting over the amnesia but now all that new found happiness had been snatched away. Now it was even more important that she remember those missing years, not only for the positive things she had forgotten but for anything which might make her ashamed. Had she been cheating on Phil? The thought was abhorrent, but there was no way of knowing. And there was very little time to think through these developments as tomorrow was Thursday and Dave had made it clear what was expected of her.

****

Charles Brown, one of Peter's partners in RBL Architects Ltd had been purposely vague on the telephone fending off questions with a laugh.

'You'll have to come in if you want to know and better make it soon before the champagne is finished.' Charles concluded the rather cryptic phone call.

'Well it must be good news for them to have champagne,' Peter thought putting down the phone and searching for a pair shoes. He found one behind the sofa but the other was missing so he made his way to the bedroom to fetch another pair, not wanting to waste time hunting for a lost shoe. The first thing he saw in the bedroom was Tara, their cat, curled up and fast asleep in the missing size nine. Smiling at the sight and wondering how on earth she had managed to drag it there, he opened the wardrobe to find another pair; there was no way Tara would give up her trophy now.

During the four mile drive to the office Peter speculated on what could be causing celebration so early on a Wednesday morning. After tossing a few ideas around in his head, the only logical conclusion was that they must have secured the contract to design the new shopping outlet on the edge of town for which they had recently tendered. If it was this it had been decided with remarkable speed, a decision was not expected for another three or four weeks, possibly longer. Pulling into the car park at the back of the RBL offices Peter had dismissed the contract idea and was no further forward in guessing the reason for being summoned to a celebration.

Walking into the office Peter could have been excused for thinking he had come across a Christmas party even though it was mid July. Stephen Roberts, the third partner in the firm, thrust a glass at him and proceeded to fill it to the brim with the last of the champagne.

'Well tell me first,' Peter pleaded, 'How can I enjoy celebrating unless I know what the occasion is?' Looking from one partner to the other and then Lucy, their relatively new secretary, they were all so much in the party mood that Peter felt quite out of the loop.

'We three...' Charles halted to correct himself giving a little bow in the general direction of Lucy, 'Sorry, four including you Lucy, have won an international award for 'Sustainability in Practice' for the eco-friendly Academy we designed three years ago.' Charles was positively beaming, an enormous smile across his usually sombre face, brought about by the excellent news or the average champagne, it was difficult to tell. 'So my friends, a huge pat on the back is in order, but no more of this stuff or else we'll not be fit to work for the rest of the day.'

Peter could hardly believe it, he remembered the project well enough, it was their first really big contract as RBL Ltd and one to which they had all contributed more than their usual hours to see the Academy up and running in record time. Their brief had been to design a building with very little 'footprint', one which would generate its own electricity through solar panels and be constructed using as much recycled fabric as possible. Peter, who was usually responsible for costing large projects, had found this one a real challenge and had spent many hours researching the best materials to use and where to source them whilst his partners designed the Academy using cutting edge technology and working closely with the engineers from very early on in the design to make the whole project as 'green' as it could possibly be. This was, as well as being their first major development, the one of which they were most proud. The Academy was built to be a prototype for future such buildings, housing a thousand pupils which although not the largest learning facility, was certainly the most economic purpose built college in the whole area. Their involvement in the build had taken up much of their time over the two years of its construction.

'The prize is irrelevant,' Stephen broke in, 'but the kudos is everything. I think from today we will be able to pick and choose which projects we want to take and dare I say, what fee we require for the work we do take

199

on. The Architect's Monthly who sponsors the award has already been in touch about a feature spread on us which will be great publicity. But there is one little hiccup to all this adulation and that is, that one of us is expected to give a lecture on sustainability in design, which my friend,' he looked directly at Peter 'we have decided should be you.'

'But I've never done any public speaking before, why not you or Charles?'

'I have already booked a holiday on the dates they have given and Charles suffers from travel sickness.'

'Travel sickness, where is this lecture to be given?'

'Well there are two venues, Las Vegas and then New York, the big apple no less, but don't worry you can deliver the same lecture in both places.'

Peter's partners were both smiling as this information sank in.

'All expenses paid, naturally.' Stephen added 'and it's in three weeks time, so you had better order your visa and Maggie's too, I expect she'll want to go with you.'

'I couldn't, surely one of you should go? I'm not up to speed on many of the aspects of the build, you know I'm a real dinosaur when it comes to computers and you used technology for so much of the design.'

'You could waffle?' Charles suggested with a grin.

'No', Stephen laughed, 'the design process was more than computer generated; you put in equally as many hours as we did and became somewhat of an expert in recycled materials and where to source them. And take no notice of Charles, you wouldn't need to waffle, that's the champagne talking. Your input was every bit as valuable as ours, besides we thought you would enjoy the chance of a trip to the states, we know things haven't been easy for Maggie lately. Just accept graciously and go home to begin writing that lecture.

You know either of us will be happy to write up a piece on the computer generated design, so you'll be able to weave it into your lecture no problem.'

'Well.' Peter hardly knew what to say, 'I didn't expect that the good news you insisted I came in for was this. Thank you both for your generosity, I shall accept it in the manner it is offered and now I'll ring Mags and surprise her.'

****

Maggie had to ask Peter to repeat the news again but still could barely take it in. For the firm to win such an award was wonderful but to be whisked off to America and in only three weeks time was incredible. Yes, she assured him, her diary at work could be re-arranged; they had been planning to take a holiday in the near future in any case but intended going no further than Scotland.

'We can have a good chat about it tonight,' Maggie's mind was already trying to work out the logistics of a trip at such short notice. Who would look after Ben and Tara was the first consideration followed by whether or not their visas could be arranged in time.

'No, can't wait, I'll pick you up at lunch time and we can grab a sandwich or something, okay?' Peter was keen, his enthusiasm infectious.

'Fine, it will have to be at one though, I have a client at twelve.' Placing the phone back onto its cradle, Maggie smiled. Peter sounded so animated and alive it was good to hear that in his voice. There was however a little niggle at the back of her mind as to whether such a gruelling trip would be too much for him, but it was a fantastic opportunity, she had never been to America and didn't think Peter had either. They would cope;

201

when they married it was understood that they would take each day as it came and live for the moment. So far, Peter's condition had been manageable and he seemed excited about this trip, she would travel beside him on the strength of his enthusiasm and they would enjoy every minute

Chapter 25

Ellie hadn't slept all night and was making coffee in the kitchen when her mother came in, glancing in her direction with concern.

'Do you think you should see the doctor love? You're looking very peaky, not well at all.'

'I'll be fine, I just didn't sleep much that's all.'

'But what about that headache yesterday, it came on quite suddenly didn't it?'

Forcing herself to smile in an attempt at reassurance, Ellie poured coffee and offered some to her mother. The two women sat at the little pine table in the kitchen, the early morning quiet almost tangible, broken only when Grace spoke again,

'If you're not feeling well I could take Sam for the day, it would be no trouble.'

'Thanks Mum, that's kind of you but we're in a routine now, best keep to what he knows.'

'Then I'll come with you and can at least take him out for a while so you can have a break.'

Ellie studied her mother; Grace was still an attractive lady for her sixty four years with only a few wrinkles which seemed to have the effect of enhancing an already expressive face. Ellie had caused so much anxiety lately albeit unintentionally, but was she about to cause more? Forcing a smile, and then deciding the idea might be exactly the right thing if Dave came round as he had threatened, the reply was positive,

'I'd appreciate that, thanks Mum'

The quiet took over once more, mother and daughter content with the silence, a precursor before plunging into the day ahead.

'Hey good morning, two for the price of one I see!' Phil was in high spirits, the very sight of him making Ellie shudder, would his happiness be shattered yet again and all because of something that couldn't even be remembered? Sam began patting on the sofa against which he stood; his chubby round face alight with pleasure, ready for another fun packed day. Grace was first to pick him up, bringing him to his mother, saying,

'Have you got a kiss for Mummy Sam?' The answer was yes as the little boy almost leapt from his grandmother's arms to squash his face into Ellie's cheek, who happily lifted him up, burying her face into his soft sweet neck and breathing in the scent of soap and talcum powder. Grace began to explain her presence, which immediately changed Phil's happy go lucky mood. His brow furrowed with concern as he asked Ellie what was wrong.

'I'm fine, really. I had a headache yesterday which is why mum and dad stepped in and I didn't sleep too well so I'm a little tired now, that's all.' She forced a smile which wouldn't come naturally but the last thing she wanted was for them both to begin the questioning again. Her emotions were all over the place as it were, being frightened that Dave would call again or that he might become angry and tell Phil they had been having an affair. Strangely it was her husband whose comfort she craved. There had been very little between them in the way of physical contact, the odd peck on the cheek and a brief hug, the closest time had been in the restaurant when Ellie had reached out for his hand and Phil had kissed hers. How she needed that physical comfort now; another sign perhaps that the old feelings towards him were being rekindled?

Soon Phil had to leave for work; kissing Sam he gave Ellie a squeeze on the shoulder,

'Take it easy today love, you are still not up to full strength you know so don't overdo things.'

'I won't.' Standing at the door to watch him go Ellie instinctively looked across to number 40 and was sure the curtains were falling back into place as if someone had been watching.

For the first hour Grace made her daughter sit down to watch Sam play while she found a small pile of ironing to do. Sam wanted a hundred per cent attention which normally would have been no problem but Ellie's mind was elsewhere, straining to hear any portentous noises from outside. It was when Grace had gone into the kitchen to put the kettle on that the door bell eventually did ring. A feeling of dread almost froze Ellie to the spot but she forced herself to go to the door, if it was Dave then he probably knew she was in.

'Hello, you're looking rather sexy today' were his first words, which charged her with a new emotion as she glared at him and hissed,

'Shut up' with a force which surprised even her. 'My mother's in the kitchen and Sam's awake, there is no way you are coming in here so go, go away and leave me alone!'

Dave was visibly surprised at this response but gathered his wits enough to retort,

'Don't think I can be dismissed so easily, we have a history you and I, there are things we need to talk about. Now, will you agree to meet me next Thursday when I'm off or shall I come in and begin by telling your mother what her precious daughter gets up to when she's bored?'

Ellie felt trapped and needed time to think.

'All right, I'll be in the park at ten thirty on Thursday morning, with Sam on the swings.' She glanced round to see if her mother was within hearing distance, fortunately she wasn't. Dave again grinned, moving his eyes slowly up and down her body, making her flesh crawl. Turning to leave, he had the audacity to blow a kiss, at which point Ellie firmly closed the door.

'Who was that dear?' Grace asked coming from the kitchen with two steaming cups of coffee.

'It was a neighbour wanting to see Phil about something. I told him he was at work.'

'Strange, you'd think he would know that.'

'Hmm' Ellie felt only mild relief at having managed to stall Dave today but he seemed persistent and she would have to think up some way to get rid of this awful man. Perhaps she could explain that if they had been having an affair it had been a mistake and it would have to end now. No, that was tantamount to admitting an affair and she wasn't completely convinced that they had. Having Grace there bought a few days' reprieve but on the flip side there was more time to worry about what might have been going on before the accident, about which she was now totally unaware. Tomorrow would bring the next session with Maggie; could they discuss this dilemma or would it ruin the respect they seemed to already have developed for each other? It was going to be a long week and Ellie was unsure if she could handle the pressure.

****

Maggie and Peter had talked until well after midnight, the chief topic of conversation being their visit to the States. At breakfast Peter resumed the conversation with an impish grin,

'I once heard New York described as a sucked orange, whatever that means, but I'll happily take my chance if you're still keen. I thought if you were free this afternoon we could go into the travel agents to book

206

our tickets, opportunities such as this don't come along very often.'

'You won't put me off with descriptions like that; I'm even more excited after sleeping on it and I only have one client this morning so after that my Friday afternoon will be all yours. '

The morning's client was Ellie Graham, someone whom Maggie was beginning to admire enormously. This was one of the worst case scenarios imaginable, yet it was a reality to Ellie and Maggie could hardly begin to understand how strange it must be to have lost a decade of your history. Yet the young woman seemed to be rapidly coming to terms with the amnesia, even looking for positive aspects and dealing with the situation pragmatically and with a degree of humour. It was therefore a surprise when Ellie arrived, seeming to have lost some of the sparkle and personality which had been visibly developing on previous occasions. Wearing no make-up and with eyes framed by dark circles, her expression was doleful, not at all what Maggie had been expecting.

'Hi Ellie, it's good to see you again.' Her smile received little response. Maggie let the silence hang between them for a while, sometimes quiet can be soothing and Ellie certainly looked as if she needed a little tranquillity. After two or three minutes Maggie asked softly,

'Do you feel up to talking today?'

For the first time Ellie looked up, a brief moment of eye contact, then turning away she drew in a deep breath.

'Perhaps you could tell me how you are feeling right now?' Maggie tried again.

'I wish I was dead.' An edgy almost angry voice was again incongruent to her attitude on previous occasions.

'You wish you were dead? Do you want to tell me why?' A few more moments of silence stretched out between them which Maggie felt could become a wedge separating them, yet still she waited until Ellie was ready to talk.

'I don't know who I am anymore,' this voice was quieter, laden with grief, and then more silence filled the little room. Maggie was the one to speak next,

'Is this the amnesia or has something else happened more recently to make you feel this way?'

Ellie's eyes widened and as she lifted her head there was an expression almost approaching fear etched on her face.

'I've been confronted with something... something that makes me feel that the 'me' before my accident may not have been a very nice person. It seems I've done... things which I feel ashamed of now, but apparently didn't then, and I was beginning to enjoy my life too...my baby...my husband.' The tears came and great sobs shook her whole body. Maggie moved beside her sliding an arm around the younger woman's shoulder, an instinctive gesture of comfort. Unable to guess what had happened to Ellie to set her back like this, it still wasn't entirely unexpected. Her client had been improving so quickly, perhaps too quickly, and now whatever it was she had learned about her past was threatening to reverse the progress already achieved. It was one thing to learn, or re-learn, things about others and be tolerant and accepting of them. But to find out something distasteful about herself was certainly, it seemed, unforgivable. Maggie had often perceived how people could accept faults in others which would be wholly unacceptable in themselves, which appeared to be the case with Ellie now.

'Don't be hard on yourself Ellie. I'm assuming this is something you have learnt from someone else and not information that you've remembered?'

Ellie nodded, blowing her nose in an effort to compose herself. Maggie waited, not wanting to rush or make her feel obliged to explain. Moving back to her own seat, Maggie was wishing there was some way of taking away this young woman's pain. The temptation in such situations was to offer advice or try to make the problem seem less of a stumbling block than it actually was, but this was Ellie's hour, Ellie's life, and she must find her own answers. Finally she spoke.

'I've had a terrible weekend. I met someone who I didn't like at all, but apparently who I had...spent time with before the accident. I have learned things about myself, things I've done which...well, which I find appalling.' She looked directly at Maggie with something akin to hope in her eyes, a longing for her counsellor to take away the problems, to make everything right again. Maggie saw this many times and ached to be able to wave a magic wand, but of course that was impossible, there was very little she could do other than to listen, to reflect her client's words and explore all the options of how to deal with situations and emotions. She could not and would not want to tell her clients to take a particular course of action; her role was one of support not direction.

'Have these things you've learned come from one person or a number of people?'

'Just one.' Ellie whispered.

'Then perhaps you should be looking at why this person has told you these things and what kind of person he or she is. My supervisor told me a few years ago that if I received criticism I should look at who it was offering the criticism. If it was someone for whom I had a high regard and a measure of respect, then I

209

should ask myself if the remarks were valid and if they were, take them on board. If it was from someone whom I knew to be unreliable, envious perhaps, or even a gossip, then I should take the remarks with quite a liberal pinch of salt. I don't know if this would apply to your situation, but maybe you could somehow check these things you are supposed to have done with someone else, someone whose judgement you do respect?'

Ellie was listening intently, taking in Maggie's quietly spoken words as if they were a lifeline. Wondering if she could confide in her counsellor and relate all the details, she waivered, almost certain Maggie would not be shocked, but was so embarrassed her face flushed even thinking about it. Putting it into words simply wasn't an option so she remained silent. To try to confirm what Dave had said was almost impossible, the only people she trusted and had respect for at the moment were her parents and Phil and these were the very people she would not want to know such things. Ellie remained pensive and withdrawn for the remainder of their time together and Maggie felt it right to remind her that she would always try to be available in between appointments and that Ellie could ring the surgery if necessary.

Chapter 26

The two of them were down on the rug on all fours, heads swaying from side to side with a pile of cushions in between them. To anyone watching this impromptu game of peek-a-boo between father and son it would have raised a smile, if not all out laughter, but to Ellie the scene playing out before her tugged at something deep inside, causing her to gasp and swallow hard in an effort to stem the threatening tears. Besides experiencing the sting of anxiety, her primary emotion was one of love, not only for her son who had stolen her heart in such a short space of time, but also now for Phil.

'I love him.' The words were not spoken aloud but brought with them such a tangle of emotions. 'How could I have risked hurting these two wonderful people? I must have been mad.' The thoughts brought such pain that she had to turn away, making some feeble excuse to leave the room. It was Saturday and Phil had the weekend off work and was delighted when Ellie had agreed to share the two days with him and their child. Not seeming to pick up on the anguish his wife was feeling, the game continued, Phil delighting in his son's laughter and childish pleasure.

Ellie busied herself in the kitchen. Grace had sent a dish of chicken casserole which would suffice for the whole weekend and Ellie lifted it into the oven then proceeded to set the table for their meal. Inevitably thoughts of Dave returned, bringing with them a sickening feeling of revulsion, not only for him but for herself too. Whatever had caused her to enter into a relationship with another man was now unfathomable. Had marriage to Phil not been happy? If not, then her parents and even Phil himself had certainly not picked up on it. Had she actually had feelings for Dave which had led her down the disastrous path of an affair? One thing was clear and that was that it needed sorting out and quickly too. Rightly or wrongly Ellie had agreed to meet Dave on the following Thursday, a meeting she dreaded but had to go through with, or risk the alternative of Phil finding out. Ellie had no idea how that meeting would go or what on earth she could say to Dave. Could he be reasoned with and accept that whatever had transpired between them was in the past? Or would he insist on carrying on their elicit relationship, forcing her to choose himself or Phil finding out how badly she had behaved? There were too many questions with not a single answer. If this Dave felt anything at all for her perhaps he would leave her in peace? Yet judging from their last encounter she could expect nothing as chivalrous from him. It was a mess, a complete and utter disaster, apparently of her own making and now there was so little time to find a solution to a problem which she didn't fully understand.

****

Sarah's weekend had dragged, and the arrival of Monday morning was a blessed relief. Mark had vacillated between the usual mix of moods, one minute angry over some trivial incident and the next all sweetness and light. Sarah could not decide which was preferable. One thing however was becoming clear and that was the fact that she could not carry on living this way much longer. Maggie had asked what her goals were in life, a simple enough question which had prompted a measure of soul searching. Drawing those houses had also given Sarah a jolt; having earnestly drawn the tall, dark, unfriendly house, the one she now acknowledged as representing her present life, it had been difficult to explain to Maggie why she accepted living this way when it was the twenty first century and not pre emancipation days. It was hard enough to understand her own feelings, never mind expressing them and explaining how things were when, theoretically, it was within her power to change her circumstances. Maybe it was something to do with her upbringing. Sarah's parents had instilled their own moral values in their daughter; not only by what they said but by example, therefore her idea of marriage was one of total compatibility, underpinned by selfless love and respect. Perhaps such a view was immature, too simplistic. If she thought about it there were not many marriages as successful as her parents. And then there was Sue, straight talking, indomitable Sue. Hers was a happy marriage and she had more than hinted that Mark was the one at fault; ergo it was he who should change. But then Sue had not met Mark and might think otherwise if she had. Still at the back of Sarah's mind was the nagging fear of dementia or insanity. The doctor, Maggie and even Sue offered reassurance that this was not the case, but there were so many inexplicable instances, things that only Mark had witnessed, which made Sarah wonder if he was right and she did need looking after. It was all too confusing and the more her thoughts dwelt on it the more confused she became. At least there was her job, perhaps not the most exciting in the world but it was somewhere she felt safe and confident, a job which Sarah knew she was good at and where the banter with colleagues and patients provided a refuge; life was comfortingly predictable at work, which most certainly could not be said about life at home with Mark.

By mid morning Sarah's mood had lightened. Marie had recounted an unbelievable tale of her weekend and a date with the latest boyfriend. Sarah had been brought out of herself and almost descended into an uncontrollable fit of laughter until remembering that patients were waiting who would not appreciate the two receptionists giggling like schoolgirls whilst they anticipated their fate in the dentist's chair.

It was just before lunch when the woman in the green raincoat came in. Marie had left for her break and Sarah was alone on reception.

'Hi, can I help you?' The lady looked familiar but then most patients did. The woman looked into Sarah's eyes as if deciding whether to speak or not, which again was not unusual, many patients were nervous, no one actually enjoyed visiting the dentist.

'Do you have an appointment?' She tried.

'Are you Sarah?'

'Yes.'

'Sarah Beecham?'

'Er... yes, I'm sorry should I know you?'

'No, but I think we should get to know one another.'

The stranger was beginning to unnerve Sarah now, whatever could she want? Before there was time to ask, the woman leaned closer and speaking in a low, almost threatening voice said,

'Meet me in half an hour at the Coffee Bean,' before spinning sharply around to leave. Sarah didn't know what to make of the brief, unsettling encounter. Half an hour would be the start of her lunch break and the cafe the woman had mentioned was nearby, the one where she often met Sue. How did this woman know her name as well as other things, such as where she worked and perhaps even what time she took her lunch break? A sudden cold shiver ran through her body, fearfulness, but also curiosity. The waiting room was quiet with only two patients waiting for late running appointments, Marie would be back soon but telling her about the woman would only prompt questions, and some vague instinct was telling Sarah not to confide in her colleague, yet some advice would certainly help. Sue would be the one to ask, so quickly picking up the telephone she rang the surgery number. Fortunately it was Sue who answered and Sarah, turning away from the waiting patients, quietly began to describe the perplexing visit. Sue would normally have laughed at such a mysterious event, but hearing the tremor in her friend's voice and knowing how low she was feeling at this time, Sue tried to see things from Sarah's point of view.

'You don't have to go you know?'

'But if I don't she might come back here, or I'd probably drive myself crazy wondering what it was all about.'

'That's true. Look, why don't you go. It's a public place, probably quite busy by now; I would think you'll be safe enough.'

'Do you think... no, you're busy I'm sure.'

'Do I think what, that I could come too?'

'Well, yes, I'd feel much happier having a friendly face around.'

'Okay, I can manage that, I'm due to break for lunch myself soon. But I think it would be better if I sat somewhere else and you didn't acknowledge me, or your stranger might be spooked and not come in.'

'Oh thanks Sue, I should have known I could depend on you, I don't feel half so anxious knowing you will be there.'

'Yeah, I can always throw my weight around if needs be, I've plenty of that these days.'

215

Sarah pushed the door of the High Street cafe open twenty minutes later and immediately saw the woman in the green coat sitting by the window nursing a cup of coffee, with a second one on the table. As she sat down the woman pushed the extra cup across the table.

'Here, this is for you, you're going to need it.'

****

Maggie's mind buzzed with of thoughts of America. They had booked their tickets on Friday afternoon and the weekend was spent in trying to solve the practical issues of such a long trip. Maggie had never been away from home for more than two weeks at a time and was a little concerned that she might be homesick. Ringing her parents in Scotland to tell them their news, her biggest problem was solved immediately.

'We'll come down to take care of Ben and Tara.' Helen Price volunteered as if doing no more than offering to make her daughter a cup of tea.

'Oh Mum, would you? That would be wonderful, I won't worry half as much if they can be here with you, thanks, you are an angel.'

'I hope not, the last I heard you had to be dead to be one of those!' Helen laughed. 'It will be a holiday for us too and I'm assuming this means we won't be having you and Peter up here for a while.'

'I'm sorry Mum but this uses up most of my holidays from work and I wouldn't want to push for more, they have been so good to me when I needed time off lately.'

'It's okay love, I understand, anyway we can maybe stay on a while when you come home?'

'Wonderful, I'd love that, I'm dying for you to see the house, I know you'll love it.'

Maggie was now flicking through her diary. Another Monday morning and less than three weeks to let her clients know she would be going away and to rearrange their sessions. Pangs of guilt always washed over her when telling clients about forthcoming holidays, as if she was deserting them, yet common sense told her it was important to look after herself as well and this particular time away would be special for her and Peter. The thought of three weeks in the States with him was quite exciting; it would be more of a honeymoon than they had managed to have after their wedding and of course any time spent with Peter was cherished. His health problems meant that Maggie never took him for granted, her own life experience had taught her to live each day to the full, a mantra she encouraged clients to adopt.

As Maggie was working out how best to rearrange her diary, Peter was at home trying to make a start on writing the lecture he was to deliver in the States. He too had never been there before and the prospect of sharing this experience with Maggie was certainly pleasing. He had only read about Las Vegas and New York in the American crime novels he enjoyed reading and so was pleased to be visiting a few of the locations in which they were set but his mind needed to focus on the lectures. Until confident that he had produced the standard of material expected of him, there would be no peace. The lecture would somehow have to incorporate the same enthusiasm they had felt for the project when designing the academy in the first place. So much seemed to have happened since then but it was important to turn his mind back to the excitement of the original design which won the tender and set them the task of cutting edge sustainability in architecture. He would take Ben for a walk; their new surroundings never failed to uplift his spirit and would hopefully inspire him to recapture the essence of nature which was at the heart of their award winning design. Perhaps then the words would come to express the thoughts which had been tumbling around his brain since finding out about the trip.

****

Ruth Duncan had not made another appointment to see Maggie; they had parted on the understanding that the counselling sessions could be picked up again if necessary but the morning's post brought Maggie a letter with news which was not entirely unexpected and confirmed that her role in helping Ruth was at an end.

Dear Maggie

I really don't know how to begin to thank you for your patient and wise counsel over the last couple of months. You have been such a help to me in sorting out my feelings and moving on to the next stage of my life and I am sure you won't be surprised at all that the next stage is to go ahead with adoption. Now that I have made the decision I'm as keen as Andy! We wish there was some kind of fast-tracking in the process but like all bureaucracy these days the wheels move at a snail's pace. Still we are trying to use the waiting time for preparation and we're also hoping to have a 'grown up' holiday before our child arrives. We are off to Italy in the summer holidays to do the whole culture bit, art galleries, museums, the full works. It's the kind of holiday we'll not want to take with a child in tow, I expect then it will be all buckets and spades, sun cream and sandwiches. I can hardly wait! Actually it might be a case of two children in tow. We have agreed to take siblings, an older child and a baby. There is evidently a great need for this and not many adoptive parents want to take on two children. If I'm honest it is also a way to ensure we will be considered for a new baby. Now that the decision's made, I'd happily take on a readymade family of three if they came along, but Andy might have something to say about that!

I feel our marriage has also taken a new direction, not that we didn't have a strong relationship before but telling Andy about my past mistakes has certainly been cathartic and has strangely brought us even closer together. Again you played a big part in that situation, so can I say thank you for that too.

Well I'm sure you have better things to do than reading all my news, but I wanted you to know that you have made an enormous difference to me and I will always be grateful.

Many thanks,
Ruth Duncan

Maggie read the letter with a smile on her face; it was so good to hear from Ruth. Usually when clients finished their allotted span she never found out how they progressed, whether they were happy with life, had moved on or if her efforts been helpful. She would make a point of ringing Ruth one evening to thank her for taking the time to write, it helped to know that her work had benefitted the Duncan's, especially while the ever present doubts about Matthew West were still so raw. From Maggie's point of view, closing another client's case made it a little easier to plan for their American trip but she wanted to speak to Ruth once more to wish her well on the adventure into parenthood.

Chapter 27

Sarah was feeling cold even though the temperature outside was pleasantly warm, so, sitting opposite the stranger she wrapped her hands around the offered cup of coffee. Sue was sitting at a small table near the kitchen, neither of them had acknowledged the other as arranged but her presence was a comfort and Sarah felt a little bolder with Sue nearby.

'Who are you?' was the first and most obvious question, followed immediately by 'and what do you want?'

The stranger smiled, a rather sad smile as if completely exhausted or coming to the end of a difficult time.

'Diane, Di if you like.'

'Well Diane, what's all this about?' Strangely the woman's demeanour now made Sarah feel less intimidated and more in control. She sat upright in her chair looking directly into a pair of green eyes which gave nothing away as to why she had been summoned. Diane stirred her coffee with the plastic teaspoon, unhurried and thoughtful, as if planning what to say next.

'Diane Beecham if you want my full name.'

'Beecham... are you a relative of my husband's?'

'Not exactly, I'm his wife.' The smile was gone and she looked at Sarah now with an expression of concern or possibly even pity. Sarah's face had turned pale, her head was spinning, this couldn't be true surely, a sick joke maybe?

'That's ridiculous, I'm his wife.' Any previous confidence had now deserted her. Diane slowly shook her head,

'I'm sorry Sarah, I know how much of a shock this must be but there is no kind way of breaking this sort of news, I married Mark Beecham six years ago and we have never divorced. Why don't you ask your friend over there if she wants to join us, unless of course you don't want her to know?' Diane nodded in Sue's direction then continued,

'Yes, I've seen you together in here, in fact I've learned quite a bit about you.'

Sarah swung around to face Sue, motioning for her to join them. Sue was up instantly, a protective instinct rising in defence of her friend who, by the look on her face, needed support.

'What's going on?' Sue sat beside Sarah, pulling the chair close enough to be able to put a concerned hand on her arm. Sarah was too close to tears to speak so Diane began to explain again. Naturally Sue was shocked at this revelation but regained enough self control to begin questioning this stranger. How had she found Sarah, why had she and Mark split up, why had they never divorced? All these questions were rapidly directed to the woman sitting opposite, and to give her credit, Diane answered as best and as truthfully as she knew how.

'It was only by accident that I discovered he had married again.' Diane explained, 'A mutual friend had seen him sitting outside the dentist's where you work. He had seen Mark picking you up, thinking nothing about it at first, but later he became curious. My friend hasn't got much of an opinion of Mark, partly because of the way he treated me, so he actually went as far as following you home, then doing the maths, two and two as it were, and that's when he told me. I had been trying to find Mark for the last six months, not because I wanted to see him, but to discuss a divorce. I've met someone else you see. I swore I would never marry again, but my new boyfriend has changed my mind.'

'So why come after Sarah and not Mark?' Sue asked.

'Well, at first I was curious. Mark had left the firm where he worked when we split up and never told me where he was living, not that I cared at the time; I was in a mess, a breakdown of sorts I suppose. By the time I began to get my life back on track there was no sign of him anywhere. He had no friends and the one or two mutual friends we had were glad to see the back of him after witnessing what he'd done to me. When I was told he had been seen and given the address of the place where you work, I couldn't help but wonder what kind of marriage you had and how he treated you.' Diane was speaking to both her companions but glanced frequently at Sarah, watching for some kind of reaction and seeing the pain etched on the younger woman's face.

'Is it a happy marriage?' Diane ventured, although from the expressions on Sarah's face the answer to her question was plain. Sarah shook her head as a slow trickle of tears began to roll down her cheeks. Sue pushed a tissue into her hand and an arm around her shoulder.

'I thought as much.' Diane took no pleasure in the fact. 'But look on the bright side, you are not actually married to Mr Mark Beecham, he's a bigamist, you can walk away any time you want, I'm the one who needs a divorce.'

'And he's the one who wants locking up!' Sue added.

By this time Sarah was beginning to think coherently again.

'Look, I don't think I can go back to work after this, Sue, would you mind calling in on your way to the surgery to tell them I'm not well or something?'

'No problem.' Sue answered, 'But I'm afraid I'll have to be getting back, will you be all right?'

'I'll be fine, the shock's wearing off and I'd like to ask Diane some more questions, that is, if you've got time?' She looked at the woman in the green raincoat, no longer a threat and in some ways rapidly becoming an ally. Diane nodded then rose to go to the counter saying, 'I'll get some more coffees and some of those tempting donuts, you've had a shock, you need sugar.' Sarah smiled and when left alone with Sue reassured her friend, thanking her for the support.

'You know you will have to report this to the police don't you?' Sue prompted.

'Yes, at some point I will, but I need a little time to get my head around it first.'

'Well, I feel in a bit of a spot being married to a policeman and all. Knowing about a crime and not reporting it wouldn't go down too well with Alan.'

'Of course, I'd forgotten! Look, don't worry, I'll go to the police station this afternoon and see somebody. I don't really know what will happen then, will they arrest him do you think?'

'Probably, yes, they'll take him to the station to question him and maybe even charge him but then he will most likely be released. Sarah, do you think Mark is dangerous?'

'I honestly don't know the answer to that. I've been afraid of him, yes, but not a fear of anything physical; it's been his moods and unpredictability that's scared me. Look, I'll have a chat to Diane and then ring you later to tell you what's happening, okay? Strangely enough I feel some kind of bond with Di, I want to find out what sort of marriage they had, a bit morbid don't you think?'

'Yes, but understandable. Now, don't forget to ring, right?'

'Promise, and thanks Sue.' Sarah hugged her friend, grateful for such solid support then sat down again waiting for Diane to come back with the coffees. Sarah had that strange distant feeling, as if she was an outsider looking down on what was happening from some high vantage point. Diane returned with the coffee and donuts and they both ate hungrily, needing the sugar boost.

'So, what kind of husband has Mark been?' Diane was the one to ask first.

'Moody, unpredictable, sullen at times...my counsellor thinks he's controlling. She hasn't said so in as many words, but sometimes the way the conversation goes, I know...'

'You've been seeing a counsellor? Surely Mark would never allow that?'

'Mark doesn't know. I go in my lunch hour. I haven't been going for very long, but she is really good, doesn't judge or think anything's too trivial, you know.'

'Gosh, I think I could have done with that. Tell me Sarah, does Mark play mind tricks with you?'

'What do you mean by 'mind tricks'?'

'Oh, silly things really, has he done the shopping thing with you?'

'What shopping thing?'

'Well, we had done the shopping one evening and I'd put it away and gone to watch telly. Half an hour later Mark came through shouting about my being lazy and why hadn't I put the shopping away?'

Sarah's mouth dropped open and Diane chuckled quietly.

'You hadn't worked that one out I see.'

'I thought it was me, that I was going mad or something, I've even seen the doctor to ask if I could be getting Alzheimer's!'

'And was Mark the one who planted that 'going mad' seed? You know, the 'I'll look after you' bit.'

'He has, he did that with you?'

'Oh yes, classic Mark that one. Turn every situation round to his advantage, it's all your fault, but caring Mark will be there to look after you. Hypocrite!'

'Tell me Di, did you ever lose your purse?'

'Hmm, he's tried that one as well has he? Where did you find it, in the ironing pile?'

'No, in the fridge actually.' They both chuckled, though rather solemnly.

'Did you ever lose the contacts from your phone?' Sarah asked.

'Ah ha, more than once.'

'The pig! And all this time I thought it was me!'

'Well, the question now is what are we going to do about him?'

'I told Sue I would report it today, her husband's a policeman and she would feel duty bound to tell him if I didn't.'

'I think we should do this together.' Di said.

'That's fine with me. And there's no time like the present.'

To most people such news would be devastating and it was certainly a huge shock to Sarah, but as the reality began to sink in her feelings changed from horror to something resembling relief. She was angry, yes, but the anger was being channelled into a feeling of confidence, even hope. It was not her who was going mad, Mark had been manipulating her for his own selfish purposes, she was a victim but one who was about to fight back. A sudden energy flooded through her body, a release perhaps, a light at the end of what was becoming a long dark existence? Certainly she felt violated and revulsion towards Mark, whilst berating herself for her stupidity in being drawn into his sick ways. One thing Sarah knew for sure, she would overcome this and keep what little dignity she had left intact.

****

Peter had made a fair start on the speech, it wasn't earth shattering and he would probably edit and re-edit it a thousand times before being satisfied with it but to get a number of words down on paper was an encouraging start. The time sitting before his computer had passed swiftly and Peter had to break off to get ready for an appointment with his GP, one he had made as soon as the US trip had been thrust upon him, partly to stock up on medication and also to ask if there were other factors which needed to be taken into consideration. Until MS had struck, Peter had hardly suffered an illness in his life so regular medical appointments and 'looking after himself' was new to him. Good health had once been taken for granted but not anymore.

The appointment was with Dr. James, the man who had actually, although unwittingly, introduced Peter to Maggie and therefore someone to whom Peter was very grateful. Simon James greeted his patient with a broad smile,

'Hi Peter, good to see you, how are you?'

'Actually not too bad, and you?'

'Oh, I'm fine but thanks for asking, that's usually my role.'

Peter returned the smile and began to tell Simon why he was there.

'Congratulations! That's some achievement but a long way to go to deliver a lecture.'

'That's why I wanted to see you. Things have been going well lately and any symptoms have been minimal. When I feel any pain I use the muscle relaxants you prescribed and if I take them soon enough they seem to block a full blown attack. I'm also careful about overdoing things, if I do get tired it seems to increase the symptoms. Actually it's probably more Maggie than me who takes charge of not doing too much; she can be quite bossy at times.'

'Good, she does right. Certainly the travelling in itself will be tiring and the stress of giving the lectures could be a problem. You're still injecting aren't you?'

'Yes, which is another thing; could you give me a prescription to cover the full period of the trip?'

'Of course, no problem.' Simon James was squinting at the computer screen as he listened, and then turned his chair to face his patient, giving him full attention.

'Peter, I wanted to have a chat about your treatment so I'm glad you've come. You saw Dr. Hassen a few weeks ago?'

Peter nodded.

'Good, I've had a letter from him concerning the new drug, Gilenya, apparently you were asking about it?'

'Yes, we'd seen it on the MS website and I wondered if it might be suitable for me.'

'Well, I'm sure Dr. Hassen explained that it wasn't available then, but the good news is that it has since been passed and we are allowed to prescribe it now for suitable patients.'

Peter's wide smile was infectious and Simon found himself grinning too.

'Don't get too excited yet. The drug is suitable for Relaxing, Remitting MS, but we need to do a few tests first to see if you are a suitable candidate.'

'What kind of tests?'

'Well, mainly to check that your heart is strong and you have no problems with blood pressure. Is there any history of heart disease or strokes in your family?'

'No, none at all and I've never suffered from high blood pressure.'

'Good. Now with your trip so close, it's pointless doing these tests now, there's no way you can try a new drug whilst globetrotting, but when you get back...'

'You will be the first person I'll see!'

Simon then began a potted version of tips on being sensible whilst travelling, drinking plenty of water and resting and exercising whenever possible but Peter was barely listening, his thoughts racing ahead, anticipating sharing this exciting news with Maggie. Leaving Dr James he made his way back to the waiting room, glancing towards his wife's office to see if the door was open. It was not which he assumed meant that she was with a client. As it was nearly five, Peter decided to wait for her to finish, keen to share the good news about Gilenya. They both knew that this was not a cure for MS, there was no definitive cure as yet, but this was the most hopeful news on the research front that had been discovered for years. For him personally it could mean that the MS might not progress beyond its current level. If Gilenya was indeed effective in repairing the myelin which MS destroyed, then his future as well as that of thousands of other sufferers would be a great deal brighter. Peter knew he would be unable to concentrate on his speech that evening, he would take Maggie out for a meal so they could relax and discuss how events were unfolding in their lives, the exciting trip ahead and

the hope of a more effective medication when they
returned.

Chapter 28

Sam didn't quite understand what was going on but still entered into the jollity of the occasion wholeheartedly. When his grandma brought in a cake with a single candle burning brightly in the middle, he clapped his hands, a gesture which he now knew made everyone around him smile and join in. And he loved the singing even though this was an unfamiliar song. The candle was blown out with a little help from daddy and soon a slice of chocolate cake was set before him on the tray of his high chair. Sam poked it once or twice before picking it up with his whole hand and pushing as much as he could into his mouth. There was more laughter and after finishing the cake, grandma wiped his hands and face and lifted him down to play. Sam could now manage two or three steps unaided and was keen to show off this new skill. It was the same with talking, 'dada' and 'mama' also seemed to please the grownups so Sam gleefully repeated the words over and over. There were new toys to play with, toys which played music when he pressed buttons and felt good when he put them in his mouth to chew.

Grace and Derek Watson were both on the floor with their grandson, happily keeping him entertained. Phil was taking photographs, delighted at having Ellie and her parents sharing the birthday celebrations with them. There had been a time, not too long ago, when he was dreading this occasion, a time when he was unsure if his wife would live, and then when the miracle happened and it seemed she would, another blow came from nowhere when it became apparent she had no memory of him or their son. Phil still worried about the future. Ellie's memory had not yet returned and there was no guarantee it ever would, yet they had begun what was almost a new relationship and again his hopes had been raised. Phil knew now that Ellie loved their son, that love had been rekindled in a very short time and given him hope that her feelings for him were returning too. They had begun to feel comfortable with each other and when Ellie spent time with him he now thought it was because she wanted to, not out of any sense of duty. But yet again the delicate thread of hope appeared to be in danger of breaking as Ellie seemed once again to be withdrawing into her shell and he had no idea why, or what could be done to bring her back again. Phil was convinced he hadn't imagined her growing feelings for him; she had even begun taking the initiative in things such as the date they had been on. Watching now, Phil saw her smile, but it didn't quite reach her eyes, it was that duty smile again, there was something Ellie was struggling with and once again Phil was being left out of her confidence. If only she would trust him, allow him in, he was certain they could once again be a happy family. He would do anything for Ellie, if only she would let him.

****

The detective constable was very sympathetic. Diane and Sarah sat side by side, both a little nervous but united in their determination to have Mark brought to account for what he had done. During the lengthy interview they were both asked dozens of questions whilst the officer meticulously noted all their answers. At one point during the interview Sarah excused herself to make a phone call to Mark, letting him know she was not at work and keeping the conversation as brief as possible, giving no indication that anything was wrong other than that she was feeling unwell and had left work early. Mark sneered at this, disliking changes to his routine and so Sarah cut short the conversation for fear of inadvertently letting him know that she was not at home.

The constable was patient and did his best to inform them of the procedure they had initiated by reporting the crime. It was agreed that Sarah should go home and act normally during the evening, when the detective and a colleague would be paying Mark a visit to arrest him on a charge of bigamy. The women left and Diane gave Sarah her phone number, asking if she would ring when Mark had been charged. As they parted, Sarah was a little apprehensive about the evening ahead but still driven by anger and the disgust she now felt for the man she had thought to be her husband.

Mark, true to his pedantic tendencies, arrived home at the usual time, slamming the door behind him in obvious irritation that Sarah had left work early. Finding her in the kitchen adding the finishing ingredients to a chicken curry, he began,
'Well! What's so wrong with you that you had to leave work?'
'A migraine, but it's much better now thanks.' As if he cared, she thought. Mark stomped upstairs to change and Sarah began setting the dining room table wondering how long she would have to play along until the police arrived. They knew what time he would be home and had a description of his car which would be parked in the drive.
'I hope that curry isn't as hot as the last one you made.' Mark sniffed as he came back downstairs.
'It's ready now so you'll soon know.'

Mark sat at the table waiting for his meal to be served but no sooner had Sarah appeared with two piping hot plates than the doorbell rang.

'Who on earth can that be right on dinner time?' Mark growled.

Sarah, on her way to the table, glimpsed the shapes of the two police officers through the glass panels in the door.

'I'll get it,' she said smiling in anticipation of the shock coming Mark's way, but firstly she calmly tipped the plate of curry right into his lap. She could not agree with whoever had said that revenge was a dish best served cold, it was much more satisfying served hot, very hot.

'What the hell do you think you're doing?' Mark yelled in obvious discomfort.

Sarah turned sharply on her heels and with three nimble strides was out of the room, eager to open the door and feeling a remarkable lightness of spirit which she hadn't experienced for a long time. The expression on Mark's face gave Sarah such satisfaction that she almost felt guilty for gloating.

Leading the officers into the room they were greeted by the sight of Mark wiping rice and curry off his trousers back onto the plate. Although red with anger, when he lifted his eyes and saw the detective and his uniformed colleague his face blanched, his fear clearly visible. Sarah with folded arms leaned against the door for support. Despite taking a weird pleasure in the situation playing out before her, she was trembling. Listening to the detective constable recite the reason for the arrest, Mark cast a look of pure hatred in her direction. The police couldn't get him out of the house quickly enough for her then. Being led away, Mark surprisingly did not say a word in his defence, even though he was usually keen to voice his indignation in whatever situation. He didn't even ask to be allowed to change his trousers. Mark may have been confident enough in the role of a husband to be the bully, but with the police he seemed deflated, unable to think of a thing to say, or perhaps he was simply afraid to speak, Sarah didn't know and cared even less.

Earlier in the afternoon, Sarah had packed a suitcase with everything she would need for several days. Retrieving it now from the hiding place in the spare bedroom and carrying it downstairs there were three phone calls she must make before leaving this house, this tall, black house with its small, dark windows.

Diane experienced the same sense of relief as Sarah whilst listening to the account of Mark's arrest, embellished with the incident of the chicken curry. The women arranged to meet the next day, Sarah knowing she would need a few days off work to sort out practical issues as well as emotional ones. Sue whooped with joy when Sarah gave an account of the arrest, but then became more serious, expressing concern and offering any kind of help her friend might need. The third call was to her parents to whom she said very little other than to let them know that she was coming over and needed to talk to them both. Closing the door, Sarah's emotions were mixed. This had been her first home as an adult away from the nest of her childhood and her parent's protection. But it had turned into more of a prison, the childhood dream of a wonderful life as a married woman had been tainted. Her 'husband' had abused and humiliated her and now she was left to face the world alone, a victim of the ultimate betrayal. Walking away from the house, the tears silently began to flow. This day had been the worst one of her life and

Sarah was exhausted, unable to think straight, the only thing she could think of was to return to the safety of her parent's home. To be enfolded in their love and protection as she had been in childhood was the one thing Sarah needed now.

Chapter 29

The week had dragged yet inevitably Thursday came around. Ellie shuddered, wishing the day to be over yet dreading what it might hold. Phil had again expressed concern, aware of the subtle changes in mood; he struggled to make sense of them, eventually deciding that the recovery process had perhaps been too fast, too soon, and now a melancholy had crept into his wife's demeanour, nullifying the progress they had appeared to be making. Phil managed only a brief conversation with Grace on the day of Sam's birthday when she too admitted to noticing a change in Ellie's recovery but was equally as bewildered as to knowing the reason why. Ellie hardly noticed when Phil kissed her on the cheek before leaving for work; she was elsewhere, some distant place where Phil could not reach her.

Sam was unusually fractious, fighting against Ellie who struggled to get him into his jacket.

'Please Sam, Mummy doesn't need this today.' She begged, but the little boy had picked up on his mother's anxiety and began to cry, the only way he knew to get attention. Eventually they were ready and setting off for the park in his stroller seemed to soothe Sam but certainly not his mother, whose trembling legs threatened to fail her as she clung to the handles of the stroller grateful for its support. By the time they reached the swings Sam had thankfully fallen asleep. Having had all week to think about this meeting, Ellie was still no wiser as to what to say or do. She had thought about challenging Dave, telling him that she did not believe they'd had any kind of relationship. Pleading and trying to reach his humanity was another option but it was doubtful whether this awful man had an ounce of humanity in him.

It was a pleasant day, warm with the promise of another scorching afternoon, the kind of day which made people smile at strangers. Entering the park, stunning displays of begonias flanked by the majestic spears of red lupins greeted visitors but Ellie did not notice them; she was gripping the handles of Sam's stroller so tightly that her knuckles were white.

Dave was there, waiting, sitting on a bench at the far side of the swings. Walking slowly, Ellie was willing her heart rate to slow down, yet it did quite the opposite when a triumphant, smug smile acknowledged the small victory Dave had won in the very fact that she was there. Stopping by the bench Ellie turned the stroller around so that Sam was facing away from Dave, who patted the empty space on the bench with another little smirk of triumph as she reluctantly sat down, perching as close to the edge as possible. Dave spoke first,

'I knew you would come, you couldn't resist could you?'

Turning to look at him with disgust, Ellie's eyes narrowed,

'You didn't leave me much choice did you?'

'Aw come on, be nice. You always used to be nice to me, I'm sure you haven't forgotten that.'

'Sorry to disappoint you but I have no memories of you whatsoever and I want to keep it that way.' Sarah was feeling a little bolder now being out in the open gave a sense of safety, what could this man do in broad daylight? Perhaps escape from this nightmare was feasible after all. Dave smiled and snaked an arm around her shoulders making her recoil, feeling almost

237

physically sick at the contact. Moving as far away as possible on the bench, Ellie decided to challenge him.

'For all I know you could be making all this up. How can I know you are telling me the truth? You certainly don't act like a trustworthy person, threatening and issuing ultimatums!' Ellie's voice was raised, the emotion rising, threatening to choke her but aware of Sam, she lowered it to say,

'I don't like you Dave and if that's true now then I'm pretty sure I would not have liked you before. I cannot believe what you tell me is true, so it's probably best if I go now and have nothing more to do with you again.'

'Hey, don't be in such a hurry, and don't come the little miss righteous with me either! We have a history whether it suits you or not and if you want your grubby secrets to become public then fine, walk away, but if you do I can guarantee you will regret it.' Dave was so smug, Ellie was desperate to get up and go, but could she risk it?

The happy sound of toddlers playing with their mothers on the swings filled her ears; she should be there with Sam, carefree and having fun, not here with this loathsome man giving rise to fears about the past and what she may or may not have done. Dave spoke again, this time lifting the hair at the back of her neck and running his forefinger along her hairline.

'If we weren't having an affair how would I know about this birthmark here on your neck? Kissing that spot always got you going...'

'Don't!' Ellie pulled herself away, angry and repulsed; how on earth could he know about that?

'Well it must have been a terrible mistake and I want to end it now!'

'But what if I don't? You think you're too good for me now don't you? Well, let me tell you what is going to

238

happen next. You can go now, straight home while the boy's asleep, then in ten minutes, I will come round. Leave the door unlocked as you always used to so there's less chance of us being seen and we'll see if I can remind you of the fun we used to have.'

'No!' she mouthed a silent scream but Dave laughed and patted her knee.

'Off you go and get yourself ready for me like a good girl.'

****

'I need to see Maggie...sorry, Ms Sayer please....'

'I know there is a client with her at the moment but she'll be breaking for lunch after that, I could have a word then?' Sue spoke softly to this young mother who was plainly distressed for some reason.

'It will be another ten, fifteen minutes if you want to wait?'

'Yes, thank you, I'll do that.' Ellie moved away to take a seat.

Sue did not ask the woman's name, almost certain that Maggie would see her even if it meant skipping lunch. When Mags was finished she would pop in and tell her about the mother with the sleeping baby.

Ellie picked up a magazine but had no interest in it. Instructing herself inwardly to calm down, take deep breaths, and relax, the ten minutes wait seemed more of an eternity but then a client came out of Maggie's room and the receptionist went in. Almost immediately the counsellor was out of the office and striding towards Ellie, putting a hand on her shoulder to guide her into the little room which Ellie thought of as a haven. Sam was still asleep but had been so for nearly an hour and would probably wake soon.

239

'I didn't know where else to go.' The tears came now and Ellie took out a tissue to muffle the sound of the sobs.

'That's okay Ellie, I'm here to help.' Maggie remained silent to allow this unexpected visitor to compose herself enough to speak but Sam chose that very moment to wake up with a grizzly cry.

'Sue on reception could take him for a few minutes if that's okay with you?'

Ellie nodded consent and Maggie pushed the stroller out to reception, catching Sue as she was finishing for lunch. Instinctively understanding the problem Sue took charge of the stroller.

'I need the practise,' she nodded and began to push Sam to the corner of the waiting room where several toys were set out for babies and children. The child was easily distracted and reached out for the toys forgetting whatever had caused him to cry. His mother too had expended her tears for the moment and turned, ready with an apology for Maggie.

'There's no need to apologize, really. Do you want to tell me what has happened?'

'Yes, I have to tell someone or I'll go mad. It's related to what I told you last time, do you remember, about finding something out about my past?'

'I remember.'

'Well, it's horrible Maggie, there's a man, a neighbour, who keeps pestering me...saying we were having an affair and I don't know if it's true or not. How can I tell? He's pressurizing me into meeting him; in fact I should be at home now, he was going to come round from the park, but I came here instead. What on earth shall I do?'

'The park? Were you with him in the park?'

'Yes, he had made me promise to meet him there, to talk, but then he wanted more and told me to go home and wait for him. What can I do?'

'Well you don't have to do what he says, you have a choice here Ellie.'

'No, he said he would tell Phil and my parents.'

'Tell them what?'

'That I've slept with him! They will hate me if they find out...' Tears were flowing freely again and Maggie pushed the box of tissues nearer.

'This man is blackmailing you Ellie. Do you want him to get away with this?'

'No, of course not, but I don't want Phil to know what I have done.'

'Yet you are not sure you have done anything are you?'

'Well I wasn't until today. He mentioned a birthmark I have on the back of my neck. I have always been sensitive about it and kept it hidden. How would he have known about that if we hadn't been intimate?'

'I should think there are several ways he could have learned of it, knowing that is not conclusive proof of a relationship. Last time we met when you told me that you had learned something from your past, if you remember I asked if you respected and trusted this person? I'm assuming it was this man?'

'Yes.' Ellie dropped her head with shame.

'Do you respect him or trust him?'

'No Maggie, from what I have seen and learned about him in the last couple of weeks, certainly not.'

'Naturally you are feeling afraid of the consequences, but could you not talk to Phil or your parents perhaps? The not knowing seems to be weighing as heavily on you as bringing it all out into the open would be.'

'I don't think so. I've only just begun to really appreciate my marriage and family; I can't risk losing them.'

'Ellie, it is entirely up to you, but perhaps you should take a long look at all the possible scenarios before deciding. Put your thoughts down on paper if it helps then weigh up the options. You are the only one who can decide what to do, as you're the one who has to live with the decision, but to state the obvious you also have a son and husband whose lives will be affected too. Look, I have the time now if you're up to brainstorming and I can pop out to check on Sam if you like?'

'Would you? I'd like to make the decision here with you; I daren't go back in case Dave's there. If Sam's okay and your friend doesn't mind, there's a bottle in his bag, some rusks and a clean nappy.'

Maggie took a pad of paper and a pen from the desk and passed them to Ellie before going out to see how Sue was coping with her little charge.

'We're fine, getting to know each other really well, tell his mummy to take as long as she needs; I can feed and change him now.' Sue was enjoying herself enormously and Sam seemed happy enough with an assortment of new toys to amuse him as well as the undivided attention of this new friend. Maggie returned to Ellie with assurances that everything was under control. Her client had already begun writing and nodded a brief thank you before returning to the task in hand. Ellie had divided the paper into three sections and written down the three possible options, which she began to explain to Maggie.

'First option, I could do nothing and see what happens. Or secondly I could go along with Dave and continue to see him, or the third option is telling Phil and taking the chance that he will forgive me.'

Maggie nodded, surprised yet pleased that Ellie had been able to pull herself together sufficiently to look at her predicament objectively and impressed that she had been able to express the options so concisely. Ellie continued,

'Looking at all three, I need to choose the lesser evil but honestly I don't relish any of the choices. Firstly, to do nothing is risky. Dave might tell Phil, my parents and anyone else who would listen. But the second option, agreeing to a secret relationship, I think would make me ill in the longer term. I can't bear the man, he makes me balk. No, I really don't think I could do that Maggie. So that leaves the third option, telling Phil and throwing myself on his mercy, which sounds rather dramatic doesn't it?'

'Well, none of them are going to be easy but it sounds as if you have at least ruled out the second option?'

'Yes, I'm sure I couldn't possibly go there.'

'So, that leaves two; do nothing, which if this man is making it all up will call his bluff, or confide in Phil.' Maggie looked into her client's eyes seeing the hurt and confusion. Ellie had been through so much and certainly did not need this complication. Living with amnesia must be frightening in itself, losing your past must surely cause confusion and pain. Was this man taking advantage of Ellie's vulnerability or had she really had some kind of relationship with him? The fact was that Ellie did not know the answer to that any more than Maggie did.

Chapter 30

Sarah struggled to hold herself together on the way to her parents' house. Having chosen to travel by bus, even though her father would have readily come to pick her up, was with the hope that the journey would give some time to become more composed and work out what to tell her parents, but thinking logically proved impossible. And now standing on their doorstep, tapping weakly on the glass panel, she peered eagerly through the glass for any signs of movement.

'Sarah love, why are you knocking, you know the door's always open?' Sarah's mother pulled her into the hallway enfolding her in a warm hug, instinctively knowing that something was very wrong. Margaret and George Porter had speculated on the reason for their daughter's rather cryptic phone call and decided it must be some sort of tiff with Mark, but looking now at the state Sarah was in and seeing the suitcase, Margaret knew this was more serious than a simple marital squabble. George appeared at his wife's side and kissed his daughter's hair, patting her shoulder in an attempt to comfort, before motioning to his wife to take Sarah through to the lounge whilst he made a cup of tea. George too had noticed the case and silently carried it upstairs to her old room wondering what on earth could have happened to distress his girl so much.

On returning downstairs George made for the kitchen but couldn't help hearing Sarah's sobs from the lounge. 'It will do her good' he thought setting the kettle to boil and deciding to give the women a few minutes to themselves. Once the sobbing was over, Sarah knew it was time to explain the situation, they deserved that much. Drawing a deep breath and taking the hot tea her father passed, Sarah attempted to tell them everything she had found out about her husband. It seemed a lifetime ago, yet it was only earlier that day when Sarah had discovered that Mark was not legally her husband, a huge shock in itself, but then to learn how he had been manipulating her throughout their short 'marriage' had been devastating. It was embarrassing to have to admit to what kind of life she had been living with Mark and realising how gullible and naive she had been added shame to an already complicated situation. George and Margaret listened quietly which in itself was difficult, especially for George who was becoming angrier by the minute. They too experienced a gamut of emotions, primarily a feeling of having let their daughter down and regret that they had not been more insistent on keeping in touch on a regular basis.

'With hindsight, we were all duped; Mark played the situation so cleverly, gaining our trust and even love.' Sarah tried to verbalize her thoughts. 'I only wish I had known the difference between love and infatuation, he had me fooled big time!'

'Mark was clearly adept at deceit; we were taken in as well.' Margaret added, 'But what about this other wife, his real wife I suppose?'

'Diane? I was quite afraid initially; it seemed as if she had been watching me which I suppose was true, in an attempt to find out as much as possible, but now I actually quite like the woman. Needless to say we have a lot in common and we will have to keep in touch to see what happens on the legal side of things.'

'Will the police keep Mark in custody?' Margaret asked.

'I doubt it, unless they think he's a flight risk. But that's why I came here; if they do release him I didn't want to be around if he came home.'

'Of course not, you did the right thing lass, this will always be your home, you remember that.' Her father was quick to speak. Sarah smiled, how she had missed spending time with her parents, they were true stalwarts whom she loved so much. They too had been taken in by Mark and the three of them would have to work through this together.

It was getting late, the darkness was closing in outside and Sarah suddenly felt achingly tired, it had been a turbulent and exhausting day. Margaret insisted on a hot milky drink and a couple of paracetamol to which Sarah meekly complied before climbing the stairs to the familiar and comforting bedroom of her childhood.

Margaret and George sat up for another hour after their daughter had gone to bed. Self recriminations were expressed then dismissed. Mark had been so believable, ingratiating himself into their family, gaining their trust and affection and so skilled at deception that there was no reason to doubt him. As George pointed out, when someone asks for your daughter's hand in marriage, you don't think to ask if they already have a wife, especially when the couple seem so happy and in love. They had missed regular contact with their daughter but had tried to be unselfish thinking that the young couple needed time alone to settle into married life. How wrong they had been but how on earth could they have foreseen such a disastrous outcome?

There were still five days until they set off for Las Vegas but Maggie had already begun to pack and their guest bedroom was covered with piles of clothes, shoes and toiletries all waiting to be placed neatly into two cases.

'We can't take all this.' Peter groaned.

'I know that, but these are the things I want to have ready until I decide which of them to take.'

'Women's logic,' Peter's comment earned a swift dig in the ribs from his wife.

'You'll appreciate my organizational skills once we are on the way' Maggie laughed. They were both looking forward to their trip although Peter knew he would be more relaxed once the lectures were delivered. Feeling comfortable with what he had written didn't stop him editing it almost every day. Stephen and Charles had been great, especially on the technology side of the designs. They helped Peter put together visual aids and gave him a crash course on how to use a lap top for a power point presentation. He in turn passed this newly acquired knowledge on to Maggie, reasoning that if there were any technical problems, two heads would be better than one. His wife however was more concerned in planning their itinerary, prioritizing the places they wanted to visit and being careful not to attempt too much, always concerned with Peter's well being. The news about Gilenya from the doctor had thrilled them both and coming home from the trip would now be equally as exciting, with the prospect of starting the new treatment for MS. Peter felt fortunate that his illness had been discovered in the early stages. If he responded well to Gilenya, the future would be much brighter than they had originally anticipated. Remembering the desperation at being diagnosed he was now so thankful that Maggie had not let him throw everything away and wallow in the destructive pit of self pity. It was amazing how well things had turned out for them and there wasn't a day went by that he wasn't grateful for the life they now shared.

Typically, Maggie had concerns about leaving some of her clients particularly Ellie Graham. She had not seen the girl for a few days, since her unexpected arrival at the surgery and Maggie wondered how things were working out and whether she had reached any decisions. Then there was Sarah Beecham, although if what Sue had recounted was accurate, Sarah was no longer called Beecham and legally never had been. Both these clients had appointments before Maggie's holiday and she was anxious to know if their circumstances had improved; she would certainly enjoy herself more knowing that things were working out well for them both. Her colleague, Steve Franks, would be available if they needed further support, but she still held regrets at not being around in what could be their time of greatest need.

****

Maggie would soon be updated on the situation of one of these clients at 9.00am when Ellie Graham had an appointment. It was Monday, over three full days since Thursday to make a decision and Maggie was anxious to find out what that decision might be. Ellie looked pale and drawn, devoid of the animation which had only recently appeared to be returning to her life.

'How have you been Ellie?' Maggie enquired softly.

'Terrible, I'm at my wits end.'

'Would you like to tell me about it?'

'There's not much to tell. I suppose I chickened out, I've done nothing about the situation which I know isn't a long term solution.'

'Was it because you were unsure of which way to go?'

'Partly, with a big dollop of cowardice mixed in. I have been hiding my head in the sand, but it's quite a disheartening thing to do.'

'How have you managed practically, with looking after Sam?'

'Mum has stepped in again, she has him today and helped me last Friday and of course Phil was home over the weekend.'

'So you haven't confronted your dilemma?'

Ellie hung her head.

'Hey, I'm not trying to bully you into this you know, but after Thursday I rather thought you had decided to talk to Phil. I wondered if anything else had happened to make you change your mind?'

'No, nothing but I'm not sure if that's a good thing or a bad one.'

'Well the confrontation hasn't happened so this Dave hasn't carried out his threat to speak to Phil has he?'

'No, that's true. I haven't seen Dave around even over the weekend but I somehow don't think he will go meekly away, he seemed to be too determined for that. It's Thursday I dread, that seems to have been the day...well, you know, when he's not at work.'

Maggie could sense Ellie's weariness. Living under such a threat was draining and it was certainly evident in the young woman's demeanour now. Her immediate concern was that this situation would drag on to the detriment of her client, undoing all the progress made so far, but the decision had to be Ellie's alone; Maggie would support her whatever that decision might be.

Chapter 31

Sarah Beecham was due to see Maggie on Wednesday, which would be her last appointment before Maggie left for the states and the first time she had ventured from her parent's home since arriving there the Monday before. Margaret Porter had spoken to Sarah's employers and it had been agreed that she should take a couple of weeks leave of absence and fortunately no one enquired too much as to what the personal problems were, there would be time enough to explain when Sarah felt stronger. The police constable had been in touch to inform them that Mark had been released on bail, news which was unsettling to say the least. The previous day had been spent in a hazy round of phone calls, both received and made. Sarah's father consulted a solicitor in an attempt to discern where his daughter stood legally; the house had been in joint names and their concern was that as Sarah's name had not actually been Beecham, this technicality might prevent the sale of the house which in Sarah's eyes would help to draw a line beneath the whole sorry affair. She was more than happy for her father to take this on board liaising with the solicitor, who seemed reasonably positive although nothing could actually be done until Mark had been tried and convicted. Until that hurdle was over it would be difficult to begin rebuilding any kind of new life. Everyone offered their assurances that Mark would be convicted but there was always a seed of doubt in her mind that he might somehow worm his way out of this. Sarah also had a long telephone conversation with Diane, a woman she felt an increasing affinity towards and someone who would necessarily be part of her life, at least until this whole episode was resolved. And now, Sarah found herself entering Maggie's office, anxious to update her although aware that Sue would have probably given her the bones of the situation.

'It's been a difficult few days?' Maggie began.

'An understatement to say the least, I honestly don't know what is going to happen.'

'How about we don't speculate on that?'

'Yes, that suits me Maggie, why try to anticipate the future, in many ways it's out of my hands.'

'So, how are you feeling now, this very moment?'

'Tired, angry, humiliated, all those and more.'

'Do you think talking about the actual events of the last few days will help?'

'Possibly, but I had assumed Sue would have told you about it all.'

'That doesn't matter, Sue knew I would be concerned for you but also that I wouldn't want second hand versions, so really all I know is that you have found out that Mark was already married, ergo he is a bigamist. Only tell me if it helps Sarah, you are the one who matters at this point in time.'

Sarah wanted to talk and so began to verbalize the events to date which had filled her mind constantly, day and night.

'I was rather afraid when Diane first approached me, particularly when she knew so much about me and I was completely in the dark. I couldn't begin to guess why this stranger had turned up insisting that we meet to talk but I could tell it was serious from her solemn expression. The reality of what it could be simply didn't occur to me and I hadn't a clue what to do so I rang Sue who thankfully agreed to come with me. Well, her suggestion was that we went in separately, quite 'cloak and dagger' stuff really, but I couldn't have done it on my own. Anyway, this woman came right out with it, told me she was Mark's wife and then suggested Sue joined us, we hadn't fooled her and she knew Sue was a friend. That was a bit scary too; clearly Diane had been following me and also knew quite a bit about my routine although what she really wanted to know was if Mark and I were happily married. She seemed relieved when I said no; it wasn't as if she was breaking up a happy couple. It's so strange Maggie, in one way the news, although a shock, was welcome. I am not married to him, Mark no longer has control over me and I'm free of his nasty little ways. Part of me wants to laugh, to celebrate, but then I also feel so sad, not because I've lost him, but because I was taken in by him in the first place. I feel ashamed and humiliated at how stupid I've been.'

'It's been a shock Sarah; you are bound to feel such mixed emotions. Perhaps you could try asking yourself why you feel a particular emotion as it occurs. That's always better than trying to suppress how you are feeling.'

'I would be asking questions all day long, my feelings change so quickly.'

Maggie smiled aware of how battered and bruised Sarah must be feeling.

'Deception is a cruel thing; it is going to take time to get over this. Initially it's difficult to accept that you were specifically targeted, but there are people out there who are very skilled at deception and Mark certainly seems to be one of them.'

'But I was so gullible, how could I have not known?'

'You weren't looking for it Sarah, that is the whole thing about deception; our natural inclination is to trust people, which in general is a good thing. Remember that most people you meet are genuine and hopefully one day you will find someone you will be able to trust.'

'I don't know about that, I really think I'll never be able to trust a man again.'

'I can understand that, but to get things into perspective look at the men you do know. There is your father, can you trust him?'

'Well yes, but that's different. He's my Dad.'

'He is also your mother's husband, can she trust him?'

'Hmm, I see what you mean.'

'Just because you have been hurt and badly betrayed doesn't mean you won't recover and be a happy woman again. Look at the marriages of your friends, how about Sue, she's happy isn't she?'

'Oh yes, Sue certainly seems to have found her soul mate, its obvious how much she loves Alan.'

'And even now in this room, fifty percent of the people here have really happy marriages.' Maggie smiled and Sarah did too, understanding what her counsellor was trying to say.

'What about those houses you drew. How about re-visiting them?'

'That's so strange isn't it? When I drew those it really hit home and I knew then that what I wanted was to go back to my childhood home with its safety and security and the knowledge that I was loved. I assumed it was impossible, but now I'm there although perhaps not quite in the circumstances I would have chosen.'

'And is it a good place to be, mentally as well as physically?' Maggie gently probed, attempting to guide Sarah into looking at the positive side of her situation.

'Oh yes, Mum and Dad have been great, it's the only place I want to be for now. I don't know what I would do without them, they've taken over all the practical things, arranging time off work and seeing a solicitor, the things which need to be done but which I couldn't face. Mum's even spoiling me with food; all my favourites are suddenly appearing in the kitchen.' Sarah at last seemed to be relaxing, letting go of the tension which had been apparent on her arrival.

'There are going to be a number of practical issues to sort out, do you think you will cope alright with your parents support?'

'Well I certainly couldn't do it without them, but fortunately I don't have to. Dad hasn't said as much but he's pretty angry about the whole thing. Mark deceived them as well as me. They had thought him to be the perfect son-in-law; he was so kind and caring before we were married. I feel rather guilty about the money they spent on the wedding too; they were so generous, encouraging me to go for everything I wanted. I suppose as their only child they thought it would be a once in a lifetime event. Now it appears it was all a sham and I'm not legally married at all. Anyway, Mum and Dad will support me, they have made it clear that we are in this together which makes everything so much easier for me to handle. I suppose at least I don't have to go through a divorce which is something Diane will have to do, yet there are other legal problems, but now that Dad has found a solicitor we'll work through it.'

'So, you are no longer the occupant of that tall, dark and unfriendly house, you are back where you feel safe, not perhaps in the best of circumstances but certainly the best place to be at this time?'

'It is, although I couldn't have anticipated it happening like this. It's a positive though, I had started to feel trapped in my relationship with Mark and now I am suddenly free. I don't ever want to go back to that house, although on a practical level I suppose I will have to, but Dad will go with me.'

'Do you know if Mark has been back there at all?' Maggie wanted Sarah to be aware of her own safety, not knowing if Mark could be violent.

254

'No, I don't know where he is but if I do go back it will be when we're sure he'll not be there. I can't imagine how it would be if I saw him again.'

'You could ask your solicitor to apply for a restraining order if you are worried he may try to contact you.'

'I never thought of that but actually I don't think he will now he's been found out, especially if he thinks he might have my Dad to answer to.'

'Hopefully that will be the case. Bullies are often exposed as the cowards they really are when they're confronted.'

As their time came to an end, Maggie reminded Sarah that she would be away for a while and that her colleague, Steve, would be happy to step in if necessary.

'Thanks Maggie but I'll be okay, I'm not alone and Sue's been a really great friend to have but I would like to see you when you come back if that's alright?'

'Of course, there will be things which crop up and may be difficult to cope with so we can tackle them as and when they arise.'

Maggie said goodbye feeling happier than she had expected about Sarah. In many ways the situation which had brought this young woman to Maggie's door in the first place no longer existed, but that in itself threw up different issues and Maggie knew that her relationship with Sarah was not yet over.

****

Sue was six months pregnant and getting larger by the day, in some ways enjoying the visible signs of pregnancy but as it was the height of summer and the temperatures soared, it became rather uncomfortable. As the pregnancy continued she relished each new stage, even having a grumble could be fun particularly as

Alan would begin to fuss and try his best to make life easier. The craving for peanut butter and gherkins had been replaced by one for ice-cream, which Alan suspected to be a rather convenient excuse to indulge during the summer weather. Perhaps it was but Sue was doing her best to eat for two and would face the consequences after their baby was born. Having recently begun to attend ante-natal classes, she discovered them to be a great opportunity to meet other expectant mums and have a good old gossip and grumble about the trials of pregnancy, or at least that was Sue's perspective on them. The mid-wife who ran the classes however, probably thought they were to prepare mums-to-be for natural childbirth, to learn breathing techniques and relaxation tips in an effort to make the forthcoming birth as pleasant an experience as possible, to weigh up the options of home birth versus hospital birth or even using the birthing pool. But still to Sue the social side was the best bit coupled with the fact that they were held on Monday mornings and she missed the mad rush at work when all the patients were clamouring to fix appointments after the weekend. Alan did his best to arrange his shifts in an effort to attend with her and had managed to be at most classes. Sue, who loved a good laugh, always found something in the meeting which set her off. Often it was simply the look on Alan's face, like the time they watched a DVD of a birth, he was ashen with his jaw almost on his chest and huge glazed eyes which Sue thought hilarious. He would probably prove no help whatsoever when she was in labour but there was no way she was going through it all alone, he was there at the conception and she would make absolutely sure he would be there at the delivery too.

After Maggie's hour with Sarah, Sue joined her for a sandwich and coffee in her office, enquiring how the session had gone and receiving the usual non committal answer which she had come to expect. One thing Maggie did say was that Sarah needed the support of family and friends now more than ever.

'Okay Mags, I get the hint' Sue winked, and then went on to describe the events at their last ante-natal class.

'We had been doing relaxation techniques and learning how to breathe; ridiculous really, I've been breathing successfully since the day I was born. Anyway, we had these foam mats and were told to lie in a comfortable position and close our eyes. I lay on my side; bub's getting too heavy to lie on top of me and makes my back ache. Well Alan was on the mat beside me and the mid-wife was droning on about breathing deeply from our core, then tensing muscles from our legs right up through the body and consciously releasing them to become totally relaxed. We were all concentrating so hard when all of a sudden my buffoon of a husband began to snore. How embarrassing! Everyone laughed and I actually had to wake him up with a pretty hard dig in the ribs.'

Maggie could picture the scene and also imagine how Sue would never let Alan forget the incident.

'We're going to miss you when you go off on your adventures.' Sue changed the subject.

'Ah, but think how much more you will appreciate me when I get back.' Maggie countered.

Chapter 32

Ellie still felt every bit as hopeless as when she had seen Maggie on Monday, particularly knowing that her counsellor would be away for three weeks. Still, Maggie must really need her holidays, perhaps more than most, with such a difficult job; it couldn't be easy listening to other people's problems all day. It was Wednesday, and Ellie was almost paralysed with fear anticipating the next day when Dave would be off work and had expectations which she dare not even think about. Grace had been accompanying her daughter each day to help look after Sam for which Ellie was grateful, being in no state to have sole charge of her son. Both parents and Phil knew that something was wrong and had gently enquired if there was anything they could do to help. Eventually they tactfully stopped asking, yet were unable to disguise their concerned looks, which only served to compound Ellie's guilt about a situation which she didn't fully understand. The problem was however consuming every waking thought and keeping her up at night, preventing any release that sleep might bring.

It was the middle of the afternoon and Grace had taken Sam for a walk after which they would pick up a few items of shopping. Ellie, alone at the house, was momentarily panicked by the sound of a car pulling into the drive, but dashing to the window was relieved to see that it was Phil and not Dave, yet the panic was almost immediately replaced with curiosity as to why he was home so early. Was something wrong, or was this perhaps a contrived situation to get the young couple together to talk.

'Hi Ellie.' Phil came in purposefully bright and cheery, yet made no attempt to hug or kiss her, not even a peck on the cheek.

'Contrived' Ellie said to herself.

'What was that?' Phil asked.

'Oh nothing, what brings you home early?'

'Well, I'm up to date with everything and the office was getting unbearably stuffy so I thought I would call it a day. Where's Sam and Grace?'

'Out for a walk, they shouldn't be long.'

'Ah, right. Its lovely outside, shall we sit in the garden for a while? Is there any of that wine left?'

'I'll get it.' Ellie offered trying to decide whether this was a pre-arranged situation which seemed most likely, but was that a bad thing? Pouring two glasses of wine, Ellie wondered if she dare use this opportunity to tell her husband about the situation with Dave, having come round to thinking that anything was better than the limbo she was living in at the moment.

It was a beautiful day, not too hot but bright enough to sit outside in their garden. Phil must work hard to keep the lawn and flower beds so tidy and it suddenly occurred to Ellie that she had no idea if she enjoyed gardening, or if Phil did it all; one of scores of little things, gaps in her knowledge of who she was, would this ever be over? Carrying the wine into the garden Ellie forced a smile and took the seat next to Phil on the bench. The sadness behind the smile had not gone unnoticed and prompted him to put a protective arm around her, gently asking,

'What is it love? Something is very wrong, and I really would like to help.' His tender concern unravelled all attempts at being brave and the tears which never been far from spilling over, now came as Ellie let go of all the emotions she had been keeping to herself for the last couple of weeks and wept bitterly.

It took several minutes for Ellie to cease the flood of tears and regain some semblance of composure. Phil had patiently held his wife, stroking her hair and trying somehow to let her know how much he loved her. Eventually, pulling away, taking a deep breath and turning to face Phil, the decision was made; she would tell him. Whether this time alone together had been contrived or not, she would take the opportunity it presented and face the consequences later, nothing could be worse than living how she had been this last couple of weeks, yet unsure how to begin, Ellie would test the waters first to see how much her husband knew.

'Do you know Dave who lives across the road?' Ellie watched as Phil suddenly stiffened and his expression seemed to darken.

'Why?' was his only reply.

'He helped me lift Sam's stroller in the other day.'

'Keep away from him Ellie, he's bad news.' Phil scowled.

'What do you mean?'

'Only that he's not a nice person, that's all you need to know. His wife left him a few months ago and I can't say that I blame her.'

'That sounds a bit cryptic, tell me more.'

'No, there's nothing you need to know, trust me.'

'But maybe I should know, I had no idea if Dave was a friend or not. I need to know about the neighbours if I'm going to come back here to live.'

Phil brightened instantly,

'You're coming home to live, really?'

'Well... I meant eventually, I thought we had agreed; no timescales?'

'Sorry love, it's just that I'm so anxious for things to get back to how they were.'

'Well I need to know how things were, with regard to the neighbours I mean, were we friends with anyone in particular?'

'Well, you often had coffee with Christine from the corner house, she has been asking after you but said she wouldn't trouble you until you were up to it.'

'So what about Dave?'

'Why him? Forget him Ellie.' Phil sounded almost angry but she must pursue the conversation now that it had begun.

'Because he's said things, implied things.' Both their voices were rising.

'Oh no, Ellie! Tell me, you must tell me.'

She had done it now, there was no going back.

'Well, he's hinted that he and I were a little more than friends...I...I didn't know what to think, he's a horrible man who keeps pestering me, saying he'll tell you...things.'

'Oh my poor Ellie, is that what you have been worrying about these last few weeks. I am so sorry, I should have told you.' He reached out to hold his wife who so wanted and needed the comfort of his arms but was unsure if she had just planted a huge wedge between them.

'Told me what? Please, I don't know what to do, I've been terrified by what he said, I thought I might lose you and Sam and I couldn't bear that. Have I done something I should be ashamed of? If so tell me...please!' Even though Ellie was so distraught, her eyes were dry, all tears used up, her body screaming exhaustion and her mind grappling with fear. Had she had an affair, did Phil already know?

'Tell me Phil, please.' Ellie's voice now became a trembling whisper.

A noise from the house distracted them, Grace had returned with Sam. Phil went inside leaving Ellie anxiously waiting, hoping this conversation could be finished; if Phil didn't explain what he meant it would be unbearable, she needed to know the truth. Sam's happy laughter rang out through the open patio doors, pleased to see his father and oblivious to the pain his parents were both feeling. After three or four minutes, which felt like hours, Phil returned, closing the door behind him.

'Phil?' Ellie's eyes pleaded for an explanation of what his earlier words meant and her head ached with the tension throughout her body. Quickly he sat down, gently taking her hand in his own.

'There was an incident, last year, a few weeks before Christmas.' Phil stared down at their joined hands, unable to look into her eyes.

'What kind of incident?' Ellie's voice was shaky.

'I don't know how to say it, he...he made a pass at you, groped you, whatever you want to call it.'

Ellie's free hand covered her mouth. Phil went on,

'It was late afternoon and Dave had come over on some pretext or other, he was always doing that and was so transparent in the way he leered at you, at first we laughed about it but then he became a real nuisance. You apparently tried to keep him on the doorstep but he pushed his way in and began forcing himself on you. I came home early that day too, you were in tears trying to fight him off, and as I came through the door you had managed to knee him where it really hurt. The situation was obvious and I'm afraid I lost my temper and lashed out at him. It seems almost comical now, arriving in the nick of time to defend your honour, but I really don't know how far he would have gone if I had not come home then.' Phil lifted his eyes to meet his wife's and could see the shock this information had brought.

'Were the police involved?' her mind was racing ahead, wondering how the situation had turned out.

'No, we decided to let it drop. Perhaps we should have involved them but to tell the truth I hit him much harder that I should have and Dave left nursing a broken jaw. It was unlikely that he would report that, so we came to the conclusion that it would be better to let the whole incident drop and put it behind us. Dave never troubled you after that but somehow his wife found out, probably the jaw, and she left him almost immediately.'

'But he did seem to know things about me...' Ellie tentatively broached the subject.

'Like what?'

'Well, the birthmark on the back of my neck, how could he have found out about that?' Ellie was still unsure whether she had been entirely blameless in this whole business and desperately needed to know for her peace of mind.

'Anyone could have known that. You often wore your hair up when it had grown it longer, the birthmark was quite visible.'

'I never put my hair up; I was always embarrassed by that mark.'

'You'd got over that a long time ago. It was cooler and so much easier after Sam was born and you look good like that. You have nothing at all to reproach yourself about; I think Dave has in some sick way been trying to get revenge. He blames me for his wife leaving but he managed to mess his life up all by himself and we had decided that he was not going to mess up our lives too.'

'So what do we do now?' Ellie looked to her husband for guidance.

'I'm going to go round to have a few words with Dave; he's gone too far this time.'

'No Phil, don't. I can't bear the thought of you getting in some kind of fight. Please, let it drop.'

'We let it drop last time and look what happened. He needs to know that he has been found out.'

'Well, if you go to see him I'm coming too.'

'No, please, let me handle it. I'll be very careful but I want him to know that if he comes near you again we will report him to the police for harassment.'

Ellie nodded in agreement, even managing a smile which couldn't really convey the feeling of utter relief now flowing through her mind. She hadn't betrayed Phil and that knowledge was all she needed to reclaim some of the happiness she had so recently been feeling before it had been snatched away by that bitter man. Lacing her fingers into Phil's, they went into the house to see their son and his grandmother and to begin a new chapter in her recovery.

Chapter 33

Diane had not been able to see Sarah as originally planned and now suggested they meet at the 'Coffee Bean'. Sarah however wanted a more private meeting so invited Di to her parent's home where they could talk without being overheard. It was so unreal, sitting talking to this woman who was Mark's legal wife, a status she was by no means sorry to relinquish. It was another lovely day so they took their coffee into the garden where no one would disturb them and Diane pulled out a notebook,

'There are so many things I wanted to tell you and ask about when we first met but most of them flew out of my head, and I would imagine that now you've had time to think there are things you want to ask me too?'

'Goodness yes,' she replied, 'but I'm not so organized as to have them written down.'

Sarah felt comfortable in Diane's presence; after all they had much in common and were meeting on an equal footing now that the cloak and dagger stuff was over.

'Is it macabre to want to know about your marriage to Mark? Like you I'm curious to compare notes and I suppose it's best to present a united front on the legal side of things. I haven't a clue what sort of sentence he will get, hopefully a long custodial one, but you never know.'

'Have you found a solicitor yet?' Di asked.

'Yes, my Dad's handling that side of things for me, both he and Mum have been brilliant about everything, I think I would go under without their support.'

'I had my parents to fall back on too.' Diane looked suddenly thoughtful and asked,

'Sarah, are you an only child?'

'Well yes, why do you ask?'

'I've been reading up on psychological abuse. It's amazing how much my experiences with Mark fit into the classic examples. I'm an only child too and he certainly picked his target well with me. I met him after the breakup of another relationship and was so low in confidence that it was easy to have me eating out of his hand. I feel foolish now, but we are all a lot wiser with hind sight. Anyway, psychological abuse often follows a pattern and is well thought out by the perpetrator. The victim is nearly always someone who is vulnerable and so from Mark's point of view an only child is an easy target. He was so charming that my parents took to him readily and in a very short time frame we were engaged and planning the wedding. I was naive enough to think that Mark's first wife must have been an idiot to let him slip through her fingers...'

'Wait a minute. Did you say his first wife?' Sarah was aghast, this was the first she had heard about another wife.

'You didn't know? Well having been married before was perhaps the only thing he was honest about with me. I assumed he had told you that too.'

'No, he missed out that little fact. I believed he was a bachelor and had never been married, which was what he put on the wedding certificate. I can't believe it, how on earth has he got away with it?'

'Choosing his target carefully I expect.' Diane tried to answer. 'You are also a little younger than I am, he probably played on your romantic fantasies, you know, boy meets girl, happy ever after and all that. Anyway, only children are a better target because there's less extended family to have to deal with. He wouldn't want you to have a sister to whom you were really close, that would definitely work against his plans.'

'It all sounds so calculated and cunning.'

'It is! Did he discourage you from maintaining any friendships?'

'Oh yes, and deleting the contacts on my mobile phone was presumably part of that.'

'Yep! You're getting the hang of this Sarah. Tell me, did he ever suggest taking power of attorney for your parents?'

This was another shock for Sarah,

'No, never, but because you're asking presumably he did with you?'

'Right again. Another reason why an only child is the best target, power of attorney and then all of the inheritance will come to him, through you of course. Did he handle all your finances?'

'Yes, he convinced me that I was no good with money even though I'd managed for years without him.'

'It was exactly the same for me.' Diane smiled. 'And perhaps if you had been together longer he might have tried the power of attorney thing. I ended up feeling so incompetent about everything that in only two years, he had me exactly where he wanted me. I began to think that all I was capable of doing was holding down my part time job and looking after Mark, but at times he piled on the guilt about not being very good at that. He is nothing short of a monster, a selfish pig of a monster and he only left me when my parents intervened. They were unhappy about not seeing me regularly and then when he suggested the power of attorney they stepped in, fortunately spoiling all his plans. My parents are more than capable of taking care of their own affairs; he had gone a step too far with that. I've even thought that if he had managed to get that, his next step would have been to have me declared insane. When he was challenged he simply left one day, no goodbyes, no divorce, he even left his place of work without any notice at all.'

'It must have been so hard for you Di.'

'No more than it's been for you and things might have gone on much longer if it hadn't been for that chance sighting which led me to him and you. I'm sorry for scaring you at first. I had tried to summon up the courage to see you before and then chickened out.'

'Don't worry about it, I'm really grateful. I was getting to breaking point myself and honestly don't know how much longer I could have coped. Looking back now I can see it all as part of Mark's plan. He really had me afraid of him and believing that I was going insane. It was easier to go along with him in every aspect of our life. I'm ashamed that I pushed my parents away simply to please Mark but to avoid his moods it was so much easier to give in to him.'

'How did you manage to see the counsellor you said you had been going to?' Diane asked.

'It was Sue's suggestion, you know, my friend from the coffee shop? She works at the health centre and is close friends with Maggie. It was her suggestion that I see her and she agreed to meet me over lunch times so that Mark would know nothing about it.'

'That was a brave step; I don't think I would have dared try anything like that, if Mark had found out...'

'Yes, that fear was always with me, but I was desperate for some support and Maggie was great, I'll probably still be seeing her for quite a while.'

'You'll have to give me her number.' Diane smiled.

'Anyway,' Sarah felt the need to lighten the conversation, 'You have a new man in your life now?'

'Ah, yes, and he is everything Mark was not. It took some persuasion to agree to see him but I am so glad I did, he's gorgeous and wants to marry me.'

'You are so brave to be trying again. I'll probably be off men for quite a long time after this.'

'That will change in time. If you let Mark sour any future relationships then he has won a little victory over you. Don't give him that satisfaction Sarah, live your life as you want to now and to hell with Mark Beecham!'

Sarah knew that Diane would become a friend; after all they had so much in common. When Di had left she remained alone in the garden for about twenty minutes reflecting on their conversation. Hopefully she too would get over this terrible experience enough to trust another man, but that was a long way off. Firstly there were people to face up to, people who knew she had been deceived, which would be difficult and more than a little embarrassing. The time off work would help to get her thoughts and affairs sorted out and the support of her parents was invaluable. Sarah's father had already lined up appointments at the bank, the building society and of course the solicitor but he would be there as a guide through the obstacles of unravelling this pseudo marriage. It was a mammoth task and one she did not relish but there was an end in sight. The legal process moved slowly but Sarah wasn't destitute and had a home now with her parents, a safe, happy home with their unconditional love to support her.

****

It was Maggie's last day at work before the holiday and she had almost finished tying up loose ends. They would be setting off early the next morning, Saturday, very early in fact with a 7.30 am flight and having to be at the airport ninety minutes before to check in. Alan had offered to take them, another thirty minute drive but at least the traffic shouldn't present any problems so early in the day. The telephone broke into her thoughts, which were already in Las Vegas.

'Maggie? It's Ellie, have I caught you at a bad time?'

'No, no, it's good to hear from you, how are you?'

'Actually, I'm doing pretty well.'

Maggie heard the vitality in Ellie's voice and found herself smiling into the phone.

'That's great Ellie, have things been resolved at all?'

'Oh yes, and more than that, I think my future is now back on track. I dithered so much about what was the best thing to do that I was making myself ill. Phil came home early and I took the opportunity to try and find out about our horrible neighbour. There is, it seems a history and this Dave had caused problems last year which ended up with Phil giving him a broken jaw which is not something he is particularly proud of but was apparently in my defence and makes me feel good that he would do that for me. Anyway, Phil told me everything and I understand now that by his silence he was trying to protect me, but if he had told me it could have all been sorted weeks ago.'

'You sound pretty happy now?'

'Oh Maggie, I can't tell you! I was beginning to feel that I had been this horrible woman and was at the point of actually hating myself but now everything has been explained it's such a relief. We can actually get back to where we were and continue getting to know each other again. I hope you don't mind me ringing you, but I knew you were off on holiday and I wanted to tell you before you went.'

'Actually I'm really glad you have rung Ellie, I'll enjoy my holiday so much more knowing that things have improved for you. You've timed it well too, another half an hour and I would have left for home.'

'I'd still like to see you when you're back, having someone to talk to has been such a help, will that be okay?'

'Yes, of course. Our sessions aren't limited and it is still early days so I'll be happy to see you when I'm back, we have booked a session for then haven't we?'

'Yes, only I thought you might think I didn't need you anymore.'

'Not at all, we still have quite a bit of work to do and I'll look forward to seeing you then.'

'Thanks Maggie and enjoy your holiday won't you?'

'I'm sure I will; bye Ellie.'

Maggie truly did feel better knowing that Ellie had taken the bold step of confiding in Phil. She hated going away when any clients were facing particularly difficult issues, although Joyce always reminded her that she couldn't be responsible for everybody's problems and had to look after herself too. And now it was time to go home but Maggie wanted to say goodbye to Sue before leaving and found her friend in the office behind reception rummaging through some files.

'I'm off now Sue so I will see you in three weeks, unless we like it so much we decide to stay.'

'No chance, you'll be too frightened of missing something.'

'Yes, you're probably right there, anyway I will miss you and I'm relying on you to make sure Alan gets up in time to take us to the airport.'

In an unusual display of emotion, Sue hugged Maggie who could actually detect a few tears in her friend's eyes.

'I'll probably be twice as fat when you come back!' Sue covered her feelings with a quip as usual and Maggie laughed while turning to leave with a pang of something inside her which she couldn't quite place.

Peter was home first, busily squeezing lemon juice and black pepper on two salmon fillets before wrapping them in foil to put in the oven to poach. He almost skipped to the front door to greet Maggie, wearing a huge schoolboy grin on his face and kissing his wife before saying,

'I can't believe we're actually going.' Ben joined in the welcome thinking it a game and an opportunity for a little attention. Maggie sank down onto the sofa to catch her breath, tickling Ben's ears. Tara remained curled up on the window sill, deigning to open one disinterested eye before returning to sleep.

'Well I know someone who will miss us, won't you boy?'

'He won't miss us that much with your mother around to spoil him, which reminds me, they are on the way but are stopping for something to eat, so we can have ours as usual. It'll be about half an hour, do you want to get changed first?'

'Mm, I think I'll have a shower and slip on my pyjamas, comfort is what I need tonight and Mum and Dad won't mind. We'll probably not get to bed as early as we should but hopefully we can get some sleep on the plane.'

'Should I ring Alan to remind him about tomorrow?'

'No, I've asked Sue to make sure he gets here in time. Do you know she was quite emotional saying goodbye, it must be all those hormones swimming around her body.'

Thirty minutes later Maggie and Peter were sitting at the table eating salmon and salad and enjoying the view over the fields.

'I'll miss our home.' Maggie said. 'I love it here, the view and the tranquillity. I should think LA and New York will be a bit of a culture shock.'

'The time will probably fly and we'll be home before you know it.' Peter squeezed his wife's hand, he too would miss their home, it had been such a good move, this house gave them everything they needed and more and both of them loved it.

George and Helen Price arrived at 6.30pm. It was almost three months since Maggie had seen her parents and she greeted them enthusiastically. Coffee was made and they took time to catch up on each other's news. The visitors were enchanted with the house as Maggie knew they would be.

'It will be like a holiday for us staying here, we'll have some lovely walks out with Ben, won't we George?' Helen asked.

'Absolutely, if you can drag me away from that view.'

'Well we're so grateful that you've come, I'll rest easier for knowing you will be looking after everything for us. Oh, and Sue says if you need anything to ring, she would like to see you both so I think she will pop round anyway.'

'Yes, how is Sue, everything going well with the baby?' Helen asked.

'Fine, everything's as it should be; the middle of October is the date so at least I'm not deserting her then.'

'And Jane, how is she doing Peter?'

'Fine too thanks Helen, her baby's due in September so I can see it's going to be all baby chatter when we come home.'

'Okay Granddad, you love it really don't you?' Maggie teased.

'Guilty as charged, it's great being a granddad; I should have skipped the children stage and gone straight to grandchildren.'

Eventually Maggie and Peter excused themselves and went to bed. Her parents said they too would be turning in before long but first they would take Ben out for a short walk as it was such a lovely warm evening.

Both George and Helen were up early the next morning not wanting to miss seeing Maggie and Peter off to the airport.

'We can have a nap later if we need to.' George said when his daughter told him they should have slept on, 'or even go back now for another hour or two.'

Alan arrived early, wanting to put their minds at rest and so, a little before 5.30am, they were on their way.

'It's quite nice being up so early, hearing the birds sing, and it's so quiet on the roads.'

'I shouldn't think Alan likes being up at this time, it's not him going on holiday.' Peter remarked.

'Oh, I don't mind a bit, I have always been a morning person and as you say, we have the road to ourselves.'

The flight was on time and soon Maggie and Peter found themselves high above the beautifully white fluffy clouds on their way to the USA.

Chapter 34

Leaving the plane after an air conditioned flight they were hit by stifling heat which felt something akin to walking into a sauna, the atmosphere seeming almost solid. It was the height of summer in Las Vegas and they would very quickly learn that the thing to do was to hurry from air conditioned cars into air conditioned buildings. Maggie laughed as they left the terminal at McCarran airport on seeing a chauffeur waiting, holding a card with their names on. 'I feel like a celebrity,' she said, wondering if this was to be one of many firsts they would encounter in the USA.

The chauffeur had been sent by the 'Architect's Monthly' their hosts in America and he effortlessly navigated the labyrinth of roads leading out of the airport and soon they found themselves cruising on the highway heading to Las Vegas. Inside the car Peter watched the temperature rise above a hundred degrees. Maggie had expected it to be hot and having never been a sun worshipper, wondered if she might find the heat too exhausting. On arrival at the hotel their luggage was taken from the car to their room, leaving them the simple task of checking in. The opulence of the hotel was stunning and that was just the foyer, a space big enough to hold a ball in with a grand marble reception desk running the whole length of one wall, so highly polished that Maggie could see her reflection in it. The receptionist handed them their keys and an envelope addressed to Peter then they made their way up to their room on the fourteenth floor. 'Room' did not actually do it justice; it was a suite, beautifully furnished with a king sized bed and built in mirrored wardrobes. Two leather sofas and an armchair graced the lounge area, positioned for maximum benefit of the view, a spectacular panorama of downtown Las Vegas, now in darkness with thousands of lights competing to catch the eye. There was a large television and a bathroom which was almost the size of their bedroom at home, fitted with a whirlpool bath and separate shower. A trouser press, writing desk and side tables completed the suite, with fresh flowers, fruit and a complimentary bottle of wine.

'Our whole office could fit in this one room!' Peter remarked.

'Wow' was the best Maggie could offer and Peter grinned at her obvious pleasure before flopping onto one of the leather sofas to open and read the letter.

'It's from Nigel Carter, our host from the Architect's Monthly, suggesting we meet for breakfast here in the hotel at nine in the morning. Does that sound okay to you? There's a number I can ring if we want to change it.'

'No, that sounds fine; we need to meet him to see what, if anything has been arranged, which unfortunately means we should have an early night.' Maggie joined Peter on the sofa, winding her arms around his neck and lifting her face to kiss him, 'unless you have a better plan?'

Nigel Carter was a small, rotund man with a ruddy complexion split by a wide smile. Maggie instantly thought of Mr Fuzzywig from Dickens's 'A Christmas Carol', and they both liked him on sight. Nigel ordered eggs over easy, with bacon, grits and a side order of pancakes then nodded encouragingly for his guests to try the same.

'Why not?' Maggie shrugged and they repeated Nigel's order. Peter's first lecture was in two days time, scheduled to give him chance to recover from jet-lag, which as yet did not seem to have caught up with him or Maggie. Nigel offered to be their tour guide if they wanted to see some of the city and suggested they had a relatively quiet day then meet in the evening when Las Vegas really began to wake up, an offer they gladly accepted having swiftly come to the conclusion that walking in the heat was not an option. Neither of them relished the thought of driving in a strange city so they were content to rest and settle for exploring the locality around their hotel. Having established that his guests would be happy to spend the day alone, Nigel left after agreeing a time to pick them up that evening.

'How on earth do they manage to eat so much food, and that's only for breakfast?' Maggie commented after their host had left, she had been unable to eat even half of the breakfast put before her.

'Three weeks of this and we'll be rolling home; you will probably be bigger than Sue.' Peter's remark was answered with a swift kick under the table before they went back up to their room to freshen up and decide what to do with the day ahead of them.

****

Sunday morning brought another hot sunny day but to Ellie, even if it had poured with rain it would still be a good day. She had spent Saturday with Phil and Sam at their home, Phil had wanted to catch up on some gardening and give the lawn a well overdue mow, so Ellie played with Sam, 'helping' Daddy in the garden. When Sam tired, his mother took him for a nap then prepared their lunch. They had begun to feel like a real family again, so when Phil suggested a day at the coast on Sunday, Ellie was delighted and before going back to her parents for the night, prepared a picnic lunch to put in the fridge so that they could have an early start the next day.

It was good to wake with a positive anticipation of the day rather than a dread of what might happen. As they neared the coast and breathed in the salty tang of the sea air, Ellie felt unbelievably happy. They had sung songs with Sam during most of the journey, the little boy picking up on his parents' good mood, chuckling and clapping to their singing. Parking close to the beach, they gathered the collection of buckets, spades and fishing net from the boot of the car before they set off to have some serious fun. The beach was quiet but would probably fill up as the day got older, so the Graham family made the most of the morning with Sam attempting to dig in the sand and help Mummy to half bury Daddy. They ran down to the water's edge with Sam carried between his parents, and then began to jump over the little waves causing squeals of delight. Eating sandwiches on the beach was as pleasurable as a meal in any high class hotel would have been, and drinking lemonade from the bottle, Ellie had forgotten the cups, caused more hilarity when the bubbles tickled their noses. As the beach became increasingly crowded they decided to leave, having had a good four hours all three of them were feeling tired. Sam, as expected went to sleep in the car and his parents motored in compatible silence most of the way home.

'I told Mum and Dad not to expect me home tonight.' Ellie said quietly as they neared the end of their journey. Phil glanced at her briefly, smiling.

'Are you sure, it's okay if it's still too early for you?'

'I'm sure.' She put her hand over his on the steering wheel and squeezed affectionately, 'I want to stay.' They lapsed into silence, each with their own thoughts until they pulled into the drive when Phil gently lifted Sam out of his seat, then putting his free arm protectively around his wife's shoulder, the three of them went into their home.

Maggie and Peter lazily explored the area around the hotel, nipping into hotels, arcades or shops in an effort to keep out of the heat. Early August would not have been their choice for a trip to America but this was an opportunity not to be missed, a little thing like heat wasn't going to spoil their enjoyment. Stopping for iced tea in a hotel bar, and looking at the huge selection of donuts and pastries on offer, Maggie bemoaned the amount she had eaten at breakfast so they decided to share one, if only for the experience of eating the American way. Time seemed to pass quickly and when they would normally be having lunch neither of them could face more food so they turned to head back to the hotel, deciding to eat there in the evening.

Nigel was prompt and as cheery as he had been earlier in the day. Ushering his guests into the car he explained that although the best way to see Las Vegas was on foot, they would travel into the heart of the resort by car to explore the hotels and casinos and cut down the distance they would have to walk. Incredibly, Maggie thought, the daylight had suddenly been replaced by night with no dusk in between, the advantage of this being that outside was no longer uncomfortably hot; the darkness had brought with it a more temperate, pleasant warmth, easier for them to cope with and more agreeable for walking.

'You're going to love our city!' Nigel was passionate about his home town with eyes twinkling in the dark, reflecting the lights from every direction. His enthusiasm and grin were to continue all night becoming infectious and carrying his guests along in the trail of his fervour.

'You simply must see Caesar's Palace, we'll go there first.' Nigel drove to the side of a huge building, pulling up behind several other cars and jumped out to hand the keys to a valet. Before they could get their bearings as to where they were, their host had entered a door and motioned for Maggie and Peter to follow. An elevator whisked them up to the ground level and as the door opened Nigel announced,

'Welcome to Caesar's Palace!'

Maggie stared at their surroundings. It was a reception area far too grand to be called a lobby, one which easily surpassed the extravagance of their own hotel. The floors gleamed like mirrors as did all the polished surfaces. Sumptuous leather seating filled alcoves and corners and dramatic columns punctuated the room, inspired by the decadence of ancient Rome. Peter's eyes drifted upwards, taking in the magnificent ceiling and admiring the whole setting from an architect's point of view. Nigel watched his new friends' reactions with interest, allowing them only a few moments to enjoy their surroundings before ushering them through a wide passageway which led directly into the casino. This was really something else, a place where Maggie felt a little uncomfortable but had to admit that it was another world, poles apart from life in their little corner of England, yet she could immediately understand the attraction of the casino, the beautiful surroundings, the buzz of happy voices, hostesses plying visitors with complimentary drinks and smiling to encourage them to feel at home. It was an enchanting, glamorous world and of course there was the thrill of gambling, always the chance that the next turn of the roulette wheel will change your life forever, or that the fruit machine might spew it's jackpot on the next pull of its arm. It was alluring and enticing, total opulence from the thick pile of the carpets to the soft lighting, from the comfortable seating to the majestic displays of fresh flowers, everyone was your friend, everyone was happy.

'Shall we move on?' Nigel had so much he wanted to show his English visitors and they dutifully followed on through a maze of reception rooms, past tables of gamblers and eventually out into the pleasant evening air.

Maggie thoughts that nothing could surpass the grandeur of Caesar's Palace were soon proved wrong as they followed Nigel in the direction of the Bellagio. Their host led them to a vantage point in front of the hotel where a huge pool nestled beneath the backdrop of the hotel itself with its protective arc shielding the fountains and the splendour of the scene inviting visitors to explore its delights. Nigel's timing was perfect and almost as soon as they stopped, fountains began to rise and fall into the centre of the pool with coloured lighting adding an extra dimension, coupled with fitting classical music.

'There are more than a thousand fountains in this show.' Nigel informed his guests as they stood to admire an aquatic ballet like nothing Maggie had ever seen before. The inside of the hotel was amazing. They were led through the gaming rooms, similar to Caesar's Palace, and into the cavernous conservatory and botanical gardens.

'I think I could spend hours in here.' Maggie whispered to Peter. The scent from hundreds of blooms filled the room and as they meandered around she was amazed at the ingenious planting. Topiary had been tastefully used to theme different areas and each plant and flower seemed to be at the peak of its beauty; had she seen pictures of these scenes Maggie would have thought them artificial. They both would have been totally lost in the maze of the different rooms if it had not been for Nigel, whose grin never left his face, so happy that his city was making such an impression on his guests.

'There's so much more to see.' He reminded them, 'You guys must see The Mirage and Peter, you'll love the Luxor, it's a huge glass pyramid, certain to get you thinking about its construction.'

Maggie could have happily stayed in Bellagio's tropical gardens; they were situated beside a patisserie with handmade chocolates and all kinds of cakes which simply oozed calories. A chocolate fountain and a sculptured chocolate lady made her wish Sue was with them and they could sample some of the treats on offer. Instead Maggie set off again, following Nigel, confident that he would guide them to all the 'must see' places.

Peter did marvel at the Luxor from inside and out, it was truly a magnificent building but he was beginning to tire now, which hadn't gone unnoticed by Maggie who suggested they make their way back to the hotel.

'Are you sure? You haven't seen half the sights, you can catch up on sleep later; no one keeps regular hours in Vegas.' Nigel seemed rather disappointed, he was obviously enjoying playing the tour guide which made Maggie wish she had explained about Peter's illness and the limitations it imposed. They did however begin to trace their steps back to the car at Caesar's Palace and again Nigel drove skilfully through the night time traffic, keeping up a running commentary and pointing out so many landmarks which Maggie knew she would never remember. Finally reaching their hotel at four o'clock in the morning, both Maggie and Peter were exhausted, doing nothing more than drinking bottled water before they climbed into bed and were asleep in minutes.

Peter woke first and was surprised to see that it was almost mid-day. The heavy curtains had kept the room cool and in darkness and any noise there may have been certainly had not disturbed them. Trying not to wake his wife, Peter sat by the desk with the small reading lamp on and began to read through the lecture he would be delivering the following day. It was not long before Maggie too awoke, smiling and throwing back the covers to step onto the velvety carpet.

'You must know that lecture by heart now the number of times you've read it.' She kissed her husband then moved to open the curtains. By the stark morning light the view from the window looked like an entirely different place than it had the night before. Maggie was struck by how many boxy, concrete buildings there seemed to be and car parks with huge rubbish containers. None of this had been visible in the dark when their eyes were drawn towards the bright lights and flashing neon signs, the Las Vegas trademark. Turning away from the window, she announced,

'I'm hungry. Can we shower then find somewhere to eat?'

'Find somewhere? That won't be too difficult; there are places to eat everywhere.'

Maggie grinned,

'I think I would like to see the other side of Vegas, where the people live, do you think you would be up to that?'

'Of course, as long as we don't get lost without Nigel's services as a tour guide.'

Maggie's wish was granted and after a breakfast of fruit and bagels in a deli across from their hotel, they began to explore the other side of Las Vegas, turning off the strip to weave their way behind the hotels and find some of the concrete buildings they had seen from their room. The contrast was astounding; blocks of flats and rows of single storey houses which were nothing more than shacks, stretched as far as they could see. On almost every corner there were signs for bail bondsmen or pawn shops, competing with shabby looking 'wedding chapels' which hopefully looked better at night than they did in the stark light of day. Maggie found it all quite sad especially when she noticed an elderly woman whom she was certain had been in Caesar's Palace the night before, sitting passively at a slot machine, endlessly feeding it coins which she most probably could ill afford, with two carrier bags at her feet, spilling over with what looked like her life possessions. They did not need Nigel to tell them about the flip side of Vegas, the buildings and the people spoke volumes, the pawn shops testament to the grittier side of gambling. Maggie could almost feel the sadness of this area, an absolute contradiction of the glamour they had seen the last evening.

'I think we'll head back now shall we?' The effect their surroundings were having on Maggie had not gone unnoticed and Peter steered his wife in the direction of their comfortable hotel.

Chapter 35

Stepping down from the podium to enthusiastic applause, Peter blushed and Maggie could not have been prouder. The lecture had been concise but not short, punctuated with small bites of humour, interesting and informative and judging by the applause it wasn't only his wife who thought so. Maggie had not expected to find the lecture interesting, thinking that architectural jargon would be beyond her understanding, but surprisingly she had followed every word and absorbed some of Peter's enthusiasm for his subject. Reducing footprints and innovatively using sustainable materials seemed the ethical and progressive way to go forward in modern day architecture and planning and Peter's speech had certainly enthused his audience. She had known that beforehand he was worried about the daunting prospect of speaking to a large professional body of men and women but he had come over as relaxed and knowledgeable, and as he tried to get back to his seat was patted on the back and had his hand almost shaken off him.

'Brilliant!' Nigel gushed, 'Absolutely brilliant.'

Peter was more than a little embarrassed, having hoped his address would be adequate and appropriate for the theme of the conference this kind of adulation took him completely by surprise. He still felt a little overawed as they were driven back to their hotel later in the day, where Nigel insisted on buying them dinner, for which they arranged to meet later before heading upstairs for a well deserved rest.

'I was so proud of you.' Maggie hugged her husband, able to congratulate him herself now that they were alone.

'I must admit I didn't expect it to be so well received.' Peter was still a little shocked. 'I didn't think it was that good.'

'Well, you've underestimated yourself Peter; you have a natural easy going manner when you speak, which the audience certainly appreciated.'

'I only hope it will go down as well in New York' he sighed, 'this is quite something to live up to.'

'There's no reason why it shouldn't be equally as well received, it is the same lecture isn't it?'

'Yes, I know, but I'm amazed at the response.'

'Enjoy it my darling, everyone else did.'

With the lecture out of the way Peter and Maggie were able to relax and enjoy the rest of their time in Las Vegas. Nigel took them to dinner as promised, spending most of the time singing Peter's praises as a speaker. He even went so far as to say that if they ever wanted to move to the States there would be a job waiting for him in his firm. Blushing again, Peter thanked his host but had to be honest in telling him that there was little chance of that ever happening. Maggie smiled at this turn in the conversation, knowing that she and Peter were so happy and settled in their own home that a move would be unthinkable, especially one so far. Nigel once again thanked them profusely whilst saying goodbye, leaving them with a few more days until time to move on to New York, days which they could now spend at a more leisurely pace.

****

New York was something else altogether. The heat was a little more temperate although the air was still hot and humid. Here Maggie and Peter were able to walk to many of the places they wanted to see. Their hotel was on Lexington Avenue, close to the magnificent Grand Central Station, a perfect spot for tourists to be based. Once again they had free time before the lecture, three full days and although they had been met at the airport by a representative from the Architect's Monthly, unfortunately he was unable to spend time with them as Nigel had as their guide. Still, Maggie had her list and they were both beginning to get the hang of the grid system of streets which certainly made things easier in an unfamiliar place.

The top of the Empire State building was breathtaking. To be so high up was in itself a rarity and to see the view was incredible. Maggie could have stayed there all day but they moved along, allowing others to have the vantage points and keeping the flow of sightseers moving. Peter had taken photographs from several angles on their way round the walkway, sometimes catching Maggie in the view when she was unaware, capturing the expressions of wonder on her face which made him smile at her enjoyment. As they queued for the lift to go down, he squeezed his wife's hand, his eyes meeting hers and conveying all he wanted to say about the pleasure at being with her in such a place. Peter was secretly pleased that neither of them had been to America before, it made the trip a new and fresh experience, giving a kind of exclusivity to the whole experience. After sampling the food on offer at yet another deli, they walked to Central Park, finding the green spaces and leafy trees to be soothing on their eyes. They were persuaded by an Irish cab driver to take a tour of the park in his horse driven cab and enjoyed the surroundings whilst the driver pointed out places of interest in and around the park.

'Now this is beautiful.' Maggie said, 'The view from the Empire State building was amazing but the beauty and simplicity of nature has to beat it every time.'

They dutifully smiled as the cab driver took their photograph, then patted the horse and made their way back to Lexington Avenue.

'This has been quite an experience and I love it, but it can't beat home. I'll be ready to go back when our time here is done.' Maggie spoke the words but they were in accord as they both thought of their home and their own unique view from its windows. They ambled on, arm in arm, quietly now each with their own reflections.

The New York audience appreciated Peter's speech every bit as much as those in LA. He was pleased, but also relieved that it was over. As Maggie whispered that he might like to consider a new career in public speaking, he flashed a look of mock reprimand. This audience had been even larger than the previous one and Peter's nerves had been even more frayed, having a reputation to live up to. But now he could relax and enjoy the rest of their time without that persistent worry in the back of his mind of lectures to deliver. Their host drove them back to the hotel and after checking that they had no more need of a 'babysitter', wished them a pleasant stay in the city and left.

'I'm glad it's over.' Peter sank onto the sofa in their room with an audible sigh of relief.

'You were fantastic,' Maggie told him, 'I was so proud and so should you be.'

'It did go better than I had hoped and I'm glad not to have let the firm down.'

'You certainly didn't let anyone down, the response of the audience must have told you that much.'

'Yes, I have to admit that I was pleased with it all but now we can really start our holiday, ten days to do exactly as we please with nothing looming on the horizon to worry about.'

'Statue of Liberty tomorrow, we could take a taxi there and walk part of the way back, how does that sound?'

'Wonderful, but now I think I'm going to sleep for ten hours or more. Wake me if you need anything.' Peter wiggled his eyebrows giving another meaning to his words and making Maggie laugh.

Peter did not get his ten hours sleep. Only two hours after settling down he began to feel ill with a pain across his chest like nothing he had experienced before. It wasn't unbearable and he hoped it might simply be indigestion or even a pulled muscle. He felt hot, but then they had both been hot since arriving in America. Deciding not to wake Maggie but wait a while longer to see if the pain passed off, he tried taking deep breaths which did not seem to help; in fact it made him quite dizzy. Getting out of bed, Peter altered the controls of the air conditioning to cool the room, then went to the minibar and took out a bottle of water. The pain was still there, it felt like a tugging across his chest and he was beginning to worry. Waking Maggie was the sensible thing to do. He watched her sleeping, laid on her side with one hand under her cheek, looking so peaceful, yet he needed help and so very quietly spoke her name. She stirred then sighed continuing to sleep. Gently shaking her arm, Peter felt almost guilty but if it had been she who was ill he would want to help.

'What is it, what's wrong?' Maggie was sleepy and slightly disorientated.

'I don't feel so good.' Peter said.

She was suddenly wide awake,

'How do you mean, sickly, headache?'
'No, I've got a pain in my chest...'

****

Sarah had been off work for nearly two weeks and it was time for her to return, not relishing the prospect of telling her colleagues why she had been absent, but knowing she could not hide away forever, and still needed to earn a living. So, taking a deep breath and pulling her shoulders back she entered the dentist's surgery with a smile.

'Hi, how are you? We've missed you.' Marie's question was almost rhetorical not needing a detailed answer so Sarah went along in the same manner with a vague reply,

'I'm fine thanks Marie and I have missed you too, you'll have to fill me in on everything that has been happening.' Undoubtedly more detailed questions would follow which she would feel obliged to answer, but for now the first patient of the day had arrived and the opportunity for a more private conversation would have to wait.

When at lunchtime the chance did present itself, Sarah explained to Marie exactly what had happened. Her colleague responded with a spontaneous bear-hug and by expressing concern in a warm and genuine manner, which only served to bring a tear to Sarah's eyes but she managed to keep control.

'I know people say this glibly sometimes, but if there is anything I can do, just ask, really.' Marie's concern was sincere, taking away some of the apprehension Sarah had had about starting work again and making her feel a whole lot better and able to confide in her friend about some of the practical issues which had been thrown up by this unorthodox situation.

'The solicitor has been brilliant, as have Mum and Dad. He told me that many of the financial issues can only be finalised after the court case and Mark's conviction, the bigger things that is, like the sale of the house, but I have been able to draw on our joint bank account so I've taken out exactly half of the balance and opened a new account in my own name.'

'I would have cleared the lot, see how he likes being messed around.' Marie interrupted.

'I thought about that, but I don't want anything else to do with him at all, including taking his money.'

'Is he still at the house, have you seen him?'

'No, I haven't been back to the house so I don't have a clue if he is living there or not. I will have to go soon, there are more things I need to pick up, but Dad will go with me. He would actually like to confront Mark which I can understand, but I don't want that to happen. It would suit me best if I never see him again, although I know I'll have to face him in court.'

'When will that be?'

'We don't know yet, the solicitor's been pushing for a date but he has warned me that it could be a matter of months rather than weeks, I'll just have to be patient.' Sarah replied.

'It's incredible isn't it, how he got away with it I mean. To actually go through a marriage ceremony knowingly married to someone else, it's unreal.' Marie shook her head in disbelief; having expressed thoughts which Sarah and her parents had also voiced.

'I know, he has some nerve, or rather he had, apparently he has been rather quiet about the whole thing, not protesting innocence or causing any trouble and he's reporting in to the police to conform to his bail conditions. After Diane told me how he disappeared after leaving her, I half expected him to do the same again, but I suppose now that the police are involved and he has actually been charged with a crime, it's a whole new ball game.'

'Mark is a bully and they are usually cowards at heart.' Marie gave her opinion.

'I know that now and I think that's what my counsellor was trying to make me see all along.'

'Your counsellor, have you been seeing a counsellor?' Sarah's colleague was surprised.

'Oh Marie, I'm sorry I didn't tell you but I was getting in such a state about things. That's where I have been going on Wednesday lunch times.'

'Ah, it makes sense now. Don't worry about not telling me, it wasn't my business anyway.' Marie spoke without any sarcasm but Sarah felt the need to explain a bit more.

'I didn't tell anyone, not even my parents. I was so afraid Mark would find out, but apparently I wasn't the only one keeping secrets. Can you remember when I lost the contact numbers on my phone?'

'Yes, I do.'

'Well I hadn't made a mistake, Mark had deleted them.'

'No! Why on earth would he do that?'

'I think its part of a pattern of isolation; he was trying to make me completely dependent on him. Talking to Di has been a real eye opener; things which I had apparently done, thinking I was going mad, have been Mark all along. He tried many of the same things on me as he had on Diane, it's quite sad actually when we compare notes, like the time I lost my purse and it turned up in the fridge, with Di he hid hers in the ironing pile. One day we'll be able to laugh at this, but at the moment it feels anything but funny.'

'Look, in time you'll get over that bastard, but I want you to know that I'm here for you if you need someone to talk to or if there is anything at all I can do, please, I really mean it.' Marie was so concerned and sincere that Sarah wished she had confided in her sooner.

'Thanks Marie, it's good to know I have friends to turn to.'

'Well make sure you do whenever you need to. I won't ask any more questions, I don't want to pry but any time you need to talk, I'm here for you.'

Marie's reaction and attitude made Sarah a little ashamed that she had worried so much about returning to work. Perhaps it was another effect that Mark's undermining of her confidence had brought about. She was beginning to see how her 'husband' had, over time, chipped away at her self- assurance, changing her previous outgoing personality and making her an introverted, dependent wife. Sarah knew that rebuilding her life was going to be hard work.

Chapter 36

Peter tried to explain what kind of pain he was experiencing. Maggie had already rung reception and asked for an ambulance and was now looking intently at her husband, her own face mirroring his pain. What they were both thinking was 'heart attack' the ramifications of which could affect Peter's suitability for the new drug he was hoping to begin using when they arrived home.

'It could simply be stress, with the travelling and the lectures...' Maggie's voice trailed off, Peter tried to smile reassuringly but the pain was increasing and they were both worried now. The telephone made her jump and she almost dropped the receiver whilst picking it up. It was the night receptionist to say that the paramedics had arrived and were on their way up. Maggie opened the door to hasten their arrival then took her husband's hand whilst they waited. A man and woman appeared in the doorway, bustling in straight towards Peter. The questions came in rapid bursts, where was the pain, had he been doing anything strenuous, had he felt this way before, was there any history of heart trouble, what medication was he on? The pair appeared not to be listening to the answers as they took Peter's blood pressure and listened to his heartbeat, they were quick, efficient and calm.

'Your blood pressure is higher than we would like, but don't jump to any conclusions. We are going to take you to ER, to be on the safe side, do you want to come in the ambulance with us Mrs Lloyd?'

'Yes, thank you, I don't have any transport.'

'No problem.'

Peter was strapped into a wheelchair and rolled along the corridor to the lift, constantly attempting to reassure Maggie who in turn was trying to stay strong for him. The paramedic, aware of this little ritual, eventually asked,

'You two on holiday then?'

It gave them another focus and the conversation turned to whereabouts in England they had come from, how they liked the States and when they were due to go home.

Within half an hour Peter and Maggie were alone in a small room, Peter still on the gurney from the ambulance with his wife standing close and holding his hand. The fact that they had been left alone was, strangely, reassuring. Maggie's thoughts dragged her back to the very worst time in her life and the reason she so disliked hospitals, Chris. Her first husband had been in a room similar to this, but had been unconscious. She remembered watching helplessly as the ICU staff attempted, in vain, to save his life. There had been several staff then, unlike today; surely that difference was a good sign? She really needed to sit down, her whole body was trembling and she was beginning to feel quite light-headed. Peter patted the side of the gurney, attempting a smile so Maggie perched on the corner, taking at least some of the weight off her legs and giving her a degree of support. Raising Peter's hand to her face, she kissed his open palm, breathing in the scent of him and closing her eyes as he stroked her cheek, capturing the moment of closeness, of tenderness, silently praying that he would not be taken from her.

'I think it's wearing off love.' Peter almost whispered. Maggie opened her eyes but before she could speak, a doctor appeared in the doorway.

'Mr. Lloyd?' the tall wiry man smiled. Maggie almost jumped off the bed as the still smiling doctor moved towards his patient.

'How is the pain now?' he asked.

'Not quite as bad, it seems to be easing off.'

'But still there?'

'Yes.'

'And you have Multiple Sclerosis Mr Lloyd?'

'Yes again.'

The doctor studied the notes on his clip board and was silent for a very long minute before deciding.

'I would like to admit you for some tests. The readings the paramedics took in the ambulance are inconclusive so I would like to run some more.

'Is there nothing you can tell us now?' The concern was obvious in Maggie's face.

'Well as yet we are not sure if this episode has been some kind of heart problem, hence the tests. If it is connected to the heart we will need to keep you in for a few days to explore the extent of the problem. All I can say is that it does not at the moment seem life threatening, but that is another reason to stay put; if I was going to have a full blown heart attack I would choose to have it here. Someone will be with you soon to admit you to the ward and I'll see you again when you are all settled in. If the pain is subsiding do you think you could manage without pain killers?'

'Yes, I think so.'

'Good, well I'll see you later Mr Lloyd.'

The doctor's matter of fact attitude had been somewhat comforting but then, as they both knew, it was designed to be just that. They did not have to wait too long for an orderly to come and whisk Peter away, up several floors to a ward and into another side room with one other, unoccupied, bed.

It was three o'clock in the morning and they were both tired, a nurse had been to book Peter in, asking innumerable questions and painstakingly writing the answers on to several forms. By this time all the patient wanted to do was sleep.

'Why don't you get a taxi back to the hotel and get some sleep yourself?' He tried to persuade his wife.

'No, I can doze in the chair; I am not leaving here until I know you are going to be all right.'

It was pointless to argue. Peter had come to understand that his wife, usually of a placid disposition could be somewhat stubborn, especially while fighting the corner of someone she loved. No more was said and when the nurse left Peter drifted into a peaceful, almost pain free sleep. Maggie watched him for a long time until sleep eventually overtook her and she lay back in the chair, her tense body beginning to relax.

****

George Price's face was unreadable as he came off the phone.

'What is it, is something wrong?' Helen had come in from the garden in time to catch the tail end of the conversation.

'Peter's in hospital, they thought it was a heart attack but he's okay now. The pains have gone but they want to keep him in for tests.'

'Oh no! Maggie will be devastated.' Helen's hand covered her mouth. 'How did she sound?'

'Tired and a bit upset, but you know our girl, she's keeping strong for Peter.'

'How awful for them and when they had time for themselves too, did Maggie say how serious they thought it was?'

'She said he didn't have pain anymore but the doctors were doing tests to find out exactly what it was. They are hoping it was stress or a panic attack, if it was his heart it could prevent him from starting that new medication he was telling us about.'

'Of course, I hadn't thought of that, it would be terrible, Peter's pinned all his hopes on that. Do you think I should ring Sue?'

'You could do, she's sure to want to know and Maggie was going to ring Peter's daughters so they will know by now.'

Sue had been in the bath when Helen Price rang so Alan took the call and then climbed the stairs to break the news to Sue, knowing how upset she would be for her friends.

'I can't believe it; she'll be beside herself with worry. To lose one husband then have another with a heart attack, Maggie doesn't deserve that.'

'Nobody does love, but it hasn't been confirmed as a heart attack yet, let's wait and see, it might not be such bad news after all.' Alan did not want his wife getting unnecessarily upset and he was never one to anticipate the worst. Sue climbed out of the bath and Alan wrapped her up in the large towel he was holding and hugged her.

'Some people seem to get more than their share of bad luck.' She spoke into Alan's shoulder, her voice almost muffled by the towel.

****

'Have you heard of a phenomenon called the MS hug?' The doctor was standing at the foot of the bed, smiling at his patient. It was the third day of Peter's stay in hospital and the previous day had been filled with

298

every conceivable kind of test. Maggie had been with him most of the time, going back to the hotel only to shower and change.

'Not that I can recall' Peter answered.

'It's a symptom of MS, a kind of tightness or pain in the chest. Some people experience it more than others and some not at all.'

'Are you saying that my pains were this MS hug?'

'Well, all the tests have come back negative so it looks as if you have a pretty healthy heart. It could have been a panic attack brought on by stress, but I doubt it as you were asleep at the time, my opinion would be the hug.' The doctor was smiling, pleased to be passing on good news.

'So does this mean that I'll be able to start taking Gilenya when I get home?'

'I would think it prudent to have the tests done again when you get home. I will be sending a letter to your Neurologist and I'm sure that will be his advice too. But for now I don't see any reason to keep you here any longer, so maybe you can go and enjoy the rest of your holiday.'

Peter did not need telling twice, his feet were on the floor even before the doctor had left the room and within the hour they were in a taxi heading back to the hotel where they went straight to their room. They were both tired, Maggie particularly as she had hardly managed to sleep at all, so they ordered a light lunch from room service, and then tried to rest.

Maggie woke to find Peter sitting at the desk.

'Hey, didn't you sleep?' she asked.

'No, I've been laid on my back for so long that I needed to sit up. Are you feeling better for that?'

'Hmm, yes, I went out like a light.'

'I was wondering... I know we were going to explore New York a bit more, but would you mind terribly if we tried to get an earlier flight home?'

Maggie nodded,

'I was thinking exactly the same myself. I know the doctor gave you the all clear but I'm not going to be comfortable trailing all over now. I'm ready to go home too.'

Peter had been looking up phone numbers to change their flight and set about making the call straight away. It was less complicated than they had expected and they very soon found themselves booked onto a flight that left the following day. Going down to reception to make the changes there, they found the staff very understanding, and they even arranged to refund their money for the days to come.

It was late afternoon of what would now be their last full day and they decided to take a walk. Peter was keen to be outside again, so crossing Lexington Avenue they headed towards Grand Central Station, a place they had looked in rather hurriedly before and now took time to see properly. It was an incredible building for a station. The huge structure was impressive and although busy with travellers and shoppers was so spacious it did not seem crowded at all. A wonderful market ran adjacent to the concourse, with every kind of delicatessen stall imaginable, catering for all tastes. Seeing the variety on offer reminded Maggie of her infrequent trips to London where she had wandered round the food halls in Harrods to marvel at the goods on sale. Back in the main concourse they sat for a coffee in one of the bijou cafes, taking in the atmosphere and watching the comings and goings of the hundreds of people who must pass through each day.

'Penny for them?' Maggie asked.

'I was looking at the structure of the place; it's quite an incredible piece of architecture. How about you?'

'I was watching the people wondering what kind of lives they lead, if they are happy with city life. It's worlds apart from our sleepy little market town.'

Peter laughed out loud.

'Typical!' he said. 'Anyone reading our thoughts would immediately know that you are a counsellor and I'm an architect. Come on my love, let's go back to the hotel and get changed for dinner.

The time of their flight home could not have been better. It gave them chance to pack, eat breakfast and get to JFK without any delays. It was a relief to see their luggage checked in, knowing they need not worry about it until their arrival back in the UK where George would be waiting at the airport. The trip had been a roller coaster of a holiday with more than its fair share of highs and lows. Places which had formerly been only names in books had come to life and of course there was Peter's success in delivering the lectures. The spell in hospital had been frightening but even that had turned out well and was not the heart attack they had initially thought. Maggie was glad to be on the way home, she would still have a few days off work giving the opportunity of spending time with her parents, but even going back to work was a prospect she relished as client's problems were never far from her mind.

****

'How did you know that?' Peter looked at his colleagues who had welcomed him with cheers and cat calls, proclaiming him to have been a huge success on the other side of the pond.

'We don't only know about it, we have seen the videos.' Charles sat back in his chair, savouring the look of surprise on Peter's face.

'Videos? I didn't know it was being recorded.'

'Oh yes, we have a copy, courtesy of Nigel Carter and in all seriousness it is brilliant. I think we have found a hidden talent here.'

Peter shrugged off the comments but had to admit that he would really like to see the videos himself having been so nervous at the time he honestly could not remember much of what he said. The lectures would also be quoted in the Architect's Monthly giving more publicity for their little firm. They may even have to consider taking on another partner or two.

Maggie stood in the courtyard of her new home thinking about the events of the last few weeks. Lifting her face to the warm sun she allowed the gentle breeze to lift her hair, the sight of the green patchwork of fields and meadows soothed her eyes and fed her soul, she was glad to be home, this was where she belonged.

Returning to work after spending some precious time with her parents, the lengthy holiday, or at least the latter part of it back in the UK, had been good and she was ready for whatever work would throw at her now. George and Helen stayed with their daughter and son-in-law for a week, during which time they all had a day trip to York, a place which meant a lot to Maggie and Peter, being the place where their romance had begun. They enjoyed several long walks with Ben and the two women embarked on shopping trips, as therapy of course. Sue and Alan were invited for a meal one evening and Peter's daughters, Jane and Rachel had both managed to visit, needing to see for themselves that their father was recovered. Returning to work,

Maggie happily threw herself into counsellor mode, picking up the threads of events in her clients' lives and working conscientiously to make a difference, no matter how small that may be, knowing this to be her true vocation in life

Epilogue

'...and I wanted you to know how well things have worked out for us Maggie. We are having the boys Christened next month and I would love it if you and your husband could be there, I'll send a card with all the details. Many, many thanks for all your help and support, it has meant so much to Andy and I.

Best wishes

Ruth

The letter from Ruth Duncan was a pleasant surprise. Maggie rarely heard how clients progressed so this was welcome news. Ruth and Andy had begun the process of adopting two brothers, a five year old, and an eight month baby. She would ring Ruth later to thank her for taking the time to send an update.

It was six months since the Lloyds had returned from the USA. Clients had come and gone, some staying longer than others. Ellie Graham had continued counselling sessions until well into autumn. As yet none of those lost memories had re-surfaced but in her typically pragmatic way Ellie consciously determined to embrace life in the present. When Maggie had last seen her, she had returned home to live with Phil and Sam, enjoying a new and exciting life and claiming with a wry grin to be proving the saying, 'you only live once,' to be completely wrong.

Sarah Beecham, nee Porter, was still, as far as Maggie knew, living with her parents. Mark Beecham had been sentenced to five years for bigamy which would probably mean he would only serve two, but

Sarah had gone from strength to strength, continuing therapy and working with Maggie on issues of confidence and low self esteem. Her family and counsellor delighted in seeing the true Sarah emerge once again from the shell of a woman which Mark had done his best to turn her into.

Jane had given birth to a beautiful baby boy who they named Robert Peter, to be known as Robbie and Maggie became a very 'hands on' Grandmother, finding Jane so generous in the way she let Maggie share her new little son. Sue gave birth to a baby girl, calling her Rose and Alan became a very 'hands on' Daddy whether he liked it or not. All the proud parents and their respective offspring were thriving. Sue and Alan asked Maggie and Peter to be godparents to Rose, a kind and wonderful gift which they embraced with enthusiasm and love.

And then there was Peter. Simon James, his GP, repeated all the tests which had been undergone in America, thankfully with the same positive results. Dr. Hassen, the neurologist started him on Gilenya and although it was early days and Maggie famously never counted her chickens, Peter had not experienced any symptoms of MS since taking the drug.

This was Maggie's world and these were her people whom she loved with all her heart. Their presence enriched each day and whilst there were no guarantees that life would be smooth for any of them, her world would keep on turning and Maggie would continue to play her part as long and as well as she could.

The End

Lightning Source UK Ltd.
Milton Keynes UK
UKOW030750211212

203980UK00001B/11/P